STATE OF
EMERGENCY

STATE OF EMERGENCY

A NOVEL

JEREMY TIANG

EPIGRAM BOOKS
SINGAPORE · LONDON

Epigram Books UK
First published in 2017 by Epigram Books Singapore
This Edition published in Great Britain in May 2017
by Epigram Books UK

A CIP CATALOGUE RECORD FOR THIS BOOK IS AVAILABLE FROM THE BRITISH LIBRARY.

ISBN	978-191-2098-65-1
PRINTED AND BOUND IN	Great Britain by Clays Ltd, St Ives plc
	Epigram Books UK
	55 Baker Street
	London, W1U 7EU

10 9 8 7 6 5 4 3 2 1

www.epigrambooks.uk

for my parents, Helen and Victor Samuel

"The tradition of the oppressed teaches us that the 'state of emergency' in which we live is not the exception but the rule."

—WALTER BENJAMIN,
THESES ON THE PHILOSOPHY OF HISTORY
(TRANS. HARRY ZOHN)

I

JASON

Mollie Remedios died in the explosion that tore apart
MacDonald House on 10 March 1965. She was at her desk
in the Hong Kong and Shanghai Bank adding columns of
figures when the wall behind her shattered, followed by the
ceiling. She suffered several broken ribs, a punctured lung,
and a basal skull fracture that killed her instantly. She was
24 years old.

There were three fatalities apart from Mollie—two girls
who worked in the same office (the newspapers called
them all girls, even though one of them was nearly 40
and divorced), and a driver for the neighbouring Borneo
Malaya Building Society, killed by a drainpipe detaching
and crashing decisively through the roof of his car. Thirty-
three other people were taken to the General Hospital, where
seven were warded with serious injuries.

The three dead women, wholesomely pretty, would be
on the covers of all the newspapers the next day. Mollie in
particular was featured for her youth and promise; the tragedy

of her being so recently married, leaving a baby behind. The driver lay unconscious in hospital for five days before dying, and so missed out on most of the publicity.

Mollie's brother Jason was in his office on Connaught Drive when the first reports came on the radio, a few minutes after the explosion itself. There was a moment of absolute stillness in the room before Jason was down the stairs and on his bicycle, pedalling past the Padang and then down Penang Road. Traffic thickened on his approach to the red brick building, as drivers stopped to stare and abandoned cars littered the street.

Rain made the scene dreamlike. Bank workers stood calmly on the pavement, many of them bleeding from small cuts. The tall white men from the Australian High Commission, which occupied rooms above the bank, looked unhurt but far angrier. A thin old woman lay on a stretcher as ambulance workers tried to staunch the blood seeping from her forehead. The building looked undamaged from the outside, apart from the windows, which had sprayed their glass outward for a hundred feet around and now gaped black and empty.

A policeman in khaki shorts stood in front of Jason as he tried to approach the building. *Stop*, he said, grabbing Jason's shoulder so he almost fell off his bike—*no entry permitted*. He stumbled over the English words. *My sister*, said Jason, trying to keep his voice calm. *My sister inside*. But the policeman merely repeated, as if from a script, *Awas, danger, the building is unsafe*.

Men with notebooks and cameras circled the wreckage warily. Rumours rippled through the crowd: a burst gas main, structural defects, and then, with more and more resonance, the word *bomb*.

When the police grudgingly confirmed this, reporters formed a queue behind the two working telephone booths, and photographers sped off in taxis to get their pictures developed before the print deadline. Everyone seemed aware the story now being created would eventually work its way into the new national mythology. This was the worst incident yet of Konfrontasi, the confrontation with Indonesia. This was Sukarno tightening the screws, and there would have to be some kind of response.

Police fanned out on both sides of the road to prevent looting. Jason clung to his bicycle, saying over and over, *my sister, my sister*, until they left him alone. He found himself marooned on the black sea of rain-slick road, shards of glass glistening at his feet like stars. The British bomb disposal squad arrived, men with brave voices. They looked more confident than the local police, but there was little for them to do except mark off the perimeter with little flags and speak urgently into their walkie-talkies. They sounded like people in films.

"Where is everyone? Where are the survivors?" Jason clutched at uniformed arms as they passed, asking first in English and then Malay. The police shrugged, pointed at the crowds on the pavement. There was no order to this, no one was tallying lists of the living. There were too many to take in—human mountains, human oceans, they say in Chinese. "Are there still people inside?" Nobody could answer this. Rescue workers carted rubble out in wheelbarrows, manhandling great slabs of concrete out of the way.

When they began bringing the bodies out, he knew. He tried to get closer, to rip the concealing blankets off, but they stopped him again. *Go to the hospital,* they said. *Not here, not in the open.*

No one offered him a lift, and he had to cycle again through the slick streets, up New Bridge Road and into Outram. The morgue was in a basement, painted sickly green. The assistant made him stop shouting before he would show him the bodies of first two strangers and then his sister.

Mollie's face was crusted with blood, her familiar eyes open but filmed over. Flecks of rubble were lodged under her tongue, behind her perfect teeth. The attendant stopped him from touching the evidence. Jason was only required to nod for identification. Then the corpse was taken away to be labelled.

He declined tea and slumped in the corridor. Who would pick the children up from his parents' flat? Mollie usually got her daughter before he came for his twins. He tried to do something, call their parents, but the air seemed to press on him, keeping him immobile. There were things he wanted to say to Mollie, but of course she was not there. He was later unable to work out how long he'd spent in that basement. When he emerged, the rain had stopped and a weak sun was shining.

The bombers were arrested three days later, two Indonesian guerrillas caught trying to escape by sea. They had been given a Malaysian Airways bag containing between twenty and twenty-five pounds of nitroglycerine, and told to detonate it in any public building. They had landed at eleven in the morning and, after lunch, left the explosives up a flight of stairs in the imposing bank.

In Jason's memory, the killers died very soon after that, even though he has looked up the dates and knows it took three years for them to exhaust their appeals. They were hanged within the high walls of Changi Prison on 17 October 1968. Like many people, Jason stood at the prison gates that day, waiting for the flag to go up to indicate the executions had taken place.

Now, at a distance of fifty years, Jason's instinct for revenge feels blunted. It makes no difference what these men did, why their leaders told them to, if it could have been avoided. It doesn't matter that they were punished. Entirely irrational, he thinks if only his sister had not died, if Mollie had been in another room that day, if she had taken an early tea break, then he too might have been saved. Lying now on his iron bed, aware that he is dying, there are moments when he can think only of Mollie, can wonder only whether it was fear or peace that filled her mind as she looked up and saw the world, unimaginably, begin to fall apart.

•

In the minutes immediately after waking, Jason Low cannot remember where he is. There is no guarantee it will be morning, and in fact it often isn't—he needs so little sleep these days. He lies in the indeterminate pre-dawn gloom, squinting to make out shapes in the dark. He can hear laboured breathing, smell disinfectant. Reaching for his wife, for Siew Li, his fingers hit only the metal railing around his bed, and he thinks *prison* for a moment, before remembering he's in hospital.

The bed is in a Class C ward, which means there are seven other bodies in the room. He would rather be alone, but his Medisave account is running out after several years of lavish disease. Whenever he tentatively mentions going private, like a nice room in Mount Elizabeth, his daughter Janet's mouth snaps shut like a purse. She appears to regard her inheritance as a *fait accompli*, and any unnecessary spending as straightforward theft from his grandchildren. He could go against her wishes, but if he angers Janet and she stops visiting, then no one will. Light begins to seep into the room, and the grey walls take on their daytime shade of bilious green. Next to him is Madam Ngoh, the mouth breather, who cries out in her sleep to absent children. Although they have nothing in common—she barely speaks English—he has come to depend on her. They are both here for the long haul, surviving as the other beds fill and empty with transients, dilettantes who breeze in with cataracts and leave without. They don't even have to cut you open for kidney stones these days; a laser goes right through without breaking the skin.

None of the beds have curtains drawn around them,

which is a good sign—it means no one has died during the night. In the fortnight he's been here, he's seen three bodies removed from the ward (discreetly, under sheets). Each time, he glanced across at Madam Ngoh, and she looked as apprehensive as he felt. *Time is picking us off one by one*, he thought, *like characters in a horror film.*

There is something unseemly about the place itself. The nurses, talking amongst themselves, call it "gerry"—"I'm on gerry tonight," they say, sometimes right in front of him. He doesn't blame them, even though it's disrespectful—he knows his face is falling in on itself, his eyes dim, his mouth slack. How are they to know that there is sentience in all this drooping flesh? He has tried telling them about the dream of Gerontius, but they don't have time to listen to his old man's mumble, his old-fashioned insistence on complete sentences, just briskly assume he's mispronouncing "geriatric" and assure him, *Yes, that's where you are, Mr Low. The gerry ward.*

Before coming here, he used to enjoy this part of the day—the faint chill of the air, the light mist over the field downstairs. He would make himself a cup of tea in the dim false dawn and sit at his kitchen table, listening to the neighbours beginning to wake up. The hospital is different. There is already a tinny feeling of readiness as the night shift hands over, as tureens of Quaker oats are filled and loaded onto trolleys. He tries to sit up, but that makes his sheets rustle unnaturally loudly. Only the higher-class wards are carpeted. This room has noisy tiled floors and a ceiling fan.

Not that he's particularly eager for the day to start. After breakfast, the nurses come round with medication, and at some point in the morning he will have a sponge bath. Afternoons grind by, once the lunch trays have been cleared away and he has nothing to do. There's a television in one corner of the room but he worries about looking in its direction, alarmed at the great chunks of time that slip away in chat shows and cookery programmes. He wonders if his face in repose takes on the same deadened look he sees in the others as they gape at the machine. He wishes he could read instead, but it's too much effort to hold a book upright, to concentrate.

His daughter invariably arrives with the first wave of visitors at five on the dot. She has to leave work early to ensure this, and is always sure to let him know if this has meant walking out of an important meeting or letting a deadline lapse. He wants to say, *You didn't have to*—but what if she takes him at his word and stops coming?

Janet is a schoolteacher—at least she was, until her talent for bureaucracy was spotted by someone high up in the Ministry. She still looks like one, with her stiff cardigans and martinet's glasses, her hair tightly permed. Jason is faintly stunned every time he remembers his daughter is less than a decade from retirement. It seems wrong that she should be old.

His grandsons occasionally come with her, clearly press-ganged and eager to run away as soon as they can, citing films to see, girlfriends to meet. They are in their twenties now, tall and well-nourished, speaking the uninflected dull English the young all seem to use. Janet's husband put in a perfunctory appearance right at the start, but he's busy with his grassroots work, and as the hospital is far from his constituency there isn't much point being seen here. He has a lot of ground to cover.

Visiting hours go on till eight, and every evening Janet dutifully sits by her father's bedside until the nurses begin asking people to leave. Sometimes she tells him about her work or the boys' accomplishments, but for the most part she is happy to sit in silence, making quick notes on a policy document, as if her presence is all that's required. Each visit ends with her reading from *The Daily Bread*, a handbag-sized booklet of devotional tracts she gets free from her church. Jason has told her he's not religious, but she brushes that aside. There's nothing wrong in being reminded how to behave well, she tells him. Although neither of them will say this, both know she is thinking about the small amount of time he still has on earth, her tiny opportunity to save his imperilled soul.

•

As a civil servant, Jason ran his life along orderly tramlines—each day as like the one before as possible. His department gained a reputation for efficiency. Meetings started on time with no deviations from the agenda. Projects finished exactly when they were supposed to and never over budget. At the retirement dinner on his 65th birthday, even the Minister joked about how they'd had no need to look at their clocks with Jason around to keep them on schedule. They gave him a gold watch and engraved plaque. He'd always done everything exactly as he should. Was this his reward?

His current incarceration feels like a hellish version of this earlier life: wide empty days punctuated with regular, worthless events. Even Janet's visits, which should be the highlight of each day, feel cloying and airless as soon as they commence. He knows his daughter is prompted more by duty than affection. At least his sense of obligation has passed on to one of his children. He has tried asking for sleeping pills to get through the afternoon, but the nurse will only give them out at night, with a doctor's approval.

The main problem is in his own mind, which seems weak and spongy. He has always prided himself on his grasp of facts, but now he cannot hold anything in his head for long. More than once he has had to ask a nurse to buy him a newspaper on her lunch break as a favour, because he was too embarrassed to ask the date. It hardly matters, he has no appointments for the foreseeable future, but it feels necessary to hold on to his sense of who he is. He will not become a person so irrelevant to the world he does not know which month it is.

When desperate to make conversation with Janet, he sometimes accidentally asks her about people who are gone. *How is your mother*, he says. *How is Auntie Mollie?* The first time it happened, she glared at him as if he were a troublesome student, as if he might have been joking. Now, she simply murmurs, "Dead, Pa," then adroitly changes the subject as if to save them both from embarrassment.

He doesn't know how to explain to her that he knows they are dead. Truly, he is aware of how much he has lost. And yet, they are inside him. He cannot tell her about the long conversations he has with the departed, whiling away long afternoons, as he tries over and over to understand where they went. He cannot tell her that sometimes his sister, and sometimes his wife, come to visit him in the small hours of the morning.

"Lost in his own past," he heard her whisper once on the phone. People are becoming less cautious around him. Perhaps they think his hearing is going, since everything else is. Unlike her brother, Janet has never had time for bygones, preferring instead to focus on what she calls her goals. "You need to know where you're headed," she is fond of saying. "Otherwise how will you ever get there?"

Sometimes he thinks this is supposed to happen, his life flashing before his eyes at the end, the final moments expanding to fit everything that's gone before. But the events are not unfolding in an orderly way, which would at least make them easy to follow. He finds his attention constantly wandering, sinking into the fog of memory, meeting old enemies, replaying arguments he should have won. Afterwards, he is angry for some time without being able to remember why.

Jason has lost a great deal—more, he considers, than the usual attrition of a long life. He spends the hot sleepless nights making lists. His parents, of course, long ago. His sister and his wife, taken from him in different ways. His son in London, a city on the other side of the world. Janet, who belongs to no one but herself. And Barnaby, his brother-in-law—he decides to add Barnaby to the list of the missing, even though they were never particularly close. Gone is gone.

He talks to the nurses about the many people who have left him, and they nod with sympathy and impatience. Gerry ward is full of the abandoned, and for all his grief and anger, Jason is visited by his daughter every day. *Such a respectable lady*, whisper the staff, *and her husband an actual MP*. They don't understand what more he wants, with such a good daughter to take care of him.

Each evening, when Janet leaves, he takes stock of his body. Often it is tense from the effort of being in a room with her, both of them straining towards cordiality. He lies stiffly, listening to the other inhabitants creaking around getting ready for bed. Although he still has most of his teeth, he can't be bothered to brush them very often. He doubts he'll be around long enough to see them rot.

It is hard to accept this decrepitude, which the nurses seem to think is all you can expect at his age (he's 76, not even that old these days). Jason would really like to be one of those smiling centenarians, usually Japanese, who appear in newspapers attributing their continued good health to genes and a daily glass of brandy, lively eyes looking out from a mass of origami-fold wrinkles. A hundred seems like a good age, although the doctors have told him that he'll probably not see out the year, or even the month (in fact, he suspects they wish he wouldn't, so they can have their bed back—there are shortages). In any case, long lives are probably the domain of the guiltless, those at peace.

●

He knows he hasn't always been a good father. In his defence, it was unusual for a man to be left in charge of children back in those days. He had help, naturally, after Siew Li went away: from his mother (and hers, though he didn't like to ask after a while—she just cried all the time). Mollie helped for a while, but she had her own baby, then she was gone too. Sometimes Jason wonders if they could have stayed a family, had Mollie continued to be there. His mind slips into a familiar groove: what if Mollie had lived? What if his children had grown up alongside her Stella? He imagines them all sitting together after school, feasting on jam sandwiches.

He wonders if he should have joined forces with his brother-in-law, but he never had much time for Barnaby—even when they'd both lost their wives, and were falling apart from within, they still barely spoke. Barnaby was weak, had always been. So the two fathers brought up their children separately, sunk in isolation, even as the kids grew closer.

Janet takes pleasure in reminding him of the many ways in which he has failed them. She drops these into conversation like amusing anecdotes: the time Henry, aged seven, refused to eat his dinner, and Jason smashed his bowl of soup on the floor. The time Jason forgot to come to Janet's graduation ceremony, as a result of which she has no photographs of herself. The time he beat them both for going into his room without permission. She still has the scars.

His daughter is an unknown quantity to him. She is a good mother—at least her sons have turned out well—but she seems as closed to him as she is to the world. Implacable, armour-plated, so sleek and single-minded that she appears to have no weak points. Quite often, when he hears her crisp footsteps approach the ward, his initial reaction is claustrophobic fear. When did this happen? Surely it used to be the other way round.

Henry, his son, has been in London for decades, and seldom comes back to Singapore. It would have been easy enough for Jason to get on a plane—especially with all these cheap flights now—but something about his sense of the fitness of things made him feel it was Henry's duty to come back here, to his home, and not for others to go to him. What if Jason had gone, and been unwanted?

He allows himself to regret this. It would have been nice, at least, to know how Henry lives. His son has transformed himself, now has the patched tweed jacket and clipped accent of an English academic—he's a professor of history at one of the less exciting London colleges. How is it possible to escape your origins so utterly? Henry has a flat in Bayswater, something he vaguely imagines from the few British novels he has read to be poky, damp, and smelling of cabbage. Janet has been to London a couple of times but never says much, apart from hinting darkly that she's surprised the English did not succumb to cholera generations ago.

Large areas of his son's life are not open to him. Why has he never married or had children? Jason never asked. He hopes his son isn't damaged, afraid any woman he married would abandon him like the mother he has no memory of. Of course, Jason himself has never remarried, and couldn't tell you why either. He and Henry have simply never talked about any of this, never talked about anything that mattered.

They do speak—Janet bought him a mobile phone and calling card, and he can now talk to his son in London for surprisingly little money. He's distrustful of this, mindful of the days when an international phone call meant weeks of low-level anxiety until the phone bill arrived. His youngest grandson frequently tries to persuade him that it would be free to call the UK over the Internet, but he doesn't see how that could possibly work, and in any case doesn't own a computer.

Calls start the same way—hellos and how-are-yous, then awkward silence. "How's your health?" Henry asks.

"Terrible," he replies—he truly doesn't want to discuss his ailments, neither interesting nor fixable. Instead, he asks about Henry's work. *How are the students?*

"It's not just teaching that I do," says Henry wearily, as if he has rehearsed this argument before. Perhaps he has; Jason's porous memory forces repeats of entire conversations.

"I know. You have to do the admin as well. So does Janet, you know. In fact, the other day she told me she had a meeting that went on the whole afternoon." As he speaks, he remembers that Janet hasn't taught for at least a decade.

"I do research, I publish papers—I'm an associate professor. Dad, it's not just about face time with the students. We have postgrad monkeys to run the tutorial circus. I'm an academic." Henry, he can tell, is getting frustrated and annoyed, which in turn makes him sound like a teenager. His voice grows strangled, as if he is only a hair's breadth away from snapping at his father. He wonders how his son deals with his students, who are probably much less well-behaved these days.

"Are you going to write a book?"

"I've written a book. Three. I sent you copies."

"They're somewhere in the flat. But I don't mean some textbook. A real book. Something normal people will read."

"Dad—" Again, that clenched-throat noise. It can't be healthy.

"I saw on the news that your students are rioting," he says, trying to change the subject.

"They seem to do it every year. There's always something, some war or government policy to be unhappy about. Too much free time." Henry has always been distinctly antipathetic to any kind of political agenda. Perhaps his long view of history has given him a sense of nothing ever changing, not really, and therefore the best thing being to keep your head down and get on with the things in front of you. Jason can sympathise with this.

They are then able to discuss some of the stories on the news with reasonable civility. Henry complains about the folly of Brexit, a country cutting itself off from the world, and his father points out that Singapore did the same, albeit not voluntarily, but no one could argue with the results. Henry tries to explain that the circumstances were completely different, the populace in Singapore didn't get a real vote, but Jason is already drifting off. It was all so long ago, he's bored of it all. So much history, especially with the 50th anniversary of independence just recently. Everyone wallowing in it— all over the TV and papers, even in the streets. Why? Bad enough living through it the first time round.

Jason feels almost tender towards his son during these conversations. For all that it seems impossible to say anything without one or the other of them being offended, this at least feels more bearable than the brittle politeness he suffers with Janet. The difference in time zones doesn't help the patchiness of their conversations. When Henry answers the phone with "good morning," he takes weak pleasure in answering "afternoon."

"When are you coming to see me?" Jason now says, his voice querulous.

"It's not very long till the end of term, maybe then?" *Maybe.* "I've had a look at tickets, they're quite pricey."

"Of course they are, everyone knows it's expensive to fly in the summer. You should have booked your flight sooner."

"I didn't know you were going to fall ill," says Henry quite reasonably. "And it's term time."

"Let me know when you've fixed a date."

"Of course. I've got to go now. I'll see you soon."

"You should come now. I might die."

"I have responsibilities. You'll just have to hang on."

•

Siew Li and Mollie appear to him at different ages. Mollie sometimes comes as a little girl, demanding a leg-up onto the rambutan tree in their back garden. Siew Li was in her teens when they met, and not a great deal older when she left—still, each new glimpse startles him with how different she has become. Siew Li in her Nanyang Girls' uniform, Siew Li as a bride, then with her babies, and much later in that other uniform, when—

He knows they are not in the room with him, not really: his faculties aren't quite that gone yet. But when the alternatives are the clammy dark, the coughs and moans of his fellow inmates, he can't resist giving in to them. Mollie's cool hands on his temples, Siew Li arranging his pillows the way he likes them, folded over to support his neck. Let them be here. Let the dead return.

There was a while, early on in their relationship, when he thought he'd lost Siew Li for good. They'd only recently met, which was the worst feeling, the fear that he'd found this precious thing and it was being snatched away. She was detained indefinitely—no indication at all if she'd ever be released. It wasn't fair, a girl of fifteen with everything still to come. *But that's you too*, said his friends, *you're young, move on*. He couldn't. So he kept visiting.

He'd thought this would be the hardest time of his

life, not having her with him, not even being able to see her regularly once he started national service. He didn't tell his parents, just Mollie, who was sympathetic and kept his secret, for which he was grateful, even if her main emotion was amusement that her staid older brother was finally in love. It was even a bit exciting for her that his crush was an outlaw girl, one of the dangerous elements the government said were destabilising the country.

He'd never believed that, although he could see the establishment doing great things for the nation, and trusted them to know best. Still, he knew Siew Li—or was at least getting to know her—and she didn't want to blow anything up. The strikes she'd help organise were necessary, she said, because how else were the workers to get their voices heard? The stories she told him were horrific. He had no idea, in his clean, light-filled existence, just how most people lived. It was true, he supposed, and yet he could also see this was no way forward, paralysing the country with violence in the streets. They were both children of the 1940s, and their first memories were of the occupation. Why have yet another warzone, just a decade later?

And yet, she fascinated him. He wanted to know more, not just about her, but about everything. Even at that age, he was aware the world only made sense if he looked away from most of it. At school, history was a straightforward pageant of progress with a few unfortunate aberrations. But then there was Siew Li, who called his parents capitalists as if that were a bad thing, who looked down on their successful business precisely because of its success. Why should so many people be working, but only they get rich? He had no answer for her. But he wanted to find out.

His curiosity was how they had met in the first place. The newspapers had been full of this riot at the bus company, and on the radio it sounded like an apocalypse. This had been going on for a while, Chinese middle school students joining forces with labour unions to hold the country hostage. He thought it was important to see this historical moment for himself—though, if he was honest, he just found it exciting— but anyway there he was, on Alexandra Road, the heat and energy of the protest searing through the order of his life. And there she was, a man's handkerchief folded double and slung rakishly across her face, like she was a bandit. A banner in her hands—Marianne, brandishing a flag. On impulse he said hello.

She lifted the fabric from her face and he saw her firm jaw, her small teeth. He tried to talk to her in halting Chinese, until she took pity on him and they switched to English, which she clearly wasn't fluent in, but somehow managed to make expressively her own. He felt a flicker of shame, and wondered why. Amongst his peers, it was a source of pride not to speak Chinese, a foreign language. English was the future. His friends mocked the Chinese school students, still clinging to the language of the old country, talking about "going back" to China when they'd been born here, listening to Yao Lee instead of Perry Como. And here he was, listening patiently as she explained the banner she was holding.

"*Gaicao huandai*. Haven't you heard this before? It means change the time and, what do you call it, the Emperor."

"We don't have an Emperor."

"You know what I mean. The *zhimin*."

"The what?"

"The ang moh. Those people."

"The British? You mean the government?"

"Yes, government." She pronounced it *gahmen*. "We need change."

"Isn't this protest about bus workers unions?"

"How can you just change one thing? Everything is not working."

They kept going for a while, him tossing statistics and facts against the wall of her indignation, but she was already looking distracted, eyeing the nearby police, pulling the handkerchief back across her face. He didn't want to talk politics with her, he thought, or not just politics. He wanted to know what else was happening behind those flinty eyes.

But before he could ask for her phone number, something shifted in the air, a slight hum of tension, and self-preservation told him to slip around the corner at once. There was shouting behind him as he strolled away, trying to look casual. He wasn't the only one, he noticed—a handful of the Chinese students were also leaving the scene, not ready yet to be martyrs for the cause. He didn't blame them. Protesting was one thing, but getting arrested was serious business.

A safe distance away, he turned back and saw her, at least he thought it was her, held in an armlock by two policemen, refusing to let go of her banner—it trailed by her side. She looked serene, almost mischievous, a still point amidst this hurly-burly. Something wilted inside him. He had to meet her again. Already he was thinking how best to find her. He could still see her face. What is it, he wondered, that made you look at another human being, and somehow just know?

•

Even though he can barely manage a shuffle, the nurses encourage him to get up and walk around, because otherwise his muscles will atrophy and he might get bedsores. He obliges with his ungainly walking frame, sometimes making it as far as the rooftop garden with its reflexology path and sterile little flower boxes. The main attraction is the view—it's high enough here to look over the city, the tall colourful blocks and, in the distance, what he imagines to be the grey mass of Malaysia.

If he gets out of here, he decides, he will travel. See a bit more of the world in the time left to him. Why didn't he do it when he could? There were the children, of course, but when they were grown, when he was still healthy and could easily have afforded it, why did he never seek out the unfamiliar?

When he visited Siew Li in prison, they promised each other so many things. She needed to look forward to something, but so did he, because the present was so unbearable. He felt guilty, each time, that he got to leave her behind and go out into the bright world. He told her what he'd done and seen, embellishing the details a little if it didn't seem exciting enough. Best not to ask her about herself: it depressed her to have nothing new to report, just the dank walls of her cell, maybe a mild improvement in the food or a nastier interrogation than usual.

The pain of those three years might be why he never visited his niece Stella, not once the whole time she was put away. He feels bad about this, as he does about so much else. He could have spoken to her after, could have sent a message, but he did nothing. Luckily he was already estranged from Barnaby at that point, otherwise this would surely have been the last straw.

What would Mollie say? He conjures her up and tells her, again, *I'm sorry about your daughter. I wasn't a good uncle. I had my own children, but that wasn't an excuse. I just didn't—* And Mollie smiles, kind as ever, and takes his hand. *You can't change that now,* she says, *we all wish we'd done things differently.* Not quite absolution, but better than nothing. He holds onto Mollie, and thinks: *you didn't live long enough for me to let you down.*

Janet has left a little Gideon Bible by his bedside, and he leafs through it nervously. He can't remember when he stopped going to church, only that it wasn't a conscious decision, he was just too busy, too tired, and how could any of this be God's plan? So he let his parents bring the kids to Sunday school, which he now regrets whenever the proselytising portion of Janet's visits comes round. It would be simpler if he believed, and more comforting—although what if she's right, and beyond the curtain is not the void he fears, but all the dead, not as friendly as in his memory, but ready with an accounting of all he owes them?

He shuts his eyes. It was so simple, to do nothing but lose himself in work each day, then the newspapers and TV afterwards. His children learnt not to speak to him if he was reading, and never to enter his bedroom. He put food on the table (mostly packets from the hawker centre, picked up on his way back) and paid for their schooling. That was as far as duty went. Should he have done more? And Siew Li. He could have done something to save her, couldn't he? He never tried. Those letters—he tries to remember now where he left them. He should say something to... The thought is tiring, and skitters out of reach.

He struggles to find a happier memory. The jubilation when Siew Li was released, that's always good. Watching her re-enter the world, taking her place in it again. Being with her, properly, without a table between them—it felt special now, like they had to treasure it because they'd waited so long. "Were you about to give up?" she asked him once. "Or would you have waited forever?" And of course he said forever, but it was impossible to know. He introduced her to his parents, afraid they would say something about her background or her imprisonment, prepared to defend her.

Jason had always been one of those people with a plan— initially marked out for him by ambitious parents (the right schools, the right clubs), and later the well-defined path of the civil service. Siew Li was an aberration, but at the time it felt exhilarating, to be with people trying to change something outside of themselves. Mollie was standoffish at first. Then perhaps inevitably, they became friends. Siew Li took to coming earlier than announced, so by the time Jason emerged from his room, they were comfortably ensconced on the sofa, chattering away slightly too fast for him to follow. Siew Li assured him that she hadn't said one word about her ideology, not to worry, and Mollie claimed to be talking only about clothes and music, nothing embarrassing.

There was talk about Jason going away to university, to England, like all the other clever boys. He made it clear he'd rather be here, with Siew Li, and his parents were secretly relieved. Money was not as plentiful as it had been—the Japanese had run their factory into the ground during the occupation, and it was a struggle to get the business back on an even footing. His father was certain he did not want his son to take over the company—it was a lamed creature, and besides, his child was destined for better things than trade.

In the end only Siew Li's name became a sticking point. His mother addressed her variously as Sue and Sally, only trying to wrap her tongue around the flat Chinese syllables after Jason put his foot down. "Hurry up and get married," she finally said. "Then I can just call her daughter."

•

They did get married, and had the twins. Jason tries to remember this as a happy time, but with the distance of years it is overshadowed by what came next. There must have been a good few months, maybe as long as a couple of years, when everything proceeded as it should. Janet has left a selection of old family pictures by the hospital bed, in the apparent belief that this will make him forget how they have fallen apart since, and Jason cannot recognise himself in them. He sees a painfully young man, awkward, bespectacled, hair carefully slicked down. Beside him is a girl, her eyes fierce. They each have a baby in their arms.

He would like to have a period of time to cling onto as purely good—but is he just fooling himself? He knows the tragedy of happiness is that you often don't recognise it till it's gone, but surely never having had it in the first place is worse? When he thinks of himself as a young man, a young father, it feels hollow, tainted.

At the time it was pleasant enough, coming home and hearing about Siew Li's day, kissing the twins, marvelling at how they changed. There was so much to do, it seemed, to keep the household running. Mollie visited often, even after she got married. Then she was pregnant, excited to have her baby meet its cousins.

The conversations of those days are now impossible to recover. He remembers them never fighting, the babies never being difficult. Surely that couldn't be? Siew Li had settled down, her radical days behind her, her English improving through regular use. She was still working for a union, but not agitating, just carrying out very sober contract negotiations. Which was fine, he was as staunch a supporter of workers' rights as the next man. She got wrapped up in politics, campaigning during the election, but this was supposed to be a democracy after all, and it wasn't like she was standing for office herself.

His father was in the process of winding down the family business. It was too labour-intensive, having roomfuls of women hand-stitching beads onto dresses. The modern taste was for imported frocks, cheaply machine-sewn printed fabrics. The fast girls around town, the ones who read the European fashion magazines, all knew what they wanted— the New Look. Modernity; soft, clean lines; subtle luxury after the dull, discoloured war years. No one wanted to take on the business, so eventually they sold off the premises and got what they could. There was enough money for his parents to live off, but not much more.

When Siew Li departed, his parents' mouths clamped shut. The effort not to say I-told-you-so was visible in their clenched jaws, and he knew he could rely on them for dutiful support, but nothing else. They would take care of the twins while he was at work. They would not tell him he hadn't been foolish, that loving Siew Li hadn't been a mistake. At first they tried to introduce him to other girls from good families, but he tartly reminded them he was still married, and they backed away.

It was an awful day. He'd had a frantic phone call at work to say Siew Li had gone out with a friend and never come back. He'd rushed home to find Mollie in tears, the children howling. They turned on the radio and heard there'd been more arrests, though when they went to the station, the police swore they didn't know anything. "We wouldn't mind speaking to her, though. Let us know if you see her," said a sergeant, and he thought *like hell, like hell I'll turn her over to you.*

Yet she was gone, and so was that other woman, Lina. Their office was locked up tight, and no one knew anything. He felt implacable rage, unfairly, that she should be able to just disappear like that. He was stuck here, there was nowhere he could vanish to. All of them, with their grand plans. They'd stolen her, and she'd let herself be taken. Why hadn't he been enough for her?

The next weeks were unbearable. He showed up at work, but sat in meetings glowering into empty air. His boss didn't have the authority to send him home, and so put him on filing duties instead. This just fed his bottomless rage. Relegated to busywork, as if he were already useless! He'd had their future planned out, their fortunes set to rise along with the new country's. All she'd had to do was play along. Was even that beyond her?

After work, he'd stop off at the kopitiam for a consoling bottle of beer or two, then show up to collect the kids late, eyes bloodshot. One time, he showed up after ten, and his mum said, kindly but firmly, "You might as well leave them here, you'll just be dropping them off again in a few hours." This was the closest she'd come to a rebuke. "Why not just let us take care of them until you can cope again?"

Some weeks later, Mollie showed up at his flat. Without

saying anything, she opened all the windows wide, found a broom and dishcloth, and started meticulously cleaning the place. He watched her from the sofa, a detached part of his brain noticing how hard she had to scour the grime. It hadn't taken long to get ingrained. She drank from the tap, lapping like a cat, but otherwise took no breaks until the place was set to rights, grunting a little when she had to bend or stretch. He shouldn't let a pregnant woman pick up after him, he thought, but couldn't make himself move. She didn't ask him where anything belonged, and he wouldn't have known anyway. It was all Siew Li's system.

Three hours after she'd arrived, she flopped down next to him. He wondered if he should thank her, or if she was angry with him. *This isn't fair,* he thought. *I'm the one left behind.*

"This won't do," she finally said. He turned to look at her, but no response seemed possible. "Did you have dinner?"

"I don't know. Probably not."

She rolled her eyes, stomped into the kitchen, and came back with a slice of white bread thickly spread with strawberry jam, right up to the edges. "Eat."

He took a cautious bite. She'd toasted the bread just a little, so it had a faint crunch but remained pale. It was delicious. He was famished, he realised. While he chewed, she went back to the kitchen to get him a glass of water.

"What's going to happen?" He didn't realise he'd said anything till, belatedly, he heard the words leave his mouth.

"I can't tell you that." Mollie smoothed her skirt. "Maybe she'll come back, or maybe she won't be able to. Siew Li's a good person. She didn't look like she planned to leave with Lina. Didn't even take anything with her. Something must have happened, suddenly. She must have had her reasons. I don't think we ever knew her, really."

"Obviously I did, I think I knew my own wife."

"This isn't school. You don't need to have all the answers."

He sank back against the cushions. She took his empty plate and glass into the kitchen, came back and stood staring at him from across the coffee table.

"I'm not here to say the obvious things. You've already heard them from Ma and Dad. Be strong for the children. You'll find someone else. I mean, it's all true, sort of, but I know it's not helpful. And maybe you won't find someone else."

"Thanks, thanks."

"Well, you might not want anyone else, I don't know. If Barnaby got run over by a bus tomorrow—he might, he's terrible at crossing roads—I'd be sad, but I'd keep going. For Stella."

"Stella?"

"The baby. It's a girl; I've decided. I'd probably marry another guy eventually, because they're useful to have around, but in the meantime I'd just keep going."

"So I should just keep going? Excellent advice."

"You don't have to listen to me if you don't want to, and I can't really help. You're in pain. It might never stop hurting. But try to let her go. Forgive her, if you can. For your own sake. I know it's not easy, but if you possibly can, I wish you would."

He nodded, suddenly feeling very tired. Mollie was a good person. Would he ever have her moral certainty?

After that conversation, she never brought any of this up again, but was simply there, never stepping away. For so much of his life, she'd been his annoying little sister. Now he knew her quiet presence was loyalty.

Siew Li's letters started coming, all addressed to the children, not a single one to him. As if he'd never existed. He read them anyway, every word, saw the pictures of her in her new life. It was as Mollie said, she'd been forced to flee. Still, he couldn't forgive her the abandonment. Was this unfair? He couldn't stop feeling that if she'd done something different—he couldn't say what—they'd still be together.

His life shrunk to a tiny point. No one at work had ever been particularly friendly with him, and now it was worse. He wasn't a pariah exactly, but the situation was strange enough that no one quite knew what to say. It was the same meeting old classmates—Siew Li's name had been in the papers, and everyone knew she was a fugitive. One chap made a joke about Communist honeypots, and Jason almost bit his head off. They sought him out less after that.

So there was just Mollie. The bank wasn't far from his office—she'd call now and then to say she was downstairs, come out and have some lunch. After work, she'd come round with packets of food, knowing he'd probably not bother eating otherwise. They'd eat in warm silence, then sit on the sofa listening to the radio, or else she'd play with the children as he watched, easier with them than he would

ever be. She saved him, in those first two years after Siew Li.
Having her there was an anchor. Who knew where he'd have
drifted to otherwise? And if she'd been around longer—

Here again the endless circles of thought: if Siew Li hadn't
left, if Mollie hadn't insisted on staying at her job, if Barnaby
had been enough of a man to stop her, if the Indonesians
had chosen another building—all the decisions, big and
small, that could have saved him if any one of them had been
different. All those years like a dark corridor growing steadily
narrower, returning to Mollie's death, the point at which the
last fragment of his self fell apart, the moment he gave up
hope of ever being whole again.

•

In the sickly light of the false dawn, Jason uses his fingers
to count off the events leading up to MacDonald House.
He knows them all so well; they glide through his mind like
rosary beads.

The first bomb went off at Katong Park, on 24 September
1963, a day after the Malaysian Federation was formed.
Marine commandos landed with instructions to destroy the
Britannia Club on Beach Road, but found too many people
in the building to work unobserved. Unwilling to leave
without accomplishing anything, they walked to the park
where they blew up the first car they encountered.

The next incident was at Vaughan Road, a little before
Christmas. Others followed, so many that they came to seem

commonplace. An explosion at Meyer Road shattered all the windows of the Ambassador Hotel, and a year later another caused minor damage to the Raffles Hotel. In between, there were false alarms, mistaken reports of troop landings all over the peninsula, rumours of commandos parachuting in and blanketing the east coast.

It was like a game, at first—long enough after the war for people to enjoy the whiff of danger. ("It feels like living in a novel. A thriller," said Mollie, when the news first broke. She was fascinated by the whole affair.) Yet despite the new safety measures, life had to continue for the economy to keep growing. There was so much money to be made in this new country, dazzling new buildings and wide roads funded by the ships that streamed in and out of the harbour, the planeloads of brightly-clothed visitors with full wallets. The Tourist Board waited with impatience for the British to withdraw so their military base, already surrounded by every imaginable security feature, could be turned into a fine new airport. (And Jason was busy, in his corner office, completing the paperwork for these transformations.)

The merciful thing about this time was that no foreigners were killed. With no resources to speak of, none of the rubber and tin that fuelled Malaysia, none of the oil which sent Brunei into its careless spendthrift decline, Singapore depended on its fledgling hospitality industry. This was a different Singapore, an island of white beaches and coconut trees. MacDonald House, constructed in 1946 by Palmer & Turner, was the first large office building of the post-war era, one of the tallest on the island. Perhaps its very prominence made it a target for the saboteurs who didn't know the island at all, and so headed with their fatal cargo for the bank that stood out proud and red against the grey storm clouds.

More than forty bombs in a year and a half, but the one most people remember even now was at MacDonald House. This explosion was surprising not for the mere fact that it happened, but for the success and efficiency with which it was brought off. True, had detonation been delayed ten minutes, a score of mechanics from the workshop next door would have been enjoying their coffee break in the alleyway beside the bank; and true, the culprits made a particularly amateurish job of covering their tracks (and they were killed for it, and Jason waited outside the prison for their deaths). But people had died and property was damaged, and that was seen as evidence that the conflict was deepening.

Konfrontasi was drearily familiar, after the real war with the Japanese and the false war of the Emergency; they were once again in an unreliable world. Bubbling through the murk of Indonesia's foreign policy came the idea that the new Malayan Federation would be dangerous, that it was a contrived creation of neo-colonial forces, the nekolim.

Sukarno was in charge, having reclaimed his country from the Dutch. He filled his country with a giddy unreality, a sense that there were no boundaries for them. He proclaimed *Tahun vivere pericoloso*, the year of living dangerously. At a public rally he shouted, "To hell with your aid," his voice resonating with justified anger, his audience roaring with him. It was just before monsoon season, the air chokingly hot. The crowd heaved, gilded with sunburn, cheering when Sukarno proclaimed he was tired of busybodies telling him how to run the country. Where had it got them? Their money was hardly worth anything, he shouted, flinging fistfuls of rupiah over the crowd.

They'd burnt their bridges now. Having seen off the white men, they turned their attention to their Asian neighbours. Some said Sukarno simply wanted to distract his citizens from their own problems, their hunger, their children not in school. Others thought it was the Federation who induced it, needing this external threat to shore up a shaky alliance. It was a time for grand adventures. No one could afford a proper war, it was far too soon after the last one. The small skirmishes and localised terror kept everyone on their toes.

In the end everything fell apart anyway. The alliance failed, and Singapore was ejected from Malaysia on 9 August 1965, and was admitted into the UN a month later—Indonesia having resigned at the start of the year in a fit of pique. Konfrontasi ended six months after that when General Suharto seized power from Sukarno in a bloodless coup. There were no more bombs for a long time after that, and soon no one remembered the excitements of those years except the families of the dead. (Mollie. Oh, Mollie.)

•

Madam Ngoh dies sometime in his sixth week of

hospitalisation, or perhaps the seventh. He has stopped keeping track. If he leaves, there will be plenty of time to find out where in the year he is. If not, it won't matter. Although he hardly spoke to Madam Ngoh, he finds himself missing her intensely. She was here when he arrived, and they have devised little rituals. A nod first thing in the morning, a private smile when lunch is particularly inedible. He knew she was gone halfway through the night, when her breathing stopped, without warning, no slowing down. One minute she was rattling in and wheezing out, just like always, and the next a terrible silence.

The nurses are, as always, kind but uninformative. *We can't tell you anything, Mr Low,* they coo. *You aren't her family. But isn't it sweet that you care, Mr Low. We'll be sure to pass on your condolences.*

He cannot get used to this changing roster of staff. There are too many nurses, some of them foreign and difficult to understand. The doctors are all young, and often look tired. None of them have time to listen to him, not when it takes him such a while to get the words out. It isn't his fault, he used to be very good with language—all his teachers at school were British, Oxbridge-educated, and when he drafted letters for his English superiors, they never failed to tell him how superb his phrasing was. *You might be one of us,* they said.

When Janet arrives, he tries to explain why he is upset. She gives the appearance of listening to him while staring into her compact mirror, retouching her make-up in short, angry strokes. Her cheeks are beginning to look gaunt, he notices.

"She wasn't really your friend," says Janet, before he has finished. "It's Stockholm syndrome."

"She was company."

"I'm company. I come every day. Why don't you just make some new friends?"

"They never stay long enough."

"How long do you want to stay here?"

And then they are silent, trying to pretend she has not asked how much longer he intends to live. She puts away her lipstick and roots around in her handbag. Unexpectedly, her hand emerges with a tangle of wool, which shakes out into the beginnings of a scarf.

"Knitting," she explains unnecessarily, slightly embarrassed. "Like an old woman, I know."

"It's good to have a hobby. Your mother used to sew." Although not in an arts and crafts way, he wants to add. Just to survive, just to have clothes for the baby. *For you*. There is a cloud of words he cannot fight through—he just wants to say her name, Siew Li.

Janet seems to feel something of this. "You never talk about her."

"There's nothing to say."

It is his standard response, and shuts the conversation down. Janet is used to this, and does not push. Perhaps she is glad—both she and Henry spent their childhoods asking about their mother, who was not dead, but not there either. Their questions met with evasion, and then rage. Now that they have established a routine, an unbreakable silence, Janet seems happy to accept what cannot be known. Perhaps she has her own secrets.

"She sent letters, didn't she? Those ones with the Malaysian stamps. We worked out later they must be from her."

So they knew. He thought he'd been so clever. "What does it matter now?"

"I wanted to ask you, but Henry wouldn't let me. We were so scared of you."

"I suppose I'm less scary now." What has he done to them?

"What did she write to you about?"

"I burnt them. I can't remember." He genuinely can't. Where are they? He can't bear to think how she pleaded, how he couldn't forgive her. If they're in the house, Janet will find them, or Henry. It doesn't matter. He feels this, too, slip from him.

Janet knits, her needles clacking gently. She must be making a present for her brother, he realises. No one in Singapore would need a woollen scarf. It is dark blue, almost black, with splashes of light through it.

"Has Henry—" He does not know how to continue. "Your brother, is he—"

"He's booked his plane ticket. I've got the dates written down. You'll see him soon."

"Is he happy?"

"You think I'd know that, just because we're twins? Some sort of sixth sense?"

"I thought you might have talked."

"You phone him more often than I do. I suppose he's

happy. Why wouldn't he be? He has everything he wants."
The needles are made of bamboo, and sound like chopsticks
when they click together.

They sit for a while more. He cannot say how long, his
sense of time has become totally untethered. He closes his
eyes for a moment and is no longer sure if this is the same
visit, or the next day. Janet's scarf seems to be progressing at
an impressive rate. If only there were a view in this room—the
window opens into an airwell, making it impossible to tell the
time of day from the quality of the light. He feels he should
say something, but the words seem to be going altogether. He
imagines them leaving his mind, one at a time, as they have
been steadily. Goodbye, meaning. Goodbye, thought.

Janet glances at her watch, and pulls *The Daily Bread*
out of her bag. "Almost time," she says, and reads the lesson
for that day. As usual, it consists of a few verses from the
Bible, then an anecdote translating them into a modern day
parable. It is always the impatient businessman, the arrogant
politician, ultimately humbled by the might of God.

When she has finished, she waits for a few seconds, what
she considers a contemplative pause. She does not expect
her father to respond, but feels she must give him the
opportunity. Perhaps he is praying. His body is completely
still, his eyes shut. After a while, she realises he has died, and
goes to fetch the doctor.

2

When they were newly married and acquaintances asked how they'd met, Siew Li and Jason would smile and say something non-committal about being at the same school event many years back. How fortunate, with her from a Chinese-speaking background and him virtually monolingual in the Queen's English; they inhabited such different worlds that if not for this one chance meeting, they might have gone their whole lives without encountering each other. What a loss that would have been, Jason would say, his hand possessively over his wife's. After the children were born, they discussed how much to tell them, but with no real urgency. The story would work itself out.

Later still, after all that was over, Siew Li had a lot of time to think about that meeting. About how much of her life, for all that it seemed chosen, had been determined by single moments of chance. If she'd stood in a different spot that day, Jason would never have seen her. If she'd gone home early like her mum had told her, Lina would never have spoken to her. And what would have happened to her life then? The Party told her that society would have to break free of its chains, that man's enslavement of man would inevitably have to end. Yet deep down, she didn't understand how they could be that certain about anything, when so much came down to happenstance.

Towards the end of her life, she wrote these thoughts down in rambling letters, sometimes on paper, sometimes only in her head, addressed to both her children. The beginning was always the same: *I hope you are healthy, I hope you are safe, I hope you have not been taught to hate me. Even if you have, try to understand. I made the decisions that seemed right, though at the time it didn't feel like there were decisions to be made, that there was only ever one course of action. I must write in Chinese. If you ever see these words, would you even understand them?*

Just before their 15th birthday, which she wouldn't live to see, she told them again about that first conversation with Lina. They'd heard this before, if they were getting these messages, but she wanted them to think about where they were now, at this age, and where she had been then. Perhaps that would help them to understand. Or perhaps not—and perhaps that was better. Part of her hoped they were doing so well, that they would never be able to see the world through her eyes.

At the age of 14, Siew Li was old enough to ignore her mum's instructions to come home early, and was wandering around Happy World on her own when Lina came up to her.

Lina was one of the older girls from school, taller and more popular than Siew Li would ever be. One time, she'd been in the bathroom when Lina walked in, and even though it was crowded, the girls parted at once, quietly stepping aside for Lina to walk up to the mirrors, which she did without so much as a glance at the bodies around her.

"Hey, you, I want to talk to you." Lina said, by way of greeting.

Siew Li was still young enough for this to be momentous, an older girl singling her out, but she decided to play it cool, nodding mutely in acknowledgement without looking too awestruck.

"Isn't it past your bedtime?"

"I'm not a child," Siew Li muttered.

"Just joking, don't be so sensitive." Lina took a bite of *lok-lok*, little fried things on a stick.

Uncertain if laughing was the right thing to do, she said nothing.

Lina grinned. "Hey, if you're not doing anything, come on the ghost train. I'll pay."

Siew Li hesitated, and Lina abruptly swung round. "Boo!" She jumped. "Unless you're scared."

"No. I mean, I'll come." It was a bit sad of her to be wandering around the amusement park alone, she thought. Better to be with someone. Then again, wasn't Lina also alone?

"My friends abandoned me," said Lina conversationally, popping the last *lok-lok* into her mouth and tossing the bamboo skewer in a bin. "Stupid idiots, said they were going home to sleep, but I think they're secretly meeting boyfriends or something. Hey, you ready?"

The other people in the queue for the ghost train didn't actually look scared. Most of them were couples, presumably wanting to be alone in the dark. Still, Siew Li felt a faint tickle of apprehension as the dumpy ticket collector lethargically took their little slips of paper and waved them on into the dark. They hunched into their allocated box, knees beneath the safety bar. The cars were spaced out enough that they couldn't see anyone else, just an eerie silence as they sat in the gloom, waiting to set out.

"Try not to wet yourself," said Lina cheerfully as the rails clicked and they started moving. A quick ratchety climb, then a plunge fast enough to make both girls gasp. Halfway down, a hanging corpse plopped in front of them, dangling obscenely. Lina screamed with gusto, apparently in enjoyment. They plummeted towards its gruesome grin, which whisked out of their way just in time.

"By the way," said Lina at the next level stretch, "You know we need people for the organising committee, right? I didn't see your name on the sign-up sheet. How come?"

Siew Li gaped at her. "Yes, I know who you are," said Lina, reading her mind. "You think just because we never talked, I don't know? People are always pointing out to me— that Form Two girl, Siew Li, very smart, top of every exam, but keeps to herself. And I thought, how come someone like that isn't helping to make things happen? That's the sort of person we need in the movement."

Siew Li managed to nod without turning her head, but before she could say anything, a severed arm trailed its fingers along her shoulder, and cobweb strands wrapped themselves around her face. "Just think about it," said Lina's steady voice, and they were falling again, into velvety darkness that absorbed them without a sound.

●

For the first part of her life, Siew Li only knew progress. Admittedly, she was born during the war, which was a fairly low baseline—her earliest memories were of constant discomfort. Her mother didn't like to talk about it afterwards, so she had to put the fragments together herself—a man, probably her father, running into the rubber plantation with her on his back when they heard the airplanes coming, only returning when the bombing stopped; the neighbours fighting over rations, hollow cheeks and the bow-legged walk of malnourishment creeping over everyone. She was four when the Occupation ended, so there was no context for any of these shards, just a sense that things had been terrible and then they got better, not only in concrete ways but also the sense of lightness, as if everyone had been holding their breath all this time and suddenly they had all the air they needed.

It took her a while to realise her father wasn't coming back. He'd gone away with the Japanese one day, and even after everything was back to what she assumed was normal, he didn't show up. Her mum just cried when she asked, and one time slapped her, though she was sorry afterwards. Anyway, Siew Li learnt not to ask.

The only thing she knew for sure was that the Party had been the only one fighting back. Later, when she saw photos of the British being taken prisoner, the straggly line of pallid men and women being marched east to Changi, she was struck by how ineffectual they looked, how easily they must have toppled as soon as they were challenged. By contrast, the Ma Gong, the Communists, were stealthy, operating in the cover of the jungle. No one knew how many of them there were, only that they were the one force the enemy still feared. And after the surrender, in the three weeks it took the British to return, they were the ones who kept order. The British stayed for a long time after that, trying to pretend the last few years hadn't happened, or that they'd been a mistake and this was the natural order reasserting itself. Some people went along with it, but mostly it seemed clear they were on their way out.

That was her childhood understanding, which she saw nothing to challenge as she got older. These were the agreed-upon facts on Kreta Ayer Road, where everyone spoke Chinese in one dialect or another, and the doings of the English elite seemed to come from a great distance away. One or two people they knew were trying to cram their children full of the foreign language, so they could go to the schools with fancy ang moh names and maybe get into the civil service, but that seemed incomprehensible to most right-thinking people—not just because the British surely couldn't be around much longer, but also who would want to raise kids unable to speak to their parents?

Siew Li's mother was glad her daughter was young enough that her schooling hadn't been touched by the war, unlike those in their late teens or as old as twenty only now returning to the classroom. Even better, Siew Li hadn't been forced to learn Japanese, the occupier's language. *So why would I want her to learn English now*, she was fond of saying, *wouldn't that be just the same?* She only had a primary school education herself, and was determined that her daughter would do better. She pushed Siew Li to study hard, to come back early and go over her homework instead of playing zero point with the other girls in the alleyway. Even when Siew Li's books passed the point her mother could understand them, she was happy just to see her daughter staring hard at them, making marks with her pencil.

When Siew Li got into Nanyang Girls', her mother was nothing as demonstrative as thrilled, just quietly proud. The very best school, in her eyes. Those crisp white uniforms. All that history. There'd been that unpleasant incident when some students flung acid in their principal's face, but there are bad apples in every community, and they probably did sincerely believe she was a government stooge. The years after the war were rough for everyone, and things seemed to be calming down. She thought her daughter would be all right.

For her own part, Siew Li was happy enough to be in a good school—or rather, not having a clue what one school meant over another, she was happy that her mum was pleased.

It was a long bus ride to King's Road, but she enjoyed those stretches of time, nothing to do but read till she got carsick, then stare out the window without taking in anything in particular. She didn't have many friends—too many of the girls felt like they were from a different world, from the big houses around Bukit Timah, with their businessman dads and *tai-tai* mothers. Even the ones with less money, like her, seemed somehow sharper, as if they knew things about the world she did not. On her first day at school, she'd tried to talk to the girl at the next desk, but then the conversation had turned to popular music. "You haven't heard of Yao Lee?" sneered the girl. "You must be really stupid." That pretty much set the tone for her life at this school, which was why she knew no one and was wandering round Happy World on her own.

It wasn't that she needed friends, as that she wanted to be a part of this thing that was happening. She had a sense of something big coming, a huge shift in the way the world was ordered, made possible by the chaos of war. Her childhood fantasies had been of heroism. If only she'd been old enough, during the war, what wouldn't she have done! Withstood torture, like Elizabeth Choy or Sybil Kathigasu. Gone into the jungle and waged guerrilla warfare, like those brave people in Force 136 and others whose names would never be known. She learnt all the stories.

Only now was it striking her that she was in her own time, the only vantage point she had. She knew what was happening around her, had even been present at the May

Thirteenth incident, so many of them gathered to support the boys taking a stance against the government, which was conscripting them without taking into account that their education would be interrupted. The police had turned violent without provocation, and she had no doubt that the government saw people like them as worth less, if not worthless. It was important to fight back. What was she actually doing?

It was easy to stay in a cocoon, unless someone sliced you free. And if this happened at the right moment, you emerged fully fledged, a new being. The first tug at the silk thread, the first unravelling, came when Lina spoke to her that night at Happy World.

•

The ride couldn't be all that long—there was only so far to go, even looping round themselves, in a space this small—but she felt herself losing her sense of time and movement in the dark. "I mean, what do you want to do with yourself?" came Lina's voice. "Learn shorthand and become a typist or something? Some other boring job?"

Siew Li bit back a smart-aleck retort and muttered something about not knowing what else to do, needing to support her mum, uncertain times.

"That's the point." A skeleton did a quick jig in front of them, unhinged its jaw and raised a jerky arm as if about to eat it. "The world is changing, can't you feel it? Of course nothing is certain. We need to keep up the pressure, otherwise it's too easy for the people in charge to forget we exist. Which side of history do you want to be on?"

"You make it sound so easy."

"Isn't it? Once you know the right thing to do, what else is there to think about?"

"Not everyone thinks this is right."

"They're too used to the wrong situation. Until now, it's been the British in charge, and the ones who try to be like them. But this isn't their country. They say we should be grateful, but for what? Being exploited? They weren't trying to help us, they came here to steal from us. They need us. Their country is so much smaller—"

"Smaller than Singapore?" interrupted Siew Li, whose grasp of geography was shaky, though even she could tell this was unlikely. Still, the idea of Britain being a small country was irresistibly odd.

"Than China, of course. Maybe even Malaya." She sounded less certain about this last point, but pushed ahead. "They have power because they've taken so much from us. Look what's happening around you. White men saying this is their land and making us work on it for almost no money. It's time for us to fight back. And that's just the beginning— if the Chinese tycoons take over from them, that's no better. So they do a bit of charity work and put their name on a school, that's supposed to be enough? You know what a better world could look like. You know in your heart. Why not work to make it happen?"

Siew Li had heard some of this before, but it sounded different in Lina's voice, measured and reasonable even when shouted over the grating mechanical music of the ride. It all made a lot of sense. Of course the British should get out of Malaya—it wasn't their country, and they'd given up what moral claim they had by getting defeated in the war. Of course a system where people shared and everyone had enough was the right one. Why should some be rich while others didn't have enough to eat?

Above all, she wanted to be like Lina. Turning her head, she surreptitiously glanced at the older girl's profile. Such strength and determination. She thought of the British people she'd seen, their weak chins and watery eyes. Why had her country ever thought these should be the people in charge?

They rounded a corner and suddenly were in hell. Paper flames licked at the sides of their carriage, and demons prodded sharp pitchforks at them. Siew Li smiled dreamily. None of this was remotely frightening, and seemed frivolous now. There was work to be done.

"What will I have to do?" she asked.

"Come to the study sessions, then we'll see. You have to learn proper thinking. When your mind is right, maybe you can be useful. Helping to organise. Passing messages, maybe even to the unions. You look about twelve, the police won't suspect you."

"The police?"

"Don't worry about it."

Before she could ask any more, there was a last burst of

spooky music and they were back in the open, rolling gently to a halt. In the bright glare of the carnival lights, it was momentarily hard to be sure what was real, whether that conversation had really taken place. Lina straightened her dress and strode to the nearest stall, where she bought two extravagant ice-cream cones with wafers and toppings. She handed one to Siew Li.

"Thank you."

"Don't thank me, just say you'll do it."

"You know I will."

"And read Mao Dun," added Lina. "Not the books they tell you to. Here. You can borrow one of mine." She pulled a tattered paperback from her satchel and handed it to Siew Li. "I wouldn't give it to you if I didn't think you were ready for these ideas. It's not safe."

This was the first time Siew Li had heard of a book being dangerous. "Why did you ask me?"

"To the ghost train? You were there. I didn't feel like going alone."

"No, to join you."

"We need people with brains. I was like you once, looking from the outside, too scared to take one more step. So here you are. I'm pulling in."

"Oh." Was it permission she'd been waiting for? Perhaps.

"I've seen you in the tuck shop, always sitting by yourself. You don't have any friends because you're too serious. Always thinking. Worrying. That's okay, we need serious people."

"I thought maybe you took me on the ghost train to tell

me all this without being overheard."

"Who's listening? I just like rides." Lina tossed her hair and started walking towards the exit. Siew Li scurried to keep up. "Tell you what, though. It's good to know you're not easily scared."

•

It went very smoothly after that, as if the movement was where she'd been meant to be all along, and she'd just needed a switch to flick in her head. To start with, she was happy with the occasional approving nod from Lina, then that became less important. Being on the inside felt not just good, but right—the only place she could possibly be. Impossible to imagine the person she had been, drifting through the world with no thought for anything but her schoolwork and her mum, gliding through each day without looking beyond her immediate surroundings. How could she have been so unaware?

She still wasn't sure what made Lina single her out, but to be honest she'd previously attended events because all her classmates were going, or it looked like there might be some excitement to be had. The idea of actually making a difference hadn't occurred to her. Now she was becoming enlightened, there was real fervour behind her chants. There was history behind what they were doing—they were part of a chain of progress, every link of which was vital.

Already, amongst her comrades, there was a sense of

having missed out on the headiest times. If they'd been a decade older, they would have joined Force 136 or the MPAJA, the guerrilla resistance against the Japanese; they would have gone to China to be part of the struggle, and shared in the glory of 1949. Things seemed grubbier now, less clear. It was easy to sit in a stadium as some firebrand flung strong words about, and to feel righteous and cleansed. But what good did that actually do? She listened to Lim Chin Siong, so stirring and strong. He'd been expelled for the exam boycott he organised; sitting there in her school uniform, Siew Li felt indicted, as if she'd never taken a real risk. They were under a state of emergency, and the National Service Act had been put in place just a couple of years ago, to co-opt their young men into fighting their brothers and sisters. With all this happening, how had she ever thought it was all right to be passive?

Now she was listening for it, she could hear there was also something in the air, the possibility that this was a crucible, and everything the nation could become was here in this moment. Lina was right. War had levelled everything, and here was a chance to blaze through the world and make it fair again. So much of this was obvious—of course workers ought to own the means of production, of course it was wrong that the people who did the actual labour were least likely to enjoy the fruits. She understood now, that her life had been an exercise in false consciousness. When her mum told her to be grateful for what they had, she now knew this to be propaganda spread by the ruling classes to keep the masses down. What was gratitude but complacency and quiescence? It was imperative to demand more.

She started writing pamphlets. So much of what she read was from China, and society here was different. Using local examples would surely do more to convince the Malayan people of these ideas. The things she said seemed obvious to her, and it was always startling how strongly her comrades responded. She could never put her name to these essays, which had to be copied and distributed in secret, but it was still amazing to think of her words spreading like that.

During their June holidays that year, she convinced the rest of the leadership to try the life of a worker. Didn't they want to experience the dignity of labour for themselves? How else could they truly understand the conditions they were striving to improve? Besides, they needed to be humble, otherwise there would be nothing setting them apart from the English school elites. She'd read *Animal Farm*, and knew the main thing in any movement was not to turn into the pigs.

She and a few others got jobs at a construction site by the simple expedient of lying about their ages. The supervisor didn't care, as long as they got the job done. It was shockingly simple—no thought at all required, just do as you're told, move the bricks from this pile over there, mix this batch of mortar quickly and get it to the bricklayers before it starts to set. The girls were expected to work as hard as the boys, which Siew Li approved of, even if by the end of the first day she felt like her arms would never stop hurting. And what glory there was in good, honest work. She came home each day exhausted and sunburnt, her mother hovering anxiously and offering to just give her the money. But of course the wages were hardly the point—in fact, they came to almost nothing, just a few coins at the end of each shift. The iced drink vendors at the end of the lane were irresistible after so much thirsty work, and Siew Li ended up handing over her hard-earned cash for a clear plastic bag of Pepsi-Cola, invigorated and refreshed by the cool, dark fluid. Instant relief. *You're spoilt*, she told herself sternly—if the real workers could see how frivolously she threw around her day's earnings, what would they think? Yet by the time school started again, she had to guiltily admit that she'd spent every cent she'd earned, and there was nothing left at all.

•

Her first meeting with Jason was like something from a play—though not one of their educational plays, which would have had her falling for him only to be thoroughly betrayed. Real life was more complex, and she trusted her own senses that the boy she was spending time with was funny and clever, and she felt good when she was with him. Not false-consciousness good, actually comfortable and happy. He just clicked into place next to her, and even when they argued—which was often, seeing as each hated the other's friends—it still felt like they were on the same side.

Even after she'd been forced to abandon him, she clung tight to the memory of that first instant. The scene was dramatic enough, scores of students in uniform alongside the workers, at the gates of the Hock Lee Company—which had refused to allow its employees to join the Bus Drivers Union. When they barricaded the bus routes in protest, the company had called in the police to disperse them. She'd been one of the main student organisers, working fast to pull together support and reinforcements. It was crucial to let the bosses know they wouldn't get away with this, and to force the government to come down on one side or the other, so people could see exactly what they stood for.

It had been a good day. They'd linked arms and sung defiant songs, and never before had that line in the "Internationale" about hot blood surging through their chests felt so strong, so true. More than one worker had gruffly thumped Siew Li on the back and said it was youngsters like her who would make the difference, that their future was in her hands. She felt the responsibility of it, and replied gravely that she was honoured to play her part. Who could stand by at such a time?

She'd broken away for a moment, and was fishing in her bag for her water bottle when she spotted him wandering by, in school uniform but nonetheless a different species from the rest of them. It was hard to explain how exactly she could tell—the strut of his walk, maybe, or the irony in his smile. "What's going on?" he called.

"You know what's going on," she said. No time for this.

"Yup, saw it in the papers, came to see what's happening."

"Join us?"

"I don't think I will, thanks." His Chinese was stiff, as if he'd never actually had a conversation in the language. Typical Raffles boy. She switched to English for his benefit, never mind how awkward she found it. Let him see how hard it was for her, having to live in the world of white men's words.

He was curious, so he'd come to have a look. She was torn between admiration and disgust. To be so detached, like this was nothing more than spectacle. And yet, to step inside, rather than pretending they didn't exist like most of his fellows—that was something. He was called Jason, he told her, like the leader of the Argonauts. She didn't pretend to know what that was, and he said he'd tell her another time. His hair was long, almost foppish, and kept falling into his eyes. She resisted the urge to brush it back. He offered his hand, and when she took it, held on a second too long.

"Be careful." She nodded at the police, massing a short way off. "They might not be able to tell the difference between you and us. You don't want to get arrested, do you?"

"It might be fun," he said, grinning. But she noticed he took a careful couple of steps back. Then someone flung a bottle and there was a lot of shouting. She quickly pulled her scarf across her face, before they could start with the tear gas. He disappeared, like evaporating steam, while her attention was elsewhere. Good self-preservation, she thought. And yet, the spot where he'd touched her felt warm, and there was a softness in her stomach that didn't bode well.

The unrest went on for three days, with quite a few injuries. Some of the leaders were arrested and charged with rioting. It was increasingly easy for people to get scooped up by the authorities, so this was nothing new. If they couldn't find anything to charge you with, they could simply hold you as long as they liked. Just detention, no trial.

And that might have been it, except he came looking for her. She came out of class to a flood of murmuring and giggling, the cause of which was apparent when she got to the gates—in defiance of the caretaker, who kept trying to shoo him away, Jason was on the pavement outside with an enormous bunch of flowers. Chrysanthemums, as if this were a funeral, but he wasn't to know. She smiled at him, but kept on walking. He showed up again the next day, and on the third day she agreed to go out with him. She could feel the warmth radiating off his body, the animal energy that called to something in her blood. As soon as the cinema lights dimmed, their lips were pressed together, and afterwards neither of them could have told you the plot of the picture.

She kept seeing him, lying to her mum and calling from phone boxes, but was too smart to let a boy distract her—either from her studies or the movement. They had more than ever to do, as the British prepared to leave. There were more than two hundred protests in 1955. They were doing important work, keeping the pressure up on the people in charge.

The previous Chief Minister stepped down and was replaced by a man who took a hard line on the movement. "A running dog," sneered Lina. "He just wants to keep the white men happy. What's the point of independence, if we're just going to be under people like him?" Siew Li tried to understand what was happening at the higher levels, but it felt like too many conversations were happening behind closed doors, the British speaking to the elite they'd educated, who were always flying off to London for talks there. Even without seeing through the currents of power, it was clear that the situation was about to get a lot harder for them.

Sure enough, the following September, the Chinese Middle School Students Union was disbanded by the authorities, and a short while after that, Siew Li and some others were detained.

•

She saw them from her window, swarming out of two cars parked just downstairs. All those men coming to get a schoolgirl, she thought, unless there's someone else in this block. But no, they were all hers. They seemed in no hurry, going through all her possessions, writing down the titles of books. "Read so much for what? Will Marx help you find a husband?" jeered one of them, even as he tilted the shelves to look behind them, as if there might be hidden messages there.

She stood by, calm, the light from her desk lamp striking her jaw at what she hoped was a dashing angle, her heroism spoiled by her mother, who would not stop sobbing. "Go next door to Auntie Wang, Ma," she called out more than once, but her mother refused to leave, pleading with the officers to let her off, her only daughter was all the family she had in the world, just a foolish girl who'd been led astray by her friends. She tried to shove things into Siew Li's hands, clothes or food. "They won't let me bring anything with me," she said impatiently, tears prickling annoyingly at her eyes.

Should she sing something? She wondered, as she was led from the flat. Something stirring, the "Internationale" perhaps, but she wasn't sure she'd be able to keep her voice steady, and opted instead for dignified silence. There was no one around, but she knew the neighbours were watching from dark windows. She was in a simple flowered dress, her hair just down over her shoulders. In hindsight, she wished she'd changed into something a little more formal.

The atmosphere in the car was almost jovial. The policemen laughed about what strange things people had in their flats, how scared this or that person had looked. "You not bad, right?" said one of them. "Still okay." She didn't deign to answer, just nodded a little and looked straight ahead, not wanting to give him the satisfaction. "Another late night," he said, jabbing her arm to make her meet his eyes. "Lucky you're the last one, otherwise I'd never see my kids."

At Central Police Station, she was brought into a small room and told to change into a uniform. Her things were put into a plain box and taken away from her. Something about the grubbiness of the room, its scuffed yellow walls and cheap wooden furniture, cut right through the shell of bravado. It started as softness beneath her feet, then a cold prickling from nowhere, and just like that she was terrified. She tried to pull herself together, to control her breath, but they were barking questions at her, and there was no chance to calm down. Whenever she paused to gather her wits, they shouted, "Answer! Are you thinking of a lie? We'll find out, you know."

This wasn't Hong Liniang going to the scaffold or the girl from Malacca facing the tiger, she realised. This wasn't going to play out like any of the stories in her books, the ones they told each other or acted out on stage. There was nothing to fight here, no brave stand to be taken. They would simply hold her here, and so many other comrades, until they'd all been forgotten. She thought of her neighbours. People didn't want heroes. They wanted a quiet life. What had she even been fighting for? She thought of all the causes, but none seemed so important that they should have landed her here.

It was one thing to be a martyr, to end up dead and glorious. How long would anyone remember her? She could be down here a very long time. For all she knew, that was the government's plan, to simply lock them all up out of sight until they slipped from people's minds.

Central Police Station didn't look particularly large from the outside, but beneath it was a warren of cells, grey concrete and stifling, a little larger than her bedroom at home. By the time they'd finished their interrogation, her body was soft and tired, and she could no longer be certain what she'd said to them. Had she given them something they could use against the cause? She hardly knew anything, she consoled herself, so it wasn't like there was much she could have divulged.

They left her in an almost empty cell, just a chair and a thin mattress on top of a cement slab. Still feeling hollow, she folded herself under the threadbare blanket, and even with the prickly sheet and sour-smelling pillow, not to mention the lights she had no way of turning off, she slipped into a profound sleep with no dreams, and woke feeling scrubbed clean, despite the sharp pain in her neck and the buzzing of the electric light.

She lay there for a while, trying to remember where she was, until it hit her. Never mind. Another day. There was no toilet in her cell; she had to knock on the door for the guard to come let her out and escort her down the corridor, then stand there the whole time she was inside. She tried to wash up as best she could, but didn't have a toothbrush and had to make do with rubbing a finger hard over her teeth. A couple of days later, she was moved to Outram Women's Prison.

Still, no one could explain why exactly she was there, or what would happen to her. The guards stared blankly if she asked anything. One snapped, "You should have thought of that before," no matter the question. Never mind, focus on surviving each day. She was able to piece together a sort of routine. Mostly, she was alone in the cell, her meals slid through the door on a metal tray—usually something grey and greasy, with too much salt in it. (A few weeks later, she stopped noticing, and by the time they let her out, she had acclimatised so much that normal food tasted overspiced, almost an assault.)

The only time she saw the other prisoners was during exercise time, an hour in the open yard with guards staring across at them, as if they might suddenly take it into their heads to scale the three-metre wall. It was all women here, just a handful of them—Lina and few others—though more trickled in over the coming months. They didn't know where the men were, elsewhere in this building or back at Central. Talking was only allowed if the wardens were in a good mood, so they had to communicate in patchy chunks. She knew all of them, anyway, at least by sight. Although they all believed passionately that women were every bit as capable as men, and didn't subscribe to feudal notions of patriarchy, the fact was that the movement's leadership was overwhelmingly male, and the few women in the top ranks tended to notice each other.

They traded what information they could, but there wasn't a lot to know—it seemed unlikely that the authorities themselves had much of a plan. There was no hurry, certainly, as far as the government was concerned—detention without trial had no timeline on it, and the state of emergency justified anything. It had only been five years since the assassination of Sir Henry Gurney at Fraser's Hill, and it would have been a huge embarrassment if anything similar were to take place in Singapore. Better safe than sorry.

Still, the stoicism of her comrades put the heart back into Siew Li. They seemed almost happy to be there, gleeful to have got under the skin of important people. So what if they were missing school? There was no use receiving an education while the British were in charge—Chinese speakers like them would never be employed in the colonial system. Being here, having done what they did, would stand them in much better stead for what was to come, when a mighty wave passed over the land and swept away the white men. What impoverished minds those others had, the ones who could only imagine contorting themselves to fit in rather than smashing their confines.

For a while, some of them tried to continue their studies, Siew Li amongst them—if only for something to do. But it was too difficult—they were only allowed to have three books in their cells at a time, and she needed a dictionary to make sense of anything, then kept getting stuck on this or that point, not being able to look it up anywhere because she'd used up her allocation. Finally she gave up, and just read more Lu Xun, which felt more familiar and comfortable, anyway.

They had a visit from a lawyer, a young chap who wasted no time telling them he'd been to Cambridge. He greeted them in halting Chinese and said something about how he hoped they were holding up, then switched to English and barrelled along, as if daring them to keep up—a lot of nice-sounding words about getting rid of the British and standing up for the students. "But what can you actually do, when they can hold us as long as they like without evidence?" said Lay Kuan, and a frown appeared on the lawyer's otherwise confident brow. "We're doing what we can," he said smoothly.

Lay Kuan was the natural leader of the group—a little older than the others, she'd already finished school and was mostly involved with the student union in an advisory capacity. She was the one who'd spoken to the warden and got them allowed books, and had even negotiated for them to receive newspapers (always a day late, though, and with certain articles snipped out). When she could, Siew Li tried to get close to her, wanting to learn her poise and intelligence, which made Lina's toughness seem hollow. Crucially, Lay Kuan got things done. So many ways to be a person, thought Siew Li. She felt unformed, as if she could be any shape at all.

Most of the time, though, she was alone, and that was when the air pressed down on her, when grey fog filled her mind and she couldn't make herself do anything at all, not even sleep. The only thing that helped was if she looked at a picture in one of her books, preferably a landscape, and imagined herself amongst the trees and beneath the sky, staring until she could see herself there, walking calmly and steadily into the distance until she was out of view, leaving behind just the soft rustle of leaves and the gentle wind.

•

The first time Jason came to see her, she almost didn't recognise him, and then thought she'd been in there so long that her mind had finally given way to hallucinations. It was a visitation, as if there were an aura around him, his school uniform glowing against the grey concrete floor and gunmetal chairs. He smiled when he saw her, and it was like an open window, cool, fresh air filling her lungs.

There hadn't been many visitors. Her mum had come a couple of times, but just sat there crying, saying useless things over and over—*why couldn't you just stay out of trouble, why did you have to make such a fuss*—until Siew Li grew embarrassed and told her not to bother, this wasn't good for either of them. Now she just sent what she could, clothes and books from the titles Siew Li gave her. The leadership had all been taken, of course, and no one from lower down showed up for fear of guilt by association. She couldn't blame them—who knew how many more arrests were planned, what lists had already been drawn up?

"Why did you come?" she asked, half-suspicious, and he said simply, "I kept thinking about you." And even though, to be honest, she hadn't thought about him all that much since being there, it felt good to know she meant something to a human being other than her mother. Here was Jason, head smooth with Vitalis hair oil, stolid and even a little boring, and he was exactly what she needed. He asked politely how she was, and she said she had nothing at all to report, just the four walls of her cell. So instead, he told her with great seriousness about his team's preparations for the inter-school debate competition, and about some American film he'd seen, one she hadn't even heard of. *The world keeps spinning without me,* she thought.

He didn't stay long, but came often. It was hard to keep track of days, but he had a talent for showing up just as she was starting to wonder how long it had been. It was nice to have someone. All the other girls had large families, squabbling and fussing, and she had him. None of them, she realised, had any friends outside the movement, or at least none close enough to visit now. They weren't supposed to touch, but now and then he brushed his hands against hers and she felt a tingle.

"If you weren't here, I'd probably go mad," she said to him one time, instantly regretting it in case it sounded like blackmail. He seemed to understand, nodding gravely and telling her more about the book they were reading in class, something by an old English man. She didn't mind, he had a way with these stories that let her understand, if not why they were interesting, at least why they were interesting to him.

A few months in, she found she was able to talk about what was happening to her, and then it burst from her in chunks: describing her tactics for keeping cockroaches away as she slept, speculating what animal exactly their lunch meat had come from. He nodded kindly the whole time, responding to her last point to show he'd been listening.

"But you're all right?" he'd say, after one of these monologues, and she'd have to stop and think if she was. They weren't questioned very much any more: really, it was just a matter of form, in case a confession or denunciation might suddenly have occurred to them after all this time. It wasn't clear if anything she said would earn her release, and even if that was the case, she could hardly buy her freedom at such a price. This was transitional, she told herself, the world would bend towards fairness, and soon it would be unthinkable for people to be locked up merely for their beliefs.

The outside world receded, and soon she thought of it in the same hazy way she did places she'd only read about. At least in normal prison, you knew exactly how long you'd be inside. She could be released the next day, or never. The uncertainty was killing. Once, she noticed Jason looking at her strangely. "What?" she tried to smile. "You said 'home', but you meant here," he said gently.

She told the others about her fear—that her mind was growing weak. "You mustn't," said Lay Kuan sharply. "No time to be feeble. You have to know exactly what you're going to do on the outside, so you can start right away when we're released. Otherwise you'll waste time. Like when you set a caged bird free, but it's forgotten how to fly."

Jason visited less often after starting his National Service. He seemed quite happy about having to do it, but then he'd been able to finish school—the system had been designed with him in mind. She held onto this thought, but still found herself infected with his boyish excitement. It did sound almost fun when they crawled through patches of jungle and learnt to put up tents. After his first time firing a rifle, he showed up aglow. Their trainers were Israeli, he told her. They knew about fighting.

She wondered if he'd told the other boys about her, his little Communist girlfriend. Something told her not—it would be inconvenient, and he struck her as being very good at compartmentalising. She didn't say anything. It was enough that he kept coming.

The longer they were there, the more latitude the guards gave them, allowing them to spend more time in the courtyard where at least there was sunlight, at least they could talk. It didn't help. When they spoke of what they'd do when they got out, the first things they'd eat, it never seemed real to her, though it was easy enough to join in and say what was expected of her. Lay Kuan had a seemingly inexhaustible supply of stories and quotes to keep the despair away, and the great gift of making the gleaming utopian future seem inevitable, if they just waited this out.

There were nights when Siew Li lay on her concrete slab staring at the patches of mould on the ceiling, trying hard to pull thoughts out of the overwhelming fear that filled every inch of her. If she fell asleep in this state, she dreamt that her cell was made of living flesh, that the walls contracted with each breath and pulsed with bulging veins. Waking, she'd lie perfectly still as the world realigned itself. How long had she been here? She wished Singapore had seasons, like she'd read about in books, so there'd be variations in temperature, and she could sense the passage of time by how the air was changing.

Lim Chin Siong came to visit the women—he'd been let out a couple of weeks before, and the government had sent him with a message. There was a hold-up over some paperwork, a little more investigation was needed for one of the women, but the rest of them would soon be free to go. "No," said Lay Kuan right away, "We're not leaving anyone behind." The others nodded, and so did Siew Li. She wondered if she was the one, and was glad Lay Kuan hadn't asked. Better not to know.

When she tried later to work out the sequence of events, Siew Li found she had no memory of how much time passed between that visit and being let out, whether it was days or months. She'd find it was morning, and have no idea if she'd slept that night. She started declining exercise sessions, claiming to feel unwell, and the guards left her alone. Jason must have visited during this time, but she didn't remember that either.

●

After all that, their actual release came as something of an anti-climax. A guard came to her cell and told her to get ready, then an hour later she was able to change back into the clothes she'd arrived in—which still fit, it seemed her body hadn't changed—and then they were being sent through the gate into a crowd. Lay Kuan immediately started waving and talking to reporters, and the others went to their families. Siew Li looked around for her mother, and instead there was Jason, still in his uniform. He led her away and into a taxi. They were pulling away when she realised she hadn't said goodbye to the other women, didn't even have their phone numbers, but of course they would see each other again.

Her mother was waiting at the flat, having cooked a huge amount of food. Siew Li was made to do the usual things— pour flower water over her head, to wash away bad luck; offer incense to their ancestors, for protection. Her bedroom was exactly the same, fresh sheets on the bed, although she noticed some of the books on her shelf were in the wrong order. Her mother put food on her plate and Jason told her all the news she'd missed, even things he'd already mentioned on his visits.

They were treating her like someone who'd been ill a long time. Her mother seemed quite happy for Jason to be there. She wondered if they'd been meeting while she was away.

By the end of her first week out, she was starting to feel herself again. It may have been the familiarity of her surroundings that helped her slip back into this life, or her mother's determination to behave as if the last two years had merely been an unpleasant interruption, that they could all simply pick up where they'd left off. The country was going through a big change, anyway, and everyone was unsettled.

The school wouldn't take her back, naturally, but she didn't want to go back anyway, there was more important work to be done. Too much was happening. The Emergency might be winding down, but the British were still here. She wasn't sure what she wanted to happen next, but this couldn't be the end of the struggle. The sorts of protests they'd organised before now seemed childish—they'd always been going to fail, she could see that now. Who would ever be swayed by schoolboys and girls chanting so earnestly and waving their banners? They needed to be strategic. Look at Chin Peng, the Ma Gong leader, walking away from the Baling talks and returning to the jungle because he didn't like the terms the British were offering.

For months, she applied for every job that was advertised, with no success. This might have been because she hadn't finished secondary school, or just that whenever anyone asked if she could explain the odd gap in her CV, she told them frankly. It was her comrades who helped in the end—

Lay Kuan found her a position at SATU, the new association of trade unions. Nothing too exciting, just processing papers, but it made her feel valued again. It was good to have somewhere to go, some reason to put on proper clothes and see the same people every day. Lina was working there too, having had similar trouble finding employment.

Jason had finished National Service and started at the university. He'd decided on Economics, because the country would need a lot of help finding its feet, and he was convinced this was the best way for him to make a contribution. When he explained their lectures to her, all Veblen curves and Public Sector Borrowing Requirements, it was like something from a different planet, but still she felt proud of him. She felt very grown up, seeing her clever boyfriend in the evening, being in the office during the day, looking over contracts and discussing the best way to exert pressure on bosses. Strike action felt riskier, under this Chief Minister, and while some of them spoke proudly of their time in detention, there was a quiet awareness in the group that it was best to tread with care. They were still finding their feet, and for the leadership to disappear again might be catastrophic.

Lina gave her a hard time for dating Jason, but then Lina wasn't dating anyone, and didn't seem to have time for anything but the unions. How to explain to her that the ideologically correct men were off-putting outside of work, with their strangled voices and tendency to lecture Siew Li earnestly whether she was in the mood or not? Jason was solid and unthinking, and that was a relief. She knew she was doing vital work, and someone needed to stand up to the exploiters, but she also took guilty pleasure in the world Jason showed her, the easy humour and comfort, the living rooms full of books for pleasure, not improvement.

She was nervous the first time she met his parents, bracing herself for disapproval, but there was none. "Young people have so much passion," said his father. "Look at those Fajar chaps, always making so much noise. Glad to hear you have a steady job. I approve of women working. It's a different era now."

His little sister Mollie was quiet that first dinner. When Siew Li asked Jason afterwards if she'd said something wrong, he blinked. "Oh, no. She's just shy." Mollie was a year younger than Jason, Siew Li's age, yet felt to her like a small child. She found Mollie's clothes (mostly pastels) and breathy voice infantile, though she'd never say so. But then what must Mollie think of her? Coarse, uneducated, not good enough for her brother. Mollie was even better-spoken than Jason—her vowels rounder, her vocabulary more extensive.

A few weeks later, Siew Li was running some errands on Orchard Road when she ran into Mollie outside Robinson's, holding hands with a boy, both of them still in their school uniforms. She was mid-laugh, her face more open than Siew Li had ever seen it. Mollie blanched, but then quickly recovered and, with the immaculate manners of a convent girl, introduced her companion. The boy had a cocky grin, Eurasian by the look of him, and told her to call him Barn, "or Barnaby if you're feeling formal." He offered his hand like a diplomat.

At the next Low family dinner, Siew Li casually asked Uncle Roger—as she was learning to call Jason's dad—whether he approved of student romances, and he said most certainly not, he believed schoolboys and girls should focus on their studies, and Mollie would definitely not be doing anything of that sort till she finished Form Six. Mollie held her gaze steady, but there was a ripple of panic in her eyes, and that was all Siew Li needed. She bent her head demurely over her soup, and said no more.

Somehow, that was all it took for Siew Li and Mollie to become friends, or at least friendly. They went on a cautious shopping expedition, but predictably enough they turned out to have completely different tastes and budgets. Despite the lack of common ground, Siew Li was fond of Mollie's warmth and spiky sense of mischief, now that she could see it beneath the smooth exterior. When Siew Li found out she was pregnant, she and Jason told Mollie first, and they spent a long time discussing how best to break it to the parents.

•

When she announced she was going to marry Jason, her mother said, "I hope he improves his Chinese, so he can address me properly." But then she added, "He'll treat you well." Which was something like approval. And who wouldn't approve of Jason? His neat haircut, his steady job. People seemed to assume she would give up work and just be a married woman, but she didn't think she could do that, and he never asked her to.

Jason's parents were ecstatic. Uncle Roger grabbed his son's hand and pumped it up and down, beaming. Auntie Mabel started talking about the dress—of course they'd have to do it soon, before she started showing, but even then corsetry would be necessary. To her relief, they appeared completely unscandalised at their grandchild's illegitimacy, though this would be obvious to anyone who could do basic arithmetic.

Once the process was set in motion, she had little to do but submit to it. Without any discussion, it was decided that the Lows would pay for the wedding, and that therefore it would take place in their church, though Jason would go through a tea ceremony with Siew Li's mother if it made her happy. There were meetings with the priest to be endured. They'd never discussed Jason's religion—it was just something he did on Sundays—but now she understood that as the wife, she would be expected to attend services with him, and that this child would be baptised. When she mentioned this to her mother, the only response was a shrug. "You marry a rooster, live like a rooster; marry a dog, live like a dog. That's how it is."

They talked about both English and Chinese names, but it was clear the Chinese would be just a formality, something for forms and official documents, while the English was for daily use—Henry if a boy, Janet if a girl, even if Siew Li couldn't quite get her tongue around those sounds.

She'd known Jason for months before learning his Chinese name, which he seemed faintly embarrassed by, while she'd steadfastly refused the Lows' attempts to re-christen her.

Her mother insisted on delivering pig trotters to Jason's parents—it was traditional. A whole jar of the stuff, reeking porkily of soy sauce and star anise. Auntie Mabel's face as she received this, equal parts amusement and distaste, ought to have angered Siew Li, but instead it was her mother she felt annoyed with. So many ways to be human, and most people were certain their way was best.

Meanwhile, her colleagues at SATU were giving her a hard time. It was one thing to go on dates with a class enemy, but to marry and have his child? Was she turning bourgeois? They were going at her quite hard, past the point of friendly teasing. When an anonymous note appeared on the notice board calling for her to be purged, Lay Kuan had to step in to stop the bullying. "The English-educated are not our enemies," she told the sullen office. "We'll need to build this country together, all of us. These people aren't going to leave with the British. We're stuck with them. Anyway, Siew Li can marry whoever she likes."

After work, Siew Li sought out Lina and asked what the hell her problem was. There'd been a strange tension between them for some time now. Yet Lina insisted everything was fine, it was just in her imagination. Why did it matter so much to her, anyway?

"You know I only became active in the movement because of you," said Siew Li. Something like a smile passed across

Lina's face. "I just want to know if I said something wrong."

"You're the one who's busy. I never think you'd have time for me."

"When did I ever say—"

"Forget it, okay? I don't want to talk about it." Lina lit a cigarette and drew hard from it. She'd looked insouciant doing that at school, sometimes right outside the gates in defiance of the discipline mistress, but now she merely seemed anxious, and the nicotine was already leaving faint brown stains on her teeth and fingers.

Lina, Siew Li realised, wanted to be back at school, where confidence and swagger had been enough for prominence. Now there was actual work to be done, and it was Siew Li who was better at navigating labour regulations, Siew Li who was rising faster within the movement, unsuitable spouse notwithstanding.

Siew Li was doing well. She allowed herself a moment to acknowledge this, then asked Lina if she had to be home for dinner, or if she'd like to go for fish ball noodles on Chin Chew Street. They ended up ordering far too much food and picking at it for hours, gossiping about everyone else in the office. Lina, to her relief, found the ideological know-it-all men just as annoying. She wished they'd had this talk sooner.

That seemed to do the trick, at least enough that Lina and a handful of others showed up at her wedding, a small affair at Wesley Methodist. No banquet, they'd decided, just a sandwich buffet after—better to put the money towards their new flat, which was a stretch even with Jason's family helping them.

Then there was no time to think of anything but the impending birth. Her mother came round every other day with tonics and strengthening foods, and she cut back on her days in the office as she became unfeasibly large. When her water broke, it was just like in the movies, pain and frantic joy all mixed as Jason rushed her to Kandang Kerbau in a taxi where, to their surprise, it turned out to be twins, so they needed both names after all. A boy and a girl. Henry and Janet.

Just a couple of months after the births, while she was still on leave, Lina came round and said she had to come to this rally. What rally? "I'll explain on the way. You'll want to be there, trust me, nothing in your life will matter more than this moment." So she left Jason in charge of the kids and hurried with Lina to Happy World stadium, where there were oceans of people (more than ten thousand, she later read) and banners everywhere saying "Merdeka". Over the stage was a huge flag, a blue circle with a red star at its apex, and beneath that the firebrand, Lim Chin Siong, announcing that he'd left the main party to set up Barisan Sosialis, the Socialist Front. The cheering was deafening. They controlled more seats in the assembly now. The leftists didn't need to work with the running dogs. They had strength enough on their own.

This was like the old days. If she'd ever thought having children would pull her away from all this, now she knew it was in her veins. When Lim Chin Siong spoke, he had the force and clarity of absolute truth. The government was taking them for granted, and there was no hope for a leftist future unless they took matters into their own hands. What good was it otherwise, moving from one dictatorship to another? Siew Li joined in all the chants, becoming part of something so much vaster than herself, ten thousand of them speaking as one. What on earth couldn't they accomplish together?

"What is it for?" said Jason when she got home, breathless and flushed, and told him about it. "Doesn't he think the government's doing a good enough job?" Siew Li looked around their Tiong Bahru SIT flat, and had to admit its modernity was attractive, everything designed to be sleek and functional, all rounded corners and pleasing finishes. But what about people who weren't as fortunate? She met them all the time at work, those who saw the progress around them but felt left out of it. There was still a lot to be done.

•

The Cambridge-educated lawyer who'd claimed to be fighting for them in detention was now leading the main party, and disposed to detaining people himself. For all that he'd railed against repression while in opposition, there wasn't much indication that he believed people should have the right to choose. In 1962, they had a farce of a referendum—about how they should merge with Malaysia, with no option for becoming independent instead. Barisan told their supporters to leave their ballots blank, only to have the main party counter that blank votes counted as support. What was the point of democracy, if your only options were bad or worse? That's why the struggle had to continue. Those in charge would never truly have her interests at heart.

In the middle of all this, Mollie finished school, got a job at HSBC, and abruptly announced to her parents that she'd been seeing Barnaby Remedios all this time, and had decided to accept his proposal. She was young, but so certain. Her plans were settled. Siew Li envied how sure she was in her mind. This was a path she had chosen, not something she'd fallen into, the way so many things in Siew Li's life had come down to chance.

In February the following year, more people were detained. Operation Coldstore, like the supermarket, as if they were simply being put into freezer cabinets until they were no longer dangerous. The others told her the government was on edge—between the revolt in Brunei and Indonesia's declaration of Konfrontasi, this merger they were planning was looking fragile—and that was a good sign, it meant they were running scared. But what about those who were taken? For a while Siew Li walked around with a cold buzz of fear churning through her, convinced every van that drove past was filled with plain-clothes police who might suddenly jump out and take her. It was weeks before she was able to sleep easily again.

Part of this was the twins. It hadn't been so bad when it was just her, but the thought of being taken away from them was unbearable. Jason pressed her to find another job, or just stay at home. "Don't rock the boat," he said. "Aren't things good the way they are?" And she'd feel his strong arms around her and breathe in his scent. The woody bass of his voice made everything sound so reasonable, and how could she argue, looking down at her babies, that all was not as it should be? But still she continued going to SATU, though she wasn't able to write as many pamphlets or go to as many rallies as before. It didn't matter. She wanted to be part of this thing, in however small a way.

As often as she could, she brought the children to work with her. Some of the men frowned and said this was supposed to be an office, not a nursery, but she didn't want to make her mother take care of them every day, and anyway, weren't men and women supposed to be equal in this new world? Chairman Mao said that women hold up half the sky. That wasn't going to happen if they had a baby in their arms the whole time.

Lay Kuan decided to run for the Legislative Assembly on a Barisan ticket, and asked Siew Li to run her campaign. She needed someone she could trust. Siew Li said yes, of course. It was right that Lay Kuan should run. There were already women in the assembly, but why not more? The unions were important, but they had to get their message out to the people.

The first event she organised was a rally outside the wet market in Havelock. It was a whirlwind, getting the flyers printed in time, hiring the makeshift stage and checking that the mics were hooked up to generators. The terrible anxiety on the day when dark clouds looked like they might gather, then when they cleared up but no one seemed prepared to stop and listen. Once Lay Kuan started, though, a crowd gathered. Her voice was clear and bright, and she was saying all the right things. *Aren't you tired of the government ignoring you? Don't you deserve better?* Siew Li went farther from the square to drag people over, and encouraged the other volunteers to do the same. Soon, they had a respectable crowd, and something electric was fizzing through the air.

Their picture was in the Chinese papers the next day. She was so proud, she cut out the article. The actual afternoon had been hot and sweaty, but in black and white they looked noble and determined, rather than scowling against the sun. The banners had hung limply, but someone had thought to give the flag a shake just as the shutter snapped so it waved in what might have been wind. She was looking straight into the camera, baby Janet in her arms, baby Henry in Lina's. My children, she thought, playing their part in the struggle before they can even speak, imagine what they'll do later on.

Jason complained that she was making him look bad— as a civil servant, how could he have a wife trying to bring down the government? She reminded him that he worked for the people, not just one party, and he backed down.

He would see, she thought, how much better things could be. It wasn't his fault he didn't understand, what chance did he have, with an education like that? Provided by the British—that was the hardest thing, having these people come in and run everything for a century and a half. No wonder he could only see through their eyes, valuing their opinion more than his own people's. She would change him, she was confident. In the meantime, she started work on Mollie. Nothing too overt, so as not to frighten the girl away, just a few nudges. She hung on to small signs of encouragement, like the day they were out shopping together and Mollie said, without prompting, what a shame it was that the bank workers didn't have a proper union, she would have liked to be part of something so powerful, though maybe Barnaby wouldn't have liked it.

The election took place five days after merger, their first as part of another country. The night before, the main party warned that Malaysia would send in troops and renew the state of emergency if Barisan were to win. This was scarily plausible—Emergency had only ended three years previously, why wouldn't it start again? They also claimed, spuriously, that every vote for Barisan was a vote for Sukarno, that Barisan was conspiring with the Indonesians to bring Singapore down through Konfrontasi. Perhaps that's why people voted the way they did, out of fear. Lay Kuan thought so. She won her seat, as did a dozen others from Barisan. Not enough to claim power, but something.

Staying up late for the count, her head buzzing as she stood still for the first time in days, Siew Li felt a flicker of optimism. This would just be the beginning. She wished her children could be here to witness it, but of course they were in bed. There was even more to do now. Once Lay Kuan was in parliament, she would be able to push forward legislation. Even in opposition, she would do a lot of good. Could the system be changed from within, after all? The leftists could no longer be ignored. This would be a new era, she was sure of it.

In the end, it lasted less than three weeks.

●

Later on, she would play those final minutes over and over in her mind, trying to find the break. There must have been a moment when her life cracked, actually broke wide open, falling into too many pieces to ever come back together again. But there was no single instant, or maybe it was too far back, long before she could possibly have known where this path or that would take her. Like the Chinese proverb, a thunderbolt from the clear sky. She would always remember afterwards the lack of clouds, the blue dome overhead like a promise.

She'd been double-boiling soup on a charcoal stove, hunched over on a low stool as she fanned the flames. Jason grumbled that they had a perfectly good gas cooker, and didn't she know that heat was heat, the soup wouldn't be any less nutritious if she made it on a modern appliance? Anyway no need to exhaust herself like that, they could just open a can of Campbell's cream of mushroom.

Jason didn't understand. That was fine, he would complain about the bitterness of the brew, but he'd drink it to please her. She'd asked the herbalist for something to help with stress. Jason kept getting these headaches, it couldn't be good.

Mollie had come by to play with the twins. "Might as well help while I can, before this one comes out," she said cheerfully, rubbing her gigantic belly. "Then you'll have to return the favour." She was always popping round, probably lonely with Barnaby at work. Jason encouraged this, he liked her singing nursery rhymes to the kids in English, otherwise they might pick up Siew Li's broken accent and that would never do.

Wiping the sweat from her forehead, Siew Li looked around her spick and span kitchen, its tiles so easy to wipe clean, the tidy canisters for tea and sugar on the counter. Everything in its place. After the soup was done, she'd make porridge for the children's lunch, then start chopping the vegetables for dinner. Jason liked to have it waiting on the table when he got home.

When the voice called her name, she didn't immediately register it. Again, "Siew Li!" They usually left the door open for the breeze, just the metal gate shut, and on the other side of the bars was Lina. Checking the fire, she scurried over to let her friend in. "Sorry, daydreaming. What are you doing here?"

"Come to the kopitiam with me, we need to talk."

"So serious!" she laughed, but Lina wasn't smiling. She strode through the flat, not even taking off her shoes. "We'll go out by the back door."

Siew Li glanced at Mollie, who nodded to say go, we'll be fine. Grabbing her purse, Siew Li slipped on her own shoes and hurried to catch up. Lina was already clopping giddily down the narrow spiral staircase. Siew Li ducked under a bamboo pole of wet laundry, and went after her.

"I thought we were going to the kopitiam?" she said

nervously, just to fill the silence. It was obvious now that something was wrong, it was written in every taut line of Lina's body. She was trying to walk as fast as possible whilst not drawing attention to herself.

"They're coming for you, Siew Li. Me too, probably. We have to go."

There was no need to ask who "they" was. So February hadn't been a lucky escape, just the net starting to close in.

"They came to SATU this morning," said Lina, a tight smile on her face. Anyone looking from a distance would have seen nothing suspicious, just two women out for a friendly stroll. "Took them all away. The cleaning auntie, Mui, she heard them mention your name. Shame you weren't there, they said, now they'll have to pay you a visit at home."

"We didn't do anything," said Siew Li, already knowing this was futile. They hadn't done anything wrong last time either. No point appealing to the rules. Why hadn't she learnt that lesson better? Still she was bargaining, clutching at straws. "Can't Lay Kuan stop them? She's in the government now, she must be able to—"

"They took her too," said Lina, her voice almost snapping with frustration. She took a breath, trying to get this out as efficiently as possible. "They took Lay Kuan. She's inside now. She's an MP, and still they detained her. Don't you understand, Siew Li? There isn't anything they can't do. They won't stop till there are none of us left."

Siew Li's breath stopped, and the road seemed to sway

beneath her, buckling under an enormous weight. She locked her knees so she wouldn't fall, trying to take in the words. If even Lay Kuan— But no, no time for that. Her skin prickled, and she knew she had to get out. She couldn't go back to that place.

Lina was pressing money into her hand, giving her instructions. Get to Sembawang Park any way she could, changing buses or rickshaws a few times so no one could trace her route. Wait till dusk, then find a fisherman named Feroz, he'd bring her across. It was the safest route, they'd almost certainly be keeping watch on the causeway.

"Are you coming too?" she gabbled. "How will I find you? Where should I go?"

"Remember this address," said Lina, repeating it till Siew Li could say it back to her. "That's one of the safe houses. Wait there, they'll tell you where to go next. They'll take care of you."

"Do you mean the Party?"

Lina's look was almost pitying. "Who else will help you now?"

"When can we come back?"

A brisk shake of her head. "I have to warn three more people, then I'm going myself. You'll all get out by different routes. Luckily you weren't at the office today."

"I have to—" She took a step distractedly back towards the flat.

Lina grabbed her arm. "You don't have time. Didn't you hear me? They're on the way now. Your sister-in-law will tell them you've gone out for a coffee, and they'll waste time waiting for you."

"I didn't say goodbye," said Siew Li woodenly, not as a protest, just a statement of fact. She tried to remember if she'd kissed the twins this morning. Had she ruffled Janet's hair just before going? She tried to hang on to it, that last touch.

"Unity," said Lina, clenching her fist for a moment, then she was gone in a flurry of skirts. Siew Li stared after her for a moment, then walked away as fast as she could, her face turned down in case anyone should spot her. Would they come in uniform, she wondered, or just normal office clothes? Were the others at Special Branch on Robinson Road, or had they gone straight to Outram Prison? She kept putting one foot in front of the other, no destination in mind, glancing out into the road in case a free taxi came along.

For the rest of the day, she kept forgetting to breathe. So many hours to kill. She ended up at the Galaxy Cinema, reasoning that a darkened room was probably the safest place to be. They were screening an English film, and she wasn't entirely able to follow the plot, but at least there wasn't much talking. A pretty woman with yellow hair seemed unhappy, despite apparently having lots of money, maybe because she kept getting attacked by birds. Siew Li wasn't sure what she'd done to make the birds angry, but maybe there wasn't a reason, who knows how bird brains work.

When she came out, the *kacang putih* uncle was listening to the news on a little transistor radio. She bought a cone of chickpeas as an excuse to linger, uncertain what she was hoping to hear. The stream of crisp English words flowed past, then Lay Kuan's name, and some others. Three members of parliament detained. A mopping up exercise, to get all the leftists they'd missed during Coldstore. This one was called Operation Pechah. It took her a minute to summon the meaning of the Malay word. *Pechah. Smash.* She finished her snack and moved on, quickly. Poor Lay Kuan, she thought. All that effort, and she would never take her seat.

The afternoon slipped past, somehow. She wished they'd had a phone put in, like Jason kept talking about. It would have been nice to hear the children's voices again. Maybe she could call the shop downstairs, leave a message? But she didn't know the number by heart, and anyway it was too dangerous. Time was doing strange things. She looked at her watch and two minutes had passed, then suddenly it had been almost an hour. She hoped Jason would be able to take care of the children. He'd know to ask his mother for help, and Mollie. It wouldn't be easy, and he'd blame her for that, but he was so competent. They would turn out all right.

She wondered if they would remember her.

But she couldn't think about that now. It surely couldn't be that long, she thought, not long till this was all over and she could come back to live her life. Just be normal. Hang on to that thought. It was already beginning to tip away, all the things she'd thought would be hers. It never once crossed her mind to try to see Jason before she went—he wouldn't understand, might try to turn her in. He believed the system was fair. Why hadn't she seen this, all along? He had never been hers.

By the time she got to Sembawang Park, it felt like this had always been her existence, the unsettled hollow deep in her stomach, the tingling at the edge of all her senses. Jason used to talk about an image in one of his books, a bird flying through the cold, dark sky, suddenly finding an open window into a banquet hall. A burst of warmth and activity, the aroma of rich food, then through another window back out into the empty night.

The park was almost empty, just a few straggling fishermen and one or two couples striving for romance. Her shoes left faint prints on the pale sandy path, and casuarina trees rustled around her. Why hadn't she done this more often? But of course, she'd always been busy, and as a mother of young children, could never have come here on her own, like this. Maybe these were the moments of true freedom, in between things. She had nothing, just the clothes she was in and a little bit of money. The air smelled of salt and something slimy, an undertone of decomposition. She breathed deep anyway.

Feroz didn't want to know anything, not even her name. He said a number, which turned out to be most of the cash. After he'd counted the notes solemnly a couple of times, he nodded and thumbed at the boat. She looked around, though it was dark enough now that no one could have made her out, and climbed in. Was this really happening? He pulled a tarpaulin over her, then she heard scraping as he hauled it the last few feet into the water. A sudden uplift, then a rocking stronger than she'd expected, for how calm the sea had been. When she judged they were a safe distance out, she risked poking her head out for a quick look back the way they'd come, too dark now to make out more than a faint wash of orange from the streetlamps, and otherwise just the rolling inky waves. She looked for the other shore, but it was still too far away to see.

3

NAM TECK

After that night, he mainly remembered his mother weeping, while a big man shouted something none of them could understand. Later, he would learn the man's words: *Stop crying, stop that bloody racket or I'll put a bullet through your heads.* All he knew then, aged four, was that his mother was distraught—as they all were, huddled in the dirt of the road, bruised and thirsty, shaking despite the heat of the night.

Later on, there was a lorry, and more weeping as they were dragged into the back. As they drove off, he saw their stilt house burning along with the rest of the village. They were dropped off at the next town with nothing at all. Some had to beg the headman for assistance. Nam Teck and his mother were luckier, they could stay with Auntie Poh, who lived alone and had room in her house. She was actually his father's aunt. He hoped his father would join them, but that never happened.

He'd never been anywhere—there'd only ever been "here". Now he learnt the place they left was called Batang Kali, although no one talked about it. They would never go back, and to say the name would be to invoke the bad luck of that day, the misfortune that crawled into their lives like ants into untended food. Their new home was safe and dry, and some days he forgot they'd ever lived anywhere else.

A couple of times he asked his mother where Baba was, and although she wouldn't tell him, she seemed pleased he remembered his father. In truth, he was asking because the other boys in the village had asked him. All he remembered were long brown legs, rough hands cradling him, the sour scorched stench of cigarettes.

When they were alone, Auntie Poh told him Baba was dead, shot by bad people, the government men who always made trouble. His mother would be cross, but Auntie Poh believed he has the right to know. At times like this, even the young couldn't afford to be innocent.

His mother cried less as time went by, and their life settled into a pattern. She found work nearby, tapping rubber. He watched her go out early every morning, while the sap still ran liquid from the trees, as Auntie Poh gave him his breakfast. He attended the village school. Perhaps the schoolteacher had spoken to the class, but nobody asked where his father was.

A few years later, the bad men came and moved them again. Everyone in their village was given a week to gather their belongings, then taken to a clearing in the jungle. The British man read from a piece of paper and someone translated. He said the name of each family and the number of the plot they'd been given. The land had been allocated on a grid, probably by someone who'd only seen a map. Some lucky people were on level ground, others found themselves on a slope or in a swamp.

They were given a hundred dollars and told to build themselves a house. When Auntie Poh protested there was no man in their family, all the men had been killed, she was told to use the money to hire labour. It wasn't enough, but the neighbours helped out. Their new home was a little smaller than before, neatly constructed out of wood. They hadn't been able to find hinges so all the doors slid open along grooves.

In the meantime, the bad men put up a fence around the new village, then another one farther away. These were made of barbed wire, two and a half metres high, topped with three-cornered spikes. There was only one entrance, and anyone going in and out was searched. His mother was no longer allowed to bring any food with her when she went out to work, in case she gave it to the people in the jungle. She was often pale with hunger when she came back from the plantation.

He seldom left the enclosure, and nor did Auntie Poh. It would be too difficult to get a permit to travel, and in any case they had nowhere to go. For the very young and the old, the village was big enough—a field, a school, even a couple of shops. All their food was brought in by the officials, and cooked in big pots in the common kitchen. Everyone brought their bowls and ate together in the square.

His mother and Auntie Poh would end up staying here for the rest of their lives. They'd moved too often, and even after the fences came down they couldn't bring themselves to go—like birds grown used to the cage, they found the world beyond the village too large and confusing, and were too tired to think of adapting to yet another place. They were glad they'd decided early on to spend the money on a sturdy house, rather than the jerry-rigged structures put up by people who'd thought they'd only be here a year or two.

After a few years in the new village, he announced one night at supper that he was moving to Kuala Lumpur. The city had seemed unimaginably distant as a child, a different universe, but in fact turned out to be only an hour away on the bus. He'd already bought a ticket. Having spent several years of free time tinkering with the few motorcycles in the village, he had the promise of a job for a car mechanic. Just an apprentice, and it wouldn't pay much, but he was young and could make do.

He'd timed it well, said his mother as she saw him off, trying to smile. The walls had only just come down and he was ready to leave her. She filled his arms with food—buns for the journey, medicinal herbs to reduce heatiness, dried pork—a pitiful selection from the village shops.

Surely you didn't expect me to stay forever, he said—and, receiving no answer, waved goodbye and stepped aboard the bus.

•

Nam Teck got used to introducing himself to people—in the village there'd been no need, everyone knew everyone else. He learnt to reduce his story to three or four sentences: the new village, the dead father, that was all people needed to know. They could fill the gaps in themselves. No one asked why he'd decided to move to the city. It was clearly the only choice.

Occasionally someone asked, *Was your father killed by the Ma Gong, the communists?* Their voices hushing on those syllables, because there were ears everywhere. At first he answered, *No, it was the British*—but this led to odd looks. They suspected his father of being Ma Gong himself, he realised, and started simply saying, *He died during the Emergency.*

Kuala Lumpur seemed untouched by the last dozen years of chaos. City dwellers vaguely knew it was dangerous in the rural wastelands—but why would they want to go there? There were difficulties over long journeys, and it was a bore that you weren't allowed to bring food out with you. *As if we would feed those people*, said one lady scornfully when he asked—but rules were rules, and they recognised the need for them.

On the whole, the soldiers and barbed-wire fenced villages belonged to another world. People trickled into the towns, marked by their clothes and way of speech as having come in from elsewhere, but no one liked to talk about the past. The British had driven out the Communists, and now everyone was safe again.

He had the sort of face that made strangers talk to him: waiting for the bus, sharing a table in a crowded coffee shop.

Everyone had a story. "I was a resettlement officer," said a neat middle-aged man in the square one evening. "We had to help build the barbed wire fences around the new villages. Sorry, you weren't—"

"I was in Semenyih," said Nam Teck quietly. "But it's all right." It wasn't really, not yet, but he was desperate not to cause offence.

"Well, we were just doing our job. It was mainly for your protection, you know—you were probably too young to realise." He was right, Nam Teck had hardly met any of the Ma Gong growing up, although on his few excursions outside he remembered thin, sunburnt men who ruffled his hair, Auntie Poh's face tight with polite fear as they told him to be good and study hard, then disappeared again into the surrounding trees.

"One day," continued the man, "I was driving along, near the jungle, when I got a flat. I had no idea how to change it—I'm just a civil servant, my job was to measure the perimeter and order the wire, we didn't have to work with our hands. I was so scared of the bandits—sorry, the Communists."

That correction, Nam Teck realised, was in case he knew someone in the jungle—an older brother, a cousin. Plenty of people in the village had family inside, which is why they had to be searched going out—what number of laws, however strict, could stop a mother bringing food out for her son? But Nam Teck knew no one, so could just smile and shrug.

"Well then. Those men with guns, they'd come out and kill you, just for doing your job. We were warned to be careful, but of course the British wouldn't let us carry arms, only the white men, as if we couldn't be trusted. They thought any Chinese was capable of turning. It's ridiculous, I speak good English, but they thought we were all the same.

"I couldn't have walked into town, it was miles, and I didn't want to go back through the jungle. Just as I was about to give up hope, two men in a jeep came along, planters—a Frenchman and a Dutch, very friendly. They helped me to fix the tire with a rubber patch—these planters always have a piece of rubber about their person. We had a good laugh, and I was on my way before sunset. A month later, I read in the paper that both of them had been killed. Shot in their sleep, even before the sun came up." The man sighed, absorbed in his small piece of the tragedy. "Terrible times. They pay the servants to stay away that morning. They kill the dogs, and then they come for you."

Nam Teck nodded, and made a sympathetic noise. He was becoming aware of battle lines, fainter now the war had ended but still present. As yet, there was no need for him to choose a side.

•

The garage was run out of a shophouse, with a sparse boneyard of cars next to it. Most of the shophouse was occupied by the owner's burgeoning family, with a small room off the main staircase where Nam Teck and the other assistant, Seng, slept. There was never quite silence, as one or another of the children seemed to be having a screaming fit at all times—a relay race of shrieks and howls. The rent was cheap, though, and eating with the family meant he could keep almost all of his tiny earnings.

The boss, Mr Chiam, had done quite well out of the Emergency, with a nice sideline in bulletproof cars. Steel plates tacked onto doors, special reinforced glass for clients who couldn't quite run to a fully-armoured car, but still fancied themselves important enough to be in danger of terrorist attacks. He had in his yard the wreck of a car that survived—there were holes all along the side, and the front was caved in where a grenade had landed on the bonnet. The glass was intact, though. He'd open the doors to show that the bullets never emerged into the interior, and the steel plates were only dented.

"The ang moh should have come to me," he cackled, speaking of Henry Gurney, killed by the Ma Gong whilst driving up Fraser's Hill. "His car—no protection, nothing, and he dared to drive through the jungle, with his wife next to him." Lady Gurney survived the ambush, after Sir Henry walked straight into the snipers' sights to draw fire away from her. "I wouldn't do that. What for? Get a new wife." He laughed again, pinching Mrs Chiam to show he wasn't serious.

The next High Commissioner, Gerald Templer, wouldn't take the job unless he was given an armoured limousine—purchased second-hand, it was rumoured, from Éamon de Valera. He had it fired on by a machine gun, and was impressed to find every bullet repelled. Templer didn't die in office, which could be considered a success.

Mr Chiam was full of such stories, which he told with the enjoyment of a born entertainer. Their dinner table was never silent, as he took advantage of the newcomer to recycle all his anecdotes, now embellished just enough to still be credible. Mrs Chiam laughed politely, but her mind was elsewhere. A thin, worried woman, she was always silently calculating if she'd cooked enough rice to feed these ravenous men, if there were enough buns for the children's breakfasts the next day, how much of the housekeeping money she had left that month. Seng laughed too, though it wasn't always clear how much he understood—he was Hainanese, while Mr Chiam, like Nam Teck, was a Cantonese-speaker.

Nam Teck sat with Seng in a corner of the crowded kitchen, jammed against the tiled wall by the foldable table— square, so it could be used for mahjong on festive occasions. Mr Chiam was at the head of the table, of course, and Mrs Chiam was near the stove so she could refill bowls and plates as needed. Between them were a variety of children—the oldest girl on a grown-up stool, the others in bamboo low-chairs decreasing in size like Russian dolls.

Mrs Chiam served up boiled and fried things that were simultaneously bland and too salty. Nam Teck thought of his mother's cooking, quickly put together but delicious, flavoured with wild plants from the jungle—workers weren't searched coming into the camp. The days after the common kitchen were abandoned, when the villagers were allowed to cook in their own houses again—that's when he ate well. Good fortune in the mouth, as the Chinese say. He was careful to mention nothing of this, though, afraid of coming across as a mummy's boy.

He was especially keen to seem a proper man when Seng was there—Seng, who'd come over on a ship all the way from China. He was ashamed of having complained about a childhood in the barbed-wire village, when Seng told his story, in broken Cantonese, of being crammed in the hold with almost no sunlight, having to fight for the food and water lowered down to them, of bodies piling up and being flung out to sea. Nam Teck had nightmares for days after that, imagining the trail of corpses cutting a line across the South China Sea, like the dotted-line sea routes on the oldest child's educational map of the world.

They started their day early. People were always popping by, imagining their auto problems could be solved quickly before work. Sometimes this was possible, but mostly the cars had to be left behind. Nam Teck turned out to be a quick learner—already good with tools, and vaguely aware of how engines worked, he was able to pick up from Seng what the different parts were and the peculiarities of each model. They worked without interruption for much of the day. Nam Teck was tired by sunset, a gratifying exhaustion that made him feel he had done good work. So this is life, he thought. It was 1961 and he was seventeen years old.

•

When he visited the village on a rare day off, it didn't appear any smaller, as he'd expected after six weeks in the big city. The dirt streets on a tight grid, the gaudy village temple, the sun-blistered wooden housefronts. If anything it seemed larger with the fences gone—there were still traces of metal stumps, and they'd left the watchtower, but already the people on the perimeter had extended their back gardens outwards.

His mother was a little thinner. She didn't always bother cooking, she said, now it was just the two of them, and Auntie Poh was too old to do much of anything except a bit of cleaning and sewing. Mostly she sat outside in her unravelling rattan chair, smiling at the neighbours as they went by.

He brought his mother a swan made of seashells he'd bought from a Malay girl at the market. She scolded him for wasting money, but he said the shops in KL were not as expensive as she might imagine and besides, Mr Chiam paid him well. This wasn't actually true, but compared to village wages, he still wasn't doing too badly.

His mother made far too much food, and with her usual efficiency it was all ready at the same time. She dished it up and he carried it to the table, noticing that the sheet of lino tacked to the wood was peeling and covered in burns. He invited Auntie Poh and his mother to eat, and picked bits of meat to put into their bowls. His mother grunted as if to say, *So, you haven't forgotten your manners.*

Later on, when Auntie Poh had gone to bed, his mother told him how things were improving in the village. They were thinking of putting more telephones in, so they wouldn't have to queue any more (*but we don't queue*, he thought, *because we have no one to call*). And the houses would get their own bathrooms soon, rather than the communal toilets on every street.

He realised, of course, that she was asking him to come back, even though she must know there was no future there. She talked about him opening a shop, or even going away to university and coming back to teach at the village school. *You're clever*, she said, *we'll find the money from somewhere*. He let her speak, he couldn't stop her even if he had the heart, these words had been stored up all the time he was gone.

She knew it was hopeless, he was already tainted with the big city. His voice was coarser and he walked so fast—he must think how slowly people in the village ambled, but why shouldn't they, you could cross this village in twenty minutes at a crawl. Still, she didn't appeal to him directly. If he hadn't said no, she could still hope he'd change his mind.

That night, he slept on the usual mat beside his mother's bed. He noticed she hadn't filled in the shallow pit under the bed, the one they'd been meant to dive into if they heard gunfire. It took him a while to drop off, because his head ached from how badly he wanted to come back here, and how badly he wanted to escape. He lay awake, his thoughts chasing each other in circles—Could he stay in the city even if he lost his job? Or should he think about university? He'd been one of the top students at the village school.

The next morning, his mother watched as he ate two eggs,

soft boiled in a bowl. She could neglect the rubber trees for a day, she said, they weren't going anywhere. Rubber prices had fallen since the army left, but he wasn't to worry, they had enough for themselves. He should keep his money and make sure he ate properly. She made him describe Mrs Chiam's cooking, and snorted when he said she served some dishes cold. She must be from the north, a Cantonese would never do that.

She didn't ask when he'd visit again, and didn't urge him to take more food than would fit comfortably in his bag. *Take care of yourself,* she said. *And maybe write a letter, if you have time, I'll get Auntie Poh to read it to me. Don't work too hard, you're still growing, you mustn't wreck your body.*

Her smile said: *I know I must let you go, I'm being brave about this.* He felt nothing but guilt and restlessness as she hugged him, unexpectedly tight, his mother who'd never been demonstrative. To fill the silence as they waited for his bus, he told her about KL, the wide streets and elegant candy-coloured buildings. As the bus carried him away he looked back at her waving, and in the end it was his mother who looked smaller than he'd remembered.

●

Nam Teck began to discover that he liked girls. He'd always expected that he would, but only in a theoretical way, until he arrived in Kuala Lumpur. The city teemed with alluring bodies, spilling from scoop-neck blouses, lengthened by high-heeled shoes. His feelings, sweaty and consuming, became unknown to him. He'd always been a simple kind of chap, but now he found he had to be subtle. On the bus, he looked from the corner of his eye, from behind a newspaper—never directly, never staring, knowing only that if one of them looked back at him he would die. They smelt of flowers and musk.

There were girls in the village, of course, but he'd grown up with them, and well into their teens they seemed children still. Dashing about in loose T-shirts and rubber slippers. Untamed home-chopped hair and muddy knees. Not like city girls, cool and unknowable.

He tried asking Seng if he had girlfriends, but Seng smiled mysteriously and brushed him off. *I want to know how to talk to girls*, he cried. *You're too young*, said Seng, *if you have to ask how.* This was not the answer he wanted, and now he couldn't ask again. He wished he had a father, surely this was the time when fatherly advice would be most welcome. There was Mr Chiam, of course, but Mr Chiam met his wife more than a decade ago; they probably did things differently back then.

The talk in the village school, he could now see, was hopelessly innocent. The cobbler's son, who'd seemed so risqué with his lewd remarks about the Red Cross nurse's fortnightly visits, was now revealed to be a drooling bumpkin. Even his pencil sketches of female anatomy, passed from boy to boy in the school toilets, seemed suspect and possibly inaccurate.

Because Seng was not an unkind man, he took his roommate dancing. He'd rather have been with his own friends, but Nam Teck was fairly presentable, being tall for his age, and Seng was young enough to remember the awkwardness of being suspended just short of manhood. He even lent the boy his cologne, and they headed out into the night, smelling—as Mr Chiam whispered to his wife the instant the door shut on them—like a Thai tart's bathroom.

They went to the BB Dance Hall, a striking art deco building in Bukit Bintang (an architecture student once explained "art deco" to Seng, and he liked the idea that buildings were not just buildings, but belonged to schools and had special names). At night it was festooned with bulbs, and the letters "B B" shone out of the darkness in vivid neon yellow. Young men and a handful of girls milled about at the entrance, the men in open-necked shirts and startlingly tight trousers. Nam Teck quietly promised himself that half his next wage packet would go towards new clothes. For just a moment, he considered making some excuse and going home. Instead, he spit-slicked his boring straight hair off his forehead and followed Seng in.

Seng bought a couple of booklets and handed one to Nam Teck. It was full of brown slips, each lightly printed with a couple of angular beige men playing brass instruments. There was a serial number, and across the bottom "Good for one dance." Seng had to explain this to him, though he was fairly certain Seng couldn't read English either. Someone must have told him.

Still unsure how it worked, he stood aside as Seng strode across to talk to a girl—a lady, actually, they were too poised and polished to be called anything else. He ripped a ticket from his book and, daringly, tucked it under one of the bracelets on her wrist. She deftly transferred it to a beaded purse, and as the music struck up for the next number, a cha-cha, they burst onto the dance floor, Seng moving his hips and feet with surprising dexterity, the woman matching him and appearing to have a good time.

Nam Teck waited out three more dances, before steeling himself to approach. The women were seated on a little platform across the room. He said hello to a short, kind-looking one in a purple flowered cheongsam. This was nowhere near as challenging as he'd feared. As soon as he presented her with his coupon she was on her feet, asking his name. She was called Rosie, she crooned, like the flower. He folded her into his arms and swayed, pressing the entire length of his body against hers.

He got a coke from the bar, let a couple of fast dances go, then found another lady who looked friendly. She was called Malady, she told him, and of course they could wait for a slow dance, *ooh, here's one starting now*. Her hair was piled into a high twist—a beehive, she told him, patting it—and her bosom strained disturbingly against the shiny fabric of her dress. She wriggled from side to side and uttered little squeals as they danced.

When all his tickets were gone, he didn't dare ask for another book, in case he couldn't afford one and looked a fool. Seng was nowhere to be found, so he walked home on his own, needing to put one foot in front of the other to clear a line through his thoughts and make himself tired enough to sleep. His dreams were pleasantly filled with dark rooms and pale languid arms. When Seng came in at five in the morning and noisily thumped into bed, it barely disturbed the surface of his sleep. The next day, they grinned at each other, but he already knew better than to ask for details.

•

Occasionally they had an argument at dinner about whether they were Chinese or Malayan. *Can't we be both*, asked Nam Teck, who wasn't very good at arguing and not bothered either way. Seng insisted he was Malayan. He would never go back to China and who cared if he didn't speak a word of Malay? This was his home.

Mr Chiam claimed his entire family was Chinese, even though every one of them was born here. *The British don't care about you,* he said, red in the face, *And now the Malays don't either. You know what they call us?* Pendatang, *visitor. You think they will ever let us belong?*

They had the sort of lopsided discussion where one person gets very heated and no one else cares much about the issue. Mrs Chiam looked embarrassed when her husband thumped the table, and tried to collect their plates as a distraction. Seng had a wolfish grin of amusement, as if merely baiting his employer, although Nam Teck had noticed he'd been teaching himself Malay from a little book. 1962 was turning out to be a very strange year for the country. The British were supposed to have left, but lingered awkwardly like bad guests at a party. The Chinese newspapers were a fervid mixture of nationalism and speculation about this new thing, this Malaysia. What did it mean, to carve a new thing out of chunks of land like this? Who would be in it? Would Brunei, Sarawak, Singapore? Singapore especially, with its firebrand prime minister and general mulishness, might be hard to live with. Such a small island. Cut it loose, they said. Let it drift away.

Nam Teck wondered what language they would speak in this new world. He had Cantonese and Mandarin, but only passable Malay and no English at all. Seng was trying to learn Cantonese in addition to Malay. *What's this,* he asked Nam Teck, holding up a wrench, a soup spoon, a sponge. Nam Teck obligingly said the word in Cantonese, and he repeated it thoughtfully, then in Hainanese as if to map the new word onto the old.

They should both be learning English, Mr Chiam admonished them. The future would belong to the English speakers. Don't be fooled that the British were going, didn't they see they'd leave their systems of government, and the country would still send the brightest to Cambridge, to come back speaking with a potato in their mouth? They'd have to keep up. It was a sobering thought, but neither of them had any idea how to start with this, and there was too much to do already. They could read the letters, but not much more.

Mr Chiam's own English was, as he liked to say, rather

jolly good. He could send his voice up into his nose the way some of them spoke, although when an actual ang moh came into the garage and he scurried to serve them, he was deferential, cheerful, playing the obliging servant for their entertainment. They seemed to enjoy that, watching him caper and smile with all his teeth. "Come again-ah, Mr Smiss sir. My regars to Missers Smiss." Even Nam Teck could tell that not all of his sounds were correct, but he seemed to make himself understood.

They relied on Mr Chiam to decipher the English-language news on the radio, just in case the ang moh and the Cambridge-educated Malayans had secret news that didn't make it into the Chinese press, but so far all the facts seemed to tally—there'd be a new government, a different kind (no one seemed to know different in what way), more elections, the British were definitely going, any day now, although a few might stay behind to manage the transition. And it would be Malaysia, not Malaya—in Chinese accomplished by adding that one character *xi*, "west" into the name.

When Sukarno announced Konfrontasi, it seemed like just another voice joining the party. This new country was a threat, he said, a construction of the nekolim. He roared to crowds of thousands, threatening to "Crush Malaysia," and they responded with raised fists. The Malayans affected disdain. *He's just a rabble-rouser,* they said. *He's only at large because the Japanese let him out of the Dutch prison. His ideas are crazed—he wants us to join Indonesia, and the Philippines too—Maphilindo, what a name. Who thinks up these things?*

But beneath that, there was fear. Indonesia didn't have a particularly good army, but it was large, and sheer numbers would make it unpleasant if they did invade. Malaya had just come out of twelve years of Emergency, and the Japanese before that. They didn't want any more, and worried what this charming man would persuade his people to do. Already, terrorists were sneaking in and blowing up buildings in Singapore.

Nam Teck should have been fearful too, but managed to shrug it off. There wasn't much he could personally do, and he didn't have the resources or inclination to leave. Like most of the people around him, he cultivated a wait-and-see attitude. Mrs Chiam stockpiled tinned food just in case.

Taking up rather more of his attention and energy was finally having intercourse with a woman. He learnt how ask shopgirls out in such a way that they felt flattered, not annoyed, how to win them prizes at funfairs and spend hours sipping tea, talking about nothing at all. When it finally came off, he almost woke Seng up to tell him, but the person he was becoming whispered that this would be gauche. Anyway, the fact is the first time was not entirely satisfying and frankly a little painful, but he got better at it quite quickly.

•

By his third Chinese New Year after leaving the village, his mother no longer asked him when he was coming back, or even if he was eating properly. He felt this a minor victory, that she trusted him to take care of himself. She no longer feared he'd get all his money stolen by clever city thieves and end up starving in the streets. Instead she focussed on the future: when was he getting married, when would he give her grandchildren? The neighbours joined in this chorus, having popped by to see the prodigal son and give him a token red packet. Even old Auntie Poh, now bedridden, chirped from her pallet that the city must be full of girls available to a strong young man like him.

His muscles had filled out, it was true. Already tall, he'd begun to grow sideways, his shoulders thickening from lifting heavy car tyres. He'd marshalled his thin wages to purchase gaudy printed shirts and tight jeans ("cowboy trousers", the Chinese called them), having asked Seng to show him the night markets where mysteriously cheap clothes might be bought. His hair was glossy and he kept an orange plastic comb tucked into his back pocket so he always had something to do with his hands.

This year, his mother had prepared more food than ever before. She waved away his protests—they had a fridge now, kept in the backyard and shared with the neighbours. She and Auntie Poh would live off the leftovers for a fortnight, and what a treat it would be not to cook. Besides, it was all his money. That silenced him, for it was true that he'd begun to send small sums when he was able to—he felt guilty it wasn't more, doubly so when she'd spent what looked like most of it on sea cucumber and dried scallops for him.

He had a whole two days off work, which he spent wandering

the village streets with his new louche gait, deliberately scuffed and slouchy. The other young people he saw were, like him, only back for the New Year. Nobody lived here any more. He smoked only when out of his mother's sight—he wasn't sure she'd approve, and wanted their time together to be peaceful. She must have smelt it on him, part of the new compendium of scents he'd acquired, but said nothing.

She took him on a walk into the jungle. This would have been a treat a decade ago; now he felt annoyance at the muddy paths and brushing ferns, so unsuitable for city shoes. He sulked a little, he couldn't help it, as she pointed out wild edible mushrooms, nearly-hidden paths, the small secrets of the jungle she'd gained through working in its embrace almost her whole life.

When they were well out of earshot of the village, she began to tell him things he only half suspected, about how she had brought supplies to the men in the jungle. For all that they were searched, she found ways to hide food and medicine, they all did. "If you were tapping rubber, and a man came up to you and said, *Bring me rice tomorrow*— well, then, you found a way, or you were dead." She tucked rice grains into the lining of her shoes, pills into the hollow handles of her tools. "They searched us so thoroughly. Sometimes they even made us take our clothes off." Those last few words were a rush. She was suddenly embarrassed in front of her handsome son. "But we got through. Those guards. They couldn't have been as afraid of the British as we were of the Ma Gong."

He was not as surprised by this as she'd expected, having heard enough stories in the city to know how dangerous the people in the jungle are, the way no one knew exactly how many of them there were, even now, or how many weapons they had—looted off dead Japanese soldiers during the war, it was rumoured. He remembered the rough men and women, and envied them. They were living on their own terms, fighting their own battles.

As they walked back towards the city, she began talking about her own death. This was bad luck, especially during the New Year, and he tried to stop her. "Don't worry, it won't be for a while yet," she ploughed on, sounding like she'd practised this speech. "But when it happens, I want to be buried with your father."

He couldn't say anything, he would have choked.

"He's in Batang Kali. It's less than an hour from KL. They were all thrown into a shallow grave just outside the town. If you ask around, people will be able to tell you where it is. There must still be people who remember. Twenty-four men shot, just like that, and all our houses burnt. Now the British are going, and we'll never find out why."

She brought her face close to his. "He would have been so proud of you. I know he would. If only he'd lived to see this. Bury me with him."

●

"Kali" means "many times", banyak kali, and "batang" means

"branches", like tree branches, but also branches in the river. The name of the place comes from the many streams that run through the town, criss-crossing and feeding into the main river, the Sungai Sendat. Thinking of the name recalls the river. Take this branch, or that one, it doesn't matter, the current is bearing you on in one direction only. Sometimes it's a matter of chance, the wind blowing this way or that.

This is one branch: soon after his 20th birthday, a new boy arrived at the workshop. Business was expanding, as the city prospered and more people wanted cars. Ah Lam, the new chap, was only slightly younger than Nam Teck. He'd just arrived from China, from Hainan Island, and he and Seng were able to chatter excitedly in Hainanese about the news from home. Ah Lam was now the apprentice, while Nam Teck graduated to full assistant, with slightly more money and a proper set of tools.

Although he was new in town, Ah Lam came with a ready-made circle of friends, acquaintances from the old country. When he invited Seng and Nam Teck along to a cultural evening one of his friends was organising, they went—Seng for the free food, Nam Teck because, despite his new-found confidence, he hadn't yet acquired the knack of making friends easily.

The event took place in a dingy basement hall off Jalan Kuching. The dim light managed to make the room seem murky rather than atmospheric. Even for the austere times, this was shabby, the walls peeling badly, the furniture moth-eaten and grey. When Nam Teck said something about the strange smell of the room, Ah Lam replied cryptically that these people had their minds on more important things than decorating.

A stage of sorts had been rigged in a corner of the room, packing crates shoved together densely and covered with plywood boards. A red hand-painted banner drooped overhead: "Culture Programme, Art and Music." The music component consisted of an all-girl choir, rather good, who presented some folk songs to the accompaniment of rudimentary coconut-shell percussion. They were wearing matching satin outfits that looked distinctly home-made. The ramshackle, amateur aspect of the show made Nam Teck feel at home. This was like the evening entertainments they used to get up in the village, on days when there was no travelling film show or medicine man to distract them.

There was a short break during which refreshments were served: over-diluted squash in plastic beakers and curry puffs cut into quarters. There were thirty or so people, most of whom seemed to know each other. Seng was gallantly complimenting a choir member on her singing, and brushed Nam Teck off when he tried to join them. Not having the nerve to invade one of the other bubbles of conversation floating around the room, he spent the rest of the interval nursing his soft drink and trying to look as if he was thinking deep, appreciative thoughts about the music.

The second half was a play. A pigtailed girl skipped onto the stage, which was now a jungle, winsomely addressing her woodland friends. Nam Teck didn't have a lot of time for stories, finding them childish. Kuala Lumpur was about facts, hard-edged things he was slowly collecting; when he had enough, he imagined, he'd be wise.

The play wound through a number of scenes, placing the heroine in ever greater peril. No sooner did she evade the clutches of a Japanese soldier, when a smooth-talking ang moh tried to drug and seduce her. In the last scene, an upstanding Chinese comrade rescued her, returning her to the bosom of her family—but first, he lectured her for consorting with the enemy. She wept as she acknowledged her mistake. "I forgot myself. I must strengthen my revolutionary zeal!" she cried, transformed, her eyes like stars. "England and Japan do not care for me. I must not forget that I am Chinese, I must not forget what we are fighting for."

The entire cast came on stage, the choir behind them, singing a revolutionary song. The audience was on its feet, their gaze faraway and dewy. Nam Teck was paralysed. He knew what he'd just seen—these were leftists, with their dangerous talk. The government was hunting down people like them.

He looked around for his friends. Seng had disappeared, and Ah Lam was near the front of the crowd, singing with his arm across his chest. He looked like a hero himself, as if there should be a roaring sea behind him and the wind in his hair.

Part of Nam Teck wanted to leave. It wasn't safe. If the police came—and the way they were singing, surely they were audible from the street—everyone in this basement would be taken away and locked up. He wouldn't be able to explain himself. But then, part of him thought, *You wanted adventure, that's why you came to the city.* And it was thrilling, the ideas he'd heard, the thought of a new world full of youthful energy, the past swept away. Without even realising, he'd starting singing too, his face as bright as if he believed.

●

Afterwards, it felt a bit like a party, except everyone was arguing about revolution in a terribly earnest way. Someone wondered if the play was ideologically sound to simply deplore the colonial forces, when surely it would be better to correct their thinking. Someone else was discussing fundraising, and whether it was too soon after the end of the Emergency to come out into the open again.

Nam Teck found he could join a group and just stand there nodding, and no one minded. He was new, so they wouldn't expect him to contribute. At the moment, all they were doing was giving him awareness. The ideas would inflame him, they believed, as they themselves were once set alight by this new way of looking at the world.

Almost everyone there was his age or younger. The few older people were treated with great respect, as though it was a great honour they'd turned up. The senior comrades, one girl explained to him, had fought in the war against the colonial oppressors. While the young may imagine they breathed revolution from every pore, the older ones had actually lived it.

He wondered why everyone was so keen to talk to him. Everything they said was incriminatory. If he were to tell anyone, anyone at all—but they were innocents, like children, bursting to share with him and too eager to consider he might feel differently from them. Ah Lam, he thought. Ah Lam hardly knew him, and he'd invited him to this evening of—ideology? Propaganda? He felt carefully around the edges of these new words.

One of the young women was laughing a bit too hard. Was she drunk? But no, there wasn't any alcohol here. She noticed him staring and beckoned him over. "I haven't seen you here before."

"It's my first time," he said. "I came with—" He pointed vaguely at Ah Lam, at the far side of the room.

"You don't sound like you're from around here."

"Neither do you."

"Singapore."

"Seminyih."

"The new village? Is it true there was barbed wire all around you?"

He shrugged. "Sure."

"You sound like you don't care."

"No, it was terrible, but it's over. I left."

She offered him a cigarette. He'd only ever had a couple before, but he took one now, trying to inhale in shallow breaths to prevent an embarrassing coughing fit.

"I hope you'll come again."

"I will if you're here." Almost as the words left his mouth, he wished he could take them back. The bantering flirtation that had become habitual felt inappropriate here.

She didn't seem bothered. "I'll be around a bit longer. I'm going inside soon."

"Inside?" He knew what she meant, he just couldn't picture her in the jungle, in uniform.

"The ang moh rounded up your people and put you behind a fence. Don't you want to fight back? This whole Emergency. It's an excuse to keep us down."

"What happened to you?" This felt somehow the right question to ask. She was spilling over with it, this thing she was carrying. He could smell it on her. She was avid, her eyes gleaming. And sure enough, even though they'd just met, she told him. The cement cell they'd held her in. The babies she'd had to leave behind. The fear that made her run.

"I can't go back," she said. "They'd pick me up right away. My friends are still in detention, even the MPs. So much for democracy—they were chosen by the people. This proves the government doesn't care about the people. We have to get rid of them. The only way I can do that is from inside."

Back in the village, he'd sometimes gone fishing in a jungle pond. There wasn't usually very much there, but at the right time of the year, the fish were big. Once or twice he caught one, a foot-long solid slab of muscle wriggling frantically in his hands. This was how he felt, talking to her. She was thrashing at the world to survive, and he could only watch helplessly.

"What happened to you?" she now asked. No one in the

city had ever wanted to hear, but now he told her the whole thing, everything he remembered about Batang Kali, what they'd done to his mother afterwards.

"I never went back," he said. "I don't even know where he's buried."

"Why would you? There'd be nothing there. Burnt houses. Maybe some weeds, but no trees, nothing grows back after you've scorched the earth."

"What should I do?"

"Join us," she said, simply, and it felt like the answer he'd always been waiting to hear. He took a final pull of his cigarette and slowly stubbed it out, trying to find the right words. "What else are you living for? If you aren't part of the struggle, how will things ever change?"

"Most days I feel contented."

"Are you contented, or just numb? What do you want to do with yourself? Slave away to make your Mr Chiam rich, until you have enough money to buy your own shop and enslave others in turn?"

"The struggle has already been going on so long—"

"And it will keep going, comrade. Read what Chairman Mao says about protracted war. It won't happen so quickly. We're talking about changing an entire society."

"Were you always like this?"

She looked away, and he wanted to bite his tongue off. It didn't matter how she'd been before, this was her now. No point asking about the past. He stopped himself. Don't talk about her children, and especially don't mention their father.

"I'm going in," she said quietly. "It's the only possible choice. I've been going from safe house to safe house for months. What kind of life is that? At least inside, I'll be free. You have to find where you belong, in life."

A smiling boy passed by with a tray of sausage rolls. She seized a couple and thrust them both at him. "Eat. You don't look like they're feeding you enough."

"You sound like my mother."

"She must be a very sensible woman."

A ghost of something passed between them. Understanding. No, complicity.

She brushed her hair back and tied a scarf around it, preparing to go. "You didn't ask my name. No, it's all right, it doesn't matter. We get new names inside. No point getting to know Siew Li, she'll be gone soon."

•

Ah Lam didn't resign, just disappeared one day. Nam Teck wondered if he'd gone inside, or been picked up by the authorities. No way to find out. He and Seng never talked about that evening, though he sensed his friend wouldn't be going back. Seng was too certain of what he wanted—a few more years of wild oats, then marriage, children, all those good things. And Nam Teck? What did he want?

He took a long look at Mr Chiam. Was this what it meant, to lead a good life? He was entirely self-reliant. A modest business, a large family. Was that enough? On impulse, he asked. Mr Chiam sighed, "Sure, I suppose. You're asking the wrong question. You should say: can you live with the choices you've made? And you know what, I can, every last one of them. I envy you. What are you, twenty? You still have everything ahead. By the time you get to my age, the course is set. I know what's going to happen, all of it, right up till I die. Some people would call that a blessing."

The next weekend, he went back to Seminyih to see his mother. If only he could ask her, but of course that was impossible—too risky to even mention. How would she feel, her son doing the very thing her husband had been mistakenly killed for? Would this be consolation, or betrayal? Which would be the better revenge: to thrive within this system, spiting the people who'd tried to crush you? Or to upend everything, crushing them in turn?

He gave his mum more money than usual, and said he might not be able to visit for a while. Work was getting busier with Mr Chiam expanding the business (this was true—he was buying the premises next door; not unrelatedly, Mrs Chiam was pregnant again). His mother nodded, resigned. As long as he was doing well, she said. He hugged her goodbye, which he didn't usually do, and held Auntie Poh's hand before leaving. On the bus back, his eyes dampened, as if he already knew he wouldn't see them again, even though his mind didn't feel made up yet.

Siew Li had shoved some pamphlets into his pocket. He read them over and over, whenever Seng wasn't around. They were called things like "Stories of the Comrades", and even if he hadn't known she'd written some of them (which ones, he wondered—none were credited), he'd still have been riveted. It was thrilling, this glimpse of a different world, in which the things he'd been taught to value were shown to be as hollow as he'd always suspected.

It seemed clear to him that something was brewing. There were reports of race riots in Singapore. Could that happen here? The country, hastily stitched together, was fraying at the seams—the Malays fighting to keep their hereditary privileges, the Chinese laying claim to a bigger slice of the pie. He'd been vaguely aware of all this before, but now he understood how relevant it was to his life, and how by choosing indifference before, he'd allowed himself to remain powerless.

Walking around the city those last few weeks, he looked closely at the faces around him. All hard and blank, no warmth behind any of them. Was that what he looked like, too? If not, how many years would it take? These people had no thoughts in their heads except survival, which meant only chasing after the next bit of money, the next promotion. It had been less than two decades since the end of the war, and already everyone had forgotten what it was like to work together. Without a common enemy, they were turning on each other. What kind of world was this?

The night of the next meeting, Mrs Chiam begged him not to leave the house. "The bandits are out again, everyone's saying. They stopped a bus in Jinjang yesterday, tried to take everyone's identity cards. Mrs Wong at the market told me. It's like the old days."

"I'll be all right," he said, "Don't worry about me."

"Is it a girl? There'll be time for girls later, if you don't lose your life. I dreamt there was a fire, I dreamt the house burnt down and all our children died. Stay at home tonight."

He was touched, never having realised he was more to her than a valued employee. But this was important. She was right, there was danger out there. And he knew which side of it he wanted to be on. He could be a victim forever. His father had been shot in the back, and his killer never punished. The powerless would never be safe. The system itself had to be overthrown.

A light drizzle fell as he ran through the streets, probably faster than was safe on the slippery pavement. The future was ahead of him. He could taste it. When he thought of how open and optimistic the comrades had been, he felt ashamed. Why had he thought the natural state of man was to be cynical and suspicious, like himself? That's how far he'd been deformed by the system. If everyone was selfish and mistrusting, they would all die alone. He was going to join the struggle to smash the barriers keeping everyone down, and without the oppressors forcing them to compete against each other, they'd be free to unite. It was so simple. Why had he ever been unsure?

He gave the password and slipped into the hall. Siew Li saw him and came over right away, radiant. She'd looked at him and known. "I'm joining you," he said, and she pressed her lips to his, just for a moment, so quickly it might almost not have happened. She took his hand. "Come, they'll tell you what you need to do next. I'm so happy." He followed behind her, unable to name the feelings bubbling inside him, knowing only they felt barely contained, as if he might explode at any moment.

•

Only a few of them were to enter the jungle at the same time—this was usual, going in small groups to avoid detection. A little before midnight, they arrived one by one at the meeting place, a disused petrol station some distance from the main road, knowing each other from the identifying marks: a red cloth tied around one wrist, a cigarette behind the left ear. There were four others besides him, all young men. They nodded, but no one wanted to be the first to speak. He wondered if Siew Li was elsewhere at that moment, meeting her own group, all of them droplets of water trickling towards the vast ocean.

He smelled frangipani in the air. The Malays said this meant a pontianak was in the vicinity, waiting to tear your soft belly open with her claws and devour your insides with her comely mouth. A dog howled, far away. The air was thick and heavy, heat rising like a plague from the dark tar of the road. He thought of his mother, wished he could have left her a note. He thought about the many branches of Sungai Sendat, the streams across Batang Kali he would never see again. All these years, and he'd never looked for his father's grave. That was behind him now, the river moving inexorably onwards, new lands ahead.

The pick-up truck arrived dead on time. The driver jumped from the cabin and said the password, and they each responded correctly. Piled into the back as it sped off, they could have been itinerant workers being ferried to a construction site. Hunched against the sides, knees drawn up to their chins, they knew they ought to sleep, but their eyes remained bright and open. Small bundles of possessions rattled by their feet, now and then jolted into the air by the bumpy road.

After five hours along dirt tracks, the driver pulled up. "Rest," he said. They were to start thinking of what their new names would be. This was why they hadn't shared their old names—as long as they told no one here, there'd be nothing to betray, and their families would be safe. As brothers of the same batch, they would share the same first character.

Without much thought, going by instinct, they settled on Xiong, and Nam Teck became Xiongmin, a hero of the people. They spoke Mandarin, not their hometown dialects, and managed to make themselves understood to each other. In the jungle they would speak only *Putonghua*, the common tongue, just as in China. Each camp would have former teachers to drill them in the language, and anyone too old or stupid to learn would have to be a cook or builder, not a fighter.

They slept fitfully as the full moon spilled pallid light over the uncovered truck, until the grunt of the engine starting woke them. Treetops flew by overhead, glints of sun beginning to peek through. When they stopped again, the driver grinned, "Welcome to Perak." They'd crossed the state line, using small roads to avoid police checkpoints. He tossed them a bag with their breakfast in it: rice and a small piece of fish, individual portions wrapped in leaves.

Not twelve hours after leaving Kuala Lumpur, there they were in the jungle. The next part of their journey would be on foot. A faint dawn haze rose from the ground, clammy and unwelcome. Nam Teck, now Xiongmin, felt an apprehensive sweat form down his back, and soon was uncomfortably damp. He worried about wild animals, but for all the crackling noises in the distant undergrowth, saw no other living creatures. They left the road behind, and the canopy overhead grew thicker, shading the air dark green.

They were far enough in to be uncertain of the way out, when they came to a wooden structure, an open-sided hut. Two men and a woman were waiting, all of them no older than 20. The woman welcomed them formally, saying they must now renounce their old way of living. Here they would be awake, and see the world as it was. The driver melted away—he wasn't one of them, but a sympathiser from the outside. He shouldn't see what came next. The new comrades swore an oath before a picture of Lenin, torn from a book and pinned to one of the wooden posts.

Xiongmin said his new name out loud, and already it belonged to him. One of the men made a speech full of revolutionary slogans and allusions to the glorious motherland, China. To finish the ceremony, they sang

"March of the Righteous Forces," their voices surprisingly resonant in the empty jungle. Then a sack of uniforms was produced, and they swapped around until they all had a set that fit. No insignia, no ranks. They were all Ma Gong now, all equal, all comrades. In uniform, they looked older, wearier. Xiongmin wondered if his expression was the same as the others: excitement subsiding, jaw set, as if against the hard whisper of fear.

They had a long walk ahead. The woman showed them how to tuck their trousers into their boots to guard against leeches—the big ones here could suck a man dry. They were given things to carry—supplies, groundsheets, other necessities. Weapons would come later. "We'll protect you for now," said one of the men, and with that they were led into the dark heart of the jungle.

●

He adjusted to his new life in a very short time. Everyone here was young, no one over 30 and most quite some years under. He wondered if this is what university would have been like, if he'd been the sort of person who'd gone—the camaraderie, the joy and energy of youth. The strict routine made it easy to forget there'd ever been any other way of living. He'd expected tents, but this was a sizeable compound, wood and rattan buildings housing two hundred. Dormitories, huts for storage, large lecture classrooms. Even a swimming pool, improvised by damming a section of river.

The day began before dawn with calisthenics, their vigorous voices counting out tens in unison, like youth camp. He worried that they'd be heard, but the others assured him the nearest village was dozens of miles away, and the treetop sentries would spot intruders long before they came within earshot. Siew Li was here too, to his relief—if she'd been sent to a different camp, he might not have seen her for a long time. She was now calling herself Lifeng, sharp phoenix. No one was ever alone in this place, so private conversation was impossible, but he was certain the glances they exchanged were meaningful.

They seemed to sing all the time. Even by the stream, cleaning themselves, the air was jolly with song. Mostly revolutionary anthems, but also folk tunes, to remind themselves of their connection to the people. Drying himself with a Good Morning towel, the same as he'd had in town, Xiongmin thought what a beautiful world he'd landed in. His comrades trooped along the forest floor chirping like birds, strong music buoying them. After parade each morning, they sang "The Red Flag."

Learning to use a gun was easier than he expected. His hands were steady, and he was soon able to hit a target from a couple of hundred paces. The rifles needed to be cleaned and oiled every day so the humidity of the jungle didn't rust them. They practiced marching with weapons by their sides, until he forgot he was carrying one. Compared to their heavy rucksacks, the gun weighed nothing at all.

With such an early start, by breakfast time he felt like

he'd done a full day's work. The food was indifferent, boiled tapioca with some vegetables if they were lucky. Hot water to drink. He missed coffee, but was careful not to complain. Fresh food was hard to come by, of course, though there was talk in the camp of starting a vegetable garden. They'd been there long enough that it looked like they might be able to stay.

The bulk of the day was taken up by *xuexi*—learning. Apart from Mandarin lessons (they called it "national language"), there were lectures on all sorts of subjects. They pooled their knowledge. He learnt about the geography of Russia and China, the countries they sought to emulate. There were propaganda talks to make sure they understood the ideology correctly. Weak points in their thinking were ferreted out and eliminated. Had he been damaged by his years in the city? They praised his early beginnings, marked out as a revolutionary by his treatment at the hands of British oppressors. He learnt to think of Batang Kali as a battle, his mother's village a concentration camp, his dead father a martyr in the struggle. He'd been angry before, but now his rage had a focus. Language and theory showed him how to understand what had happened. Mr Chiam was now an object of pity, so trapped in his cowardice and bourgeois preoccupations that he could think only of petty wealth, rather than using his abilities to further the cause of his race.

This was heady talk. They egged each other on, growing loud and agitated. Their patrol leader was a man known as Chengyi, perhaps 22, with a gift for whipping up patriotic sentiment and fanning discontent. It was right for them to be angry, he said. The Ma Gong had defeated the Japanese and forced the white devils from Malaya, yet this country was still not theirs. Not till they'd cleared the dead wood from the top would they be able to hold their heads up. How could they claim independence, when the government remained a lackey of foreign powers, in thrall to the parasite sultans? All around him, heads nodded. He was so wise, able to put into words the thoughts they'd had all along.

Chengyi was tall and square-jawed, exactly like the strapping heroes on the covers of their revolutionary books. He could have had any woman he wanted, but as far as anyone knew he was celibate. The camp on the whole was not expected to indulge in personal relationships, for fear it would complicate matters. This made sense to Xiongmin. Isolated in the jungle with five males to each female, the potential for jealousy was too great. Maybe after the revolution, he thought, looking at Lifeng. Anyway Chengyi didn't have the time, working so tirelessly for the good of the community, chopping wood, building huts, full of revolutionary fervour—anyone who felt themselves wavering only had to talk to him for half an hour to find their spirits renewed.

After dinner (rice, salt fish, sweet potato), they sang or read. Sometimes, there'd be a discussion before bedtime. Topics were proposed, then debated if there was sufficient interest. Was smoking tobacco ideologically sound? Would the non-Chinese have a place in Soviet Malaya? What were the lessons of the Emergency? The atmosphere was feverish. Anything could be said at these times. Rumours and complaints were damaging when covert, and murmuring was severely dealt with—but here, in the open, even the leaders could be criticised in the harshest terms. Why, Lenin himself could be questioned. The leadership was only temporary, after all, and would be dismissed after the revolution. Openness and transparency was all.

Some nights, there would be the special treat of a concert. Any excuse, any Soviet or Chinese festival, would see them rigging up a stage from tables and blankets. Food was a little more plentiful on these occasions, and the day would be given over to rehearsing. More girls in pigtails harmonising prettily, more revolutionary heroes thwarting the plans of vicious imperialists. They always finished with sponge cake, steamed over the camp fire, and the rousing "Internationale".

A whistle blew at nine, and the lamps were put out, though a fire burnt through the night to keep wild animals away. Xiongmin found himself exhausted at the end of each day, his hands callused from the unaccustomed work. He missed the moments of forgetfulness at the workshop, for it seemed that in the jungle all should be focused on revolution, every action examined for its correctness. But that was as it should be, the only way to change the world. He was committed to this new, aware way of living. Lying on his canvas bed, listening to the mysterious noises of the jungle, hooting, clicking, the warm breath of wind through the vast overhead canopy, he tried not to think of his old life. *Look forward,* he chided himself, *think of the world to come.*

•

The first killing was unexpected. The scouts had found no enemy activity, and there'd been no surveillance planes—not that they'd have been able to see through the thick treetops to the camp anyway. They were safe, in their closed world. Xiongmin took pleasure in the simple rhythms of their routines, sometimes even forgetting that this struggle meant something in the world outside.

They were marching through the jungle, a small detachment of eight. Two went ahead, clearing a path, the four in the middle had their rifles ready, and the two behind concealed their tracks. He looked back once or twice, fascinated by their thoroughness—sweeping a broad coconut frond across to eliminate footprints, then scattering dried leaves and dirt. No one could have guessed a patrol had passed through here, or that there'd ever been a path between these trees. They were forest spirits, magic, leaving nothing behind, unlike the clumsy government men whose rubbish they came across from time to time. Empty tins. Bits of torn uniform. Snapped branches.

They were hunting for supplies. On the way back they would gather firewood, but their main target was game. They hadn't had meat for a while, and one of the look-outs had reported seeing a young elephant not far from the camp. If it was separated from its herd, they'd be able to kill it without much danger. Those who'd eaten elephant said it tasted like pork. The trunk was the best bit.

This wasn't Xiongmin's first time in the jungle, but he was excited nonetheless. They were going a good ten miles from camp. It had been months, and still he felt a twinge of unreality, unable to believe he'd found his way to this extraordinary place. The petty quarrels and compromises of Kuala Lumpur seemed distant and grubby now, and he couldn't imagine why he'd allowed them to rule his life for such a long time. The only person he missed in the world outside was his mother, and he'd see her again soon enough, when the struggle was over—what pride he would bring to their reunion, having brought her peace at long last, justice for her and his father.

They tramped on through the permanent dusk of the jungle. The scouts did a fine job clearing creepers and undergrowth so they could march unimpeded. From time to time they swapped positions. No one had any experience tracking wildlife, but they'd planned to wander in a wide circle around the camp. If they got anywhere near the elephant, they'd hear it. If not, something else would present itself—a wild boar, a deer. They were definitely not returning empty-handed.

Lifeng walked in front of Xiongmin in confident strides. He was fascinated by her blunt-cut hair, swishing like a curtain over her pale neck, just touching her collar. Her backpack was as large as his, stuffed with first-aid equipment and water, plus a radio in case of emergency. He'd been surprised at first to see the women shouldering such burdens, but when he gallantly offered to help, they just laughed.

We're all equal here, they said, *don't think you can do anything we can't.*

He was still dreamily considering this, and other girls he'd known, when the front scout shouted a warning. Lifeng immediately flung herself against a tree, fading into its outline, only her rifle sticking out. Xiongmin was slower, uncertain which direction the danger was coming from. Everyone else seemed instinctively to know where to go, and someone pulled him urgently into a crouch. A half second of absolute stillness, and then he could see it: a Thai soldier in the uniform of the Royal Army, straightening up, eyes thin and alert, arm halfway to his holster.

At a shouted command, they fired. Xiongmin was closest, and managed to graze his arm, leaving a trail of blood through his shredded sleeve. The other shots went wide, thudding against the trees. He tried again, but nothing happened. His rifle was jammed. Screaming in frustration, he pumped the chamber frantically as the Thai man cocked his pistol, which was pointed right at him. Was this death? He felt very calm, dropping the rifle and reaching for his knife, but before he could even get it out a bullet had torn through the soldier's neck. He gasped, eyes bulging, like someone choking in a cartoon. Blood rushed from the torn artery, much more than you'd have thought possible.

Lifeng took a step forward, looking stunned. She'd fired the fatal shot. The entire episode had taken no time at all, and she probably hadn't even consciously decided what to do—their training was good enough for instinct to take over at moments like this. All she'd seen was a comrade in danger. Just like that, she was a killer.

Xiongmin thanked her brusquely—no time for more. One soldier meant the possibility of a battalion nearby. They'd have to abandon the hunt. Quickly, they searched the dead soldier. Food, water, a map and the pistol. Not a bad haul.

They started to move again, but Lifeng's legs suddenly went soft and she slumped, unable to walk. The others screamed at her to stop this nonsense, there was no time. Her eyes were blank, and Xiongmin understood. She was trapped in that single moment, when her body had assumed the position it had been taught in a thousand drills, and a spiderweb of red had spread across the enemy's throat before exploding horribly.

He took her shoulders. "You had to," he said. "If the Thais left us alone, we wouldn't bother them. This jungle is our home. If people come into our home, we have to defend ourselves." Plain words, he sensed, would be more use here than any number of revolutionary slogans.

"We could have taken him prisoner," she whispered. "What if he has a family? We could have kept him alive."

"How long could we hold him?" said the patrol leader. "We can barely feed ourselves. And look." He opened the map. "See what he was doing. Each red circle here is a land mine. He was laying them." The soldier's bag stood open, a tangle of metal and wires. "These ones here, they're not designed to kill. They have a charge but no shrapnel, so they'll only blow your feet off. They want to leave the victims alive, just crippled, so they become burdens on us. How could a human being think so cruelly? Are you still sorry you killed him?"

"I never—" Lifeng cleared her throat. "I never said I was sorry. Of course I'm not. It was my duty." She rose, shakily, to her feet.

"You're a good person," said Xiongmin, which seemed inadequate, but exactly what she needed to hear. She rested her hand, just for a moment, on his arm, and looked like she wanted to lean against him.

They hid the dead soldier in some undergrowth and went back the way they came. They would make their report, and be praised for their bravery. Lifeng would receive a special commendation for her part, though she would be wise to self-confess her moment of weakness too. This would make them all stronger. They tramped on, the rear line obscuring their footprints, leaving no trace behind as the jungle swallowed them again.

4

REVATHI

Revathi stomped down St Martin's Lane, cursing the frost on the pavement, the sharp chill in the air, everything. February had reached the point when it seemed entirely probable that winter might go on forever. Even the brief hours of daylight were grey and besmirched. A man in a bowler hat walked right into her, as if it were her job to get out of his way. She smiled blandly at him, tamping down the impulse to drive her umbrella into his foot, and thought *fuck it, this day can go to hell.* She'd been headed back to the office, but now swerved into the Nag's Head, where the boys were usually to be found.

Someone called her name as she stepped into the pub, but her glasses fogged up from the warmth, and she had to swipe at them with her scarf before she could see again. It was Fred Robertson, waving from the usual corner. She swabbed her boots on the mat and waved back. "Lars is looking for you," he called, as soon as she got within earshot.

Revathi shrugged. She'd had a beast of a morning,

tramping round half of Willesden chasing down a quote. Lars could wait. She brusquely asked if anyone wanted anything, and headed for the bar before they could answer. Time to lose herself in an unladylike pint.

The boys were unusually absorbed in a newspaper, not theirs. "Have you seen today's *People*?" one of them called, new chap, blond, some forgettable name. He was already shoving it across the table at her.

"Rhodesian Independence Close to Reality?"

"Below that."

"Horror in a Nameless Village? Bit melodramatic."

"Amazing what some people will believe," sneered Jim Carrington. "Listen. 'The corrupting and fearful effect of war on otherwise decent men.' Talk about purple prose."

She scanned the article. "You don't think there's any merit to this?"

"My dear girl, you have to learn not to believe everything you read."

She bristled. "Don't you dear-girl me, I've been on the pol desk longer than you have."

"So? You're still paddling round the shallows, like the rest of us. Give it a rest." He raised his glass and took a large slurp.

She looked around for support, but the others seemed happy to spectate. "Come on, you have to admit it's a serious accusation. You don't think it's worth investigating?"

"So we're meant to believe these blokes wiped out a whole village of chinks—"

"You can't say that word any more, Jim."

"And then covered it up—"

"I'm not sure it was ever okay, to be honest."

"What do you care, you're not a chink."

"Jesus, Jim. It's 1970."

"So?"

"So, if you use language like that, how do I know you're not calling me a darkie when my back's turned?"

He flushed, and she realised belatedly that perhaps she hadn't wanted to open that particular can of worms. Best not to know. "You lot will be in charge in a few years anyway," he muttered, turning away. "The whip hand, Powell said. He knows what's what."

Everyone else at the table was suddenly very busy, bent over crosswords or rolling cigarettes. *Screw you all*, she thought, downing enough of her pint that it wouldn't look abandoned. "Always a pleasure, gentlemen." Breezy as you like. She snatched up the paper and shook her hair out as she left.

The idea formed in her head as she was stomping up to Lars's office. Stopping outside to take several deep breaths before knocking, she was pleased her "Good morning, Mr Erickson" came out calm and cheerful. He started badgering her about the copy she was supposed to be turning in, and she cheerfully assured him that yes, she had doorstepped like a pro, and it would be in on time. As she spoke, she casually draped the *People* across his desk. "Seen this?"

He quickly skimmed it. "Interesting. Sounds like Pinkville *de nos jours*."

"You think so?"

"Could be major. Could be nothing." But he was turning to the inside pages, snuffling for more details.

"I thought it looked important."

He studied the lines of print. "No one's disputing those men got killed and their village burnt down, just a question of whether it was justified. Heat of war."

"You think this doesn't have legs?" *Go easy, make him think it's his idea.*

"Well, there's a story, there definitely could be a story. Wouldn't have to prove anything, just make people wonder if there's more to it."

"Lots of secrets there. It's my part of the world, you know."

"Thought you were a Brummie."

"Born out there. Parents moved to Birmingham when I was eight. They lived through the Emergency, said you wouldn't believe what the British got up to in the name of stopping the Communist bandits. Would be quite a scandal, if it got out."

"Indeed. Thanks for bringing this to my attention."

She stopped herself saying anything more. *Take it slow.* He was still staring at the paper as she left the office.

The next morning, she made sure to get in early, formidable in her boxiest jacket. When she tapped on Lars's door and went in, he was eating toffees from a paper bag, a sure sign of nervous excitement. "Good, I was going to send for you. I need you to go see Ian Spender."

"What for?"

"The Batang Kali story. We're pursuing. I cleared it with Hal yesterday, just need you to brief Spender before he heads out. Useful phrases, poisonous snakes, that sort of thing. Good thing you said you were from there. Handy to know."

"You're sending Spender?"

"He was out there a couple of years, back in the day. National Service."

"So he might have shot these chaps himself?"

"I don't believe he saw much action."

"Story of his life."

"He won't need much. Quick jaunt, interview a few natives, in and out. I made a few calls. Unnamed sources at the Home Office. Apparently there was an attempt by the locals to get compensation years ago. Nothing came of it, but someone coughed up the name of the local lawyer. He seems keen to help. Probably hoping publicity will get the case re-opened."

"Do you really think Spender's up to it? The heat, you know. Over 30 degrees, most days. He's not a young man." This was persuasive—Ian Spender reddened and started breathing hard if he sat too close to the central heating. Easy to imagine him keeling over beneath the tropical sun.

"Well maybe young Robertson would be—"

"Fred Robertson's been with us ten minutes."

"Maybe instead of shooting down my best men, you suggest someone then?"

"Me, Lars. Send me." No hesitation, deadly serious. She had his attention now. "I'm from there, I speak the local language." This was technically true, though she hoped he didn't know there was more than one. "I have all the background already. Grew up with it."

"You're a bit junior—"

"Lars, how long have I been under you? You know I'm grateful, but story after story gets passed over my head. I know, I know, you owe this chap a favour, that other chap has first dibs, there's always a reason. So here's something that's actually up my alley. You know I can do it. Have I ever turned in substandard copy? I have at least as good a shot at getting this right as the next person, probably better, and you know I won't succumb to malaria in my first hour there."

He looked like he might be swayed. "I'd really be sticking my neck out for you—"

"That's what I love about you, Lars. You're the sort of visionary who knows when to take a risk. Can you imagine the sort of story I'll bring home? My Lai is now Our Lai."

"Good thing you don't write the headlines," he laughed, but she knew she had him. Still chuckling, he thought a little more, scribbled down some notes to himself, and let fly with a string of instructions—all conditional on approval from above, of course. Head down to the morgue and get the coverage from Doris, all the way back to 1948; go talk to accounts about the plane ticket and so forth, they had a travel agent on retainer; he hoped to god her passport was up to date; he must be mad letting her do this, but after all people deserve a chance now and then, and her work was good, but dammit she'd better not let him down or they'd both be out on the street.

She listened very carefully, scarcely able to believe she'd pulled it off. This could be—but best not to imagine what this would do for her career if she nailed it. First she had to get it right, and something told her that she would only get one shot at this. Deep breath. She imagined Jim Carrington's triumphant grin if she failed, and knew this had to be on the front page.

•

One of the other girls at the boarding house was happy to lend her a suitcase. "Just take care of it, would you? It's a good one: Peter Jones." Revathi smiled and said of course she would, the tropics could be hard on luggage but she'd keep it away from monsoons and so forth.

"And send us a postcard, if they have those where you're going."

"There are postcards in Malaysia, Lucy. It's not a war zone."

"Isn't that why your parents left?"

"It was rough for a while. It's not like that now."

Lucy still looked concerned. She was a typist, and as far as Revathi could tell, hadn't left West London many times in her life. "There was a chap on *World This Weekend* I just heard, said he wiped out a whole village. Not just him, a whole battalion of them."

"A battalion is five hundred soldiers."

"Oh, it sounded like less than that. One of those smaller

ones. A company?"

"Platoon. That's the story I'm covering. But it was a couple of decades ago. During the Emergency."

"So why's it all coming up now? Hardly news."

"People are only now coming forward to say what really happened, so we have to look into it."

"Is it true? That they killed a whole village and had to lie about it?"

"It wasn't the whole village, just the men, and I don't know what's true yet, that's what I'm going to find out."

"Just seems so unlikely. All of them got together and lied about what they'd done, and then suddenly after twenty years they decide to come clean?"

"It happens. Guilty consciences. Look at My Lai."

"You think this is like My Lai? But that's huge. That's an enormous story. That makes sense, they wouldn't fly you out all the way there for anything less."

"One step at a time. I've got to come back in one piece first." Then, seeing her friend's eyes widen, "I was joking! It's perfectly safe, but after all I might not find anything worth writing about, or stuff it up some other way, you never know, and they'll never send me anywhere again."

"At least you'll get to go. Even if it's just this one time, you still have something to tell your grandchildren. And you have a hunch, don't you? You're following it into the jungle, all intrepid? If you break this story, this could be the making of you!"

Revathi blinked, suspecting sarcasm, but Lucy's eyes

actually were sparkling. Well, all right, she had a point, if this went well she would indeed be in for a different beat, something more challenging. There weren't many opportunities to get ahead. Plenty of people thought she should be grateful to be where she was, plenty more thought she shouldn't be there at all. She hadn't been to the right schools, wasn't a member of any of the right clubs, her parents spoke with an accent—and that was before you got on to the colour of her skin, or her being a woman.

She shook her head. Be a big girl, stop blubbing that you've been lonely. So no one slapped you on the back or took you to lunch when you first stepped into that newsroom, not like the boys. Never mind. Hold your own. She thanked Lucy for the suitcase and went down to call her parents.

"It's not too late to change your mind," said her mother, by way of greeting.

"It actually is, I'd get fired."

"I can talk to your boss, if you like."

"That's a terrible idea. Anyway, I want to go."

"Rev, why?"

"It's where I'm from. I want to see it again."

"When British people ask you where are you really from, I see you get annoyed. Suddenly you're from there again?"

"Well, I am, sort of. Where you're from, then."

"I'm from Singapore."

"I'll see that too. We're changing planes there."

"It's not safe."

"Things are different now, Amma. It's fine now."

"It's never fine. That's why we brought you to England. You were supposed to have a better life."

"I looked up some file pictures. Kuala Lumpur's a modern city now. Taller buildings than London, even."

"What about all those men who got killed?"

"That was decades ago! Don't you see what a big story this could be, though?"

"You are uncovering the truth after all this time?"

"I might. Don't make fun of me."

"Your father wants to speak to you."

Her father took the phone and said, gruffly, "Take care of yourself, Kutti," which was demonstrative for him. She hung up and went to bed, thoughtful.

That night, she dreamt of Malaysia for the first time in many years. Her parents had driven up north a couple of times, taking her to be cooed over by long-gone relatives. She saw the plantations they'd driven past, those tall trees blocking out the sun. Then she was running between the spindly trees, each trickling a channel of milk-white liquid into a Carnation tin. Her parents smiling as a foreman urged on his workers. She sprinted along the mathematically regular rows as they grew wider and wider, or perhaps she was shrinking, until the latex overflowed and lapped around her ankles, then knees. She struggled to get clear of it, but the viscous liquid made it hard to move. She called her father, but he'd disappeared. Amma? There was no one in sight. Out of nowhere, gunshots tore into the trees, and each wound produced a fresh stream of purest white. She opened her mouth to scream, but it filled with liquid before she could make a sound.

•

The heat was a shovel to the face, a blunt force smacking her entire body. Now she remembered. She'd braced herself for mere temperature, but this was altogether fiercer, the saturated air swaddling her so in seconds she was gasping slightly, her blouse soaked and hair clinging to her forehead. Was it possible the climate had become more hostile than in her childhood? Yet the locals seemed unbothered, moving minimally and not too fast, going about their business as if this whole country wasn't a furnace.

Mr Leng, the lawyer, met her at the airport. She was surprised he'd come in person rather than sending someone, but he brushed away her thanks, he enjoyed the drive out here anyway, there was a stall nearby with the best *nasi lemak*, always good to have an excuse to go there. Would she like some? Oh, of course, she must be exhausted, how long was her flight? Well, he'd take her directly to the hotel.

The Herald had booked her into the Hotel Merlin, a startlingly luxurious establishment, at least to her eyes: a tall slab of concrete and glass windows. From her room on the twelfth floor, she could see all the way to the horizon. Did the ringgit make things cheaper here? Or had she stumbled into a different level of her career, one in which there was somehow money where none had been before, the way the paper managed to pay Ian Spender significantly more than her, even though he took naps after his long lunches and turned in maybe two articles a week.

Mr Leng said as soon as she'd freshened up, he had a couple of people for her to meet in town.

The first visit felt like a warm-up, someone who'd already spoken to the papers at the time—the headman of the village that the women and children had been brought to after their houses were set alight. After his place, too, was razed, he'd come to the city to live with his brother. They sat in a cracked concrete courtyard, on rickety wooden stools. Everything he told her was already in the coverage, but it was useful to have it restated, and she'd be able to say it was as fresh in his mind as if it was yesterday. Readers liked that, to feel the past brought to them.

"We can walk to the next place," said Mr Leng. "It's the Royal Lake Club." This turned out to be an old colonial-type bungalow, surrounded by trees and water. The sun was starting to go down, swirling vivid purple and orange streaks through the sky that, judging by Mr Leng's nonchalance, was absolutely standard for this part of the world. As they climbed the cracked stone steps to the entrance, Mr Leng said cheerfully, "In the old days we wouldn't have been able to step inside here, you know. Especially not you. No women or locals."

The man they were there to meet looked like he rather missed those days, thought Revathi uncharitably. He introduced himself as Sergeant Cameron, late of the Royal

Scots Fusiliers, now retired and staying on in Malaya. (For the rest of the conversation, Revathi took mild pleasure in saying "Malaysia", and watching him twitch and pointedly stick to the old name.)

"Mr Cameron kindly agreed to answer some questions. He was here during the Emergency."

Revathi smiled as charmingly as she could, considering she hadn't slept at all on the plane and was feeling fairly woozy, though that could also have been the gin and tonic the sergeant gallantly ordered her without asking what she wanted.

Fortunately, she didn't need to do much talking at all. Even before she'd got her notebook out, he was regaling her with stories of the old days, the lawless frontier of the jungle and how his strapping British lads had restored order to the place. This was clearly a screed that got delivered at regular intervals, the anecdotes polished from repetition. Mr Leng melted into the background and let them get on with it.

"We were meant to be protecting the natives, but the natives were in on it. It was a mess, none of it made any sense. We locked them up in these camps, the rural people, the squatters—they lost all the land they had before, pigs and everything, right, we locked them up and they had to find a new way to keep going, where they ended up. And still they were helping the bandits. There were too many to keep track of. We searched them, but you're always going to miss a few grains of rice in someone's shoe, pills under someone's tongue. They told them things, where our defences were weak."

Revathi nodded. She'd heard this happened, and why.

"Why were we even here? If they were all doing it, who were we saving from whom? They said we'd be out of here before too long—not just the army, all of us, white skins, even the chaps up in city hall—they'd chuck us out, they wanted their country back. Can't say I particularly blamed them. We hadn't exactly covered ourselves in glory. And it happened, most of the old chaps are gone. Only stubborn buggers like me clinging on. Nothing for me back in Suffolk. Might as well stay.

"We made all kinds of mistakes. This chap, middle-aged bachelor type, he was found in the jungle with two tins of fruit, of course he got detained. Later on, his neighbours claimed he was worshipping his ancestors, that's how they do it, offerings of food. They knew they weren't supposed to bring food out, but some of them risked it, and he couldn't stand to think of his poor dead mother trapped in hell with nothing to eat. I told my commanding officer, he laughed at me for listening to the natives. Then he got serious and said, *It doesn't matter, there's nothing we can do, it's worth sacrificing some innocents if it means clearing the turf properly.* They arrested this girl, just a schoolgirl. She liked sugar in her coffee, they got coffee in her school but no sugar in it, so she brought sugar out with her in a twist of a paper. Someone found it and reported her. And they took her to court for that, girl of eleven."

He stared morosely out into the twinkling dark. It was a harsh, still night, the heat rising off the road with a smell of burnt rubber. The air must be close to blood heat, thought Revathi. She raised her hand and signalled for another round of drinks.

"Why do you think it went wrong?" she asked him gently.

"Did I say it did?" he returned. "We made mistakes, that's what I said. We won, you know, whatever that means. They surrendered in droves. We eliminated more than seven thousand. That's two-thirds of them, the ones we knew about, anyway. They're callous, the Chinese. They'll sit on the fence and wait to see which side wins." Revathi glanced at Mr Leng, but his face was stone, his body turned away slightly to make him invisible.

The drinks arrived. The waiter, clearly exhausted, patiently placed the glasses neatly in the centre of each coaster, not spilling a drop. Revathi waited till Cameron had taken a deep draught of his beer before asking, "Were you at Batang Kali? December 1948."

He refocused on her. "No, why?" She was silent. "What have you heard? I was in Perak at the time. It was the right thing to do, you know. Templer and his curfew. It looks harsh from the outside, but it worked. A fortnight's curfew, twenty-two hours a day. It did the trick, enough of them talked that they were able to find out who the Communists were."

"I suppose you're right," she said neutrally.

"You're not a sympathiser, are you?" He seemed suddenly suspicious. She could see him worrying that he'd said too much. "They were killing white men. We had to do something."

"I'm just curious." She kept her voice light, but brisk.

"I'm writing a story."

•

The next morning, Mr Leng phoned the hotel to say he was sending her to see one of the survivors in Seminyih, a new village outside KL. "I can't take you myself," he added. "I'll send Lina."

Lina turned out to be a Chinese woman a little older than Revathi. Her English was careful, correct. When Revathi complimented her, she flinched, as if this wasn't necessarily a good thing. "I grew up in Singapore."

"Oh, my parents are from Singapore," Revathi volunteered brightly. Lina nodded, uninterested.

The car was, unexpectedly, an Alfa Romeo, bright red and polished to a fierce sheen. "Not mine," said Lina. "Mr Leng's. I have to get it back to him by the end of the day. You must be very impressive, he doesn't usually lend anyone his car."

"How do you know him?"

"Lawyers always need people to help them. I'm good at helping."

Traffic was ridiculous for the first half hour, then they got to the edges of the city and suddenly everything was wide and open, the sun glaring harshly against the road so it seemed to shimmer in the distance. Here and there along the dusty verge, ramshackle wooden stands were piled with fruit she dimly remembered, dusty but still fantastical-looking, bright yellow stars and furry red bulbs, such abundance and colour. British food had come a long way since the end of rationing, of course, but how insipid it suddenly seemed, all greys and browns.

"You want some?" smirked Lina, seeing her look.

She shook her head. "I think I remember the taste."

"You've tasted durian? You talk with a potato in your mouth, I thought you must be completely ang moh."

Revathi wasn't sure what that meant, but it seemed intended as an insult. She nodded neutrally and settled back in her seat, looking out the window—they were passing by fields of occasional scrawny cows, sun so scorching it was a wonder anything grew at all, yet there was so much of it, such long, sharp blades of grass—"lalang," something whispered in her mind—and weeds bursting through the asphalt of the road.

After a while, the road became more of a dirt track, and they were moving between regular rows of trees. "Rubber?" she hazarded, and was surprised to find how pleased she was when Lina nodded. *Earning my keep after all*, she thought, scrabbling in her bag for a pencil, belatedly remembering she should be recording all this too. The air was moist and muddy, cooler now they were shaded by trees. Local colour. Readers go mad for that. Chinese and Indian restaurants in every British town these days, but who really knew anything about these countries? She was still scribbling away when the first narrow shops and houses appeared, and she understood they were in Seminyih.

The woman she was to meet was younger than Revathi

had expected, maybe about fifty, her face set in grim lines and hair tightly permed. She looked anxious, peering at them through the metal grilles of her front door. Following Lina's lead, Revathi carefully took off her shoes before entering, balancing awkwardly on one foot as she struggled with the straps of her sandals.

Lina said something, and the woman replied. "Mrs Wong says she's pleased to meet you," They shook hands, and Revathi realised Lina was also here to interpret. Well, of course she was, why had she thought anyone out here in the countryside would speak English? They all did in KL, like in Singapore, but this was a different place. Looking at the concrete floor and painted wooden walls, Revathi thought with a lurch that none of this had existed when she was last in this part of the world, not just the house but the whole settlement, where Semenyih now stood would have been nothing, jungle or grassland, all cleared for the new village. And here it was, the fences and gates removed at the end of the Emergency, but still feeling cramped and hemmed in, the trees around it just another form of stockade.

Revathi got out her notebook, her face already slipping into interview mode. This was the same as anything else, set the subject at ease, start with something inconsequential, though of course in her regular beat nothing was ever of consequence, except to the people involved and that nebulous beast the public interest, which ponderous men were fond of telling her did not mean "what the public is interested in", but then why do it? Why tell the stories of misfortune's victims, magnifying their perfectly ordinary existences for a moment, giving readers a temporary hit of sympathy, or relief that their own lives were still whole, their families intact, everything just fine for the moment at least?

The small talk took twice as long because it had to go through Lina. It was actually quite soothing, the sounds she couldn't decipher, although again the musical chirps and grunts hovered at the edges of familiarity. Was this something she might have heard her neighbours use? She genuinely couldn't remember which dialect they would have spoken, and wondered if she'd ever known, if her parents would be able to tell her.

The questions came automatically. *How long have you lived here? Tell me about the neighbourhood. What do you do for a living?* The translation gave her time for mental wandering, allowed her shorthand to be less frantic than usual. They'd moved here, or rather, been moved, just scooped up and placed behind barbed wire, they said it was an Emergency so the laws didn't matter any more, convenient how the law was so important one minute and then could just be ignored, but then when had people like them ever had any say.

"Who is 'they'?" said Revathi, automatically. Always query pronouns, you never know. Mrs Wong didn't burst into tears, but it was clear from the twitching of her facial muscles that a woman with less practice in suppressing her sorrow would have done so at this moment. She said something to Lina, who grimaced and said, "Her son."

"I'm sorry. Is he—"

More murmuring. "He's inside."

"You mean prison? What for?"

"No, no. Inside—the jungle."

She puzzled over this as they stared at her. Finally, Lina took pity. "He's with the Ma Gong. The Communists."

"He's a *bandit?*" She bit her tongue. Lina looked blankly at her but did not translate. She didn't need to. Mrs Wong's eyes were hooded. "I mean," said Revathi, trying to keep her voice level, "I thought all that was over. Isn't it? All long ago?"

"They're still fighting—up north, near the border."

"Lina—seriously? What on earth?"

"The struggle's still going on. I know it's not in the news or anything. People here don't think about it, why would you know?"

"Is she sure he's there?"

"There are sympathisers in the town. He got a message to her through one of them. Saying not to worry, that sort of thing. That's all she knows."

Mrs Wong was staring at the table, its cracked linoleum surface, as if wishing them away.

"Lina." Revathi licked her lips; her mouth was drying out. "Do you think it's all right to ask her, does she miss him? No, wait. Ask if she approves of what he's doing."

"I'm not going to ask her that."

"But it was the bandits, wasn't it? Their fault. That her husband—"

"The Ma Gong didn't shoot him."

"But they created the conditions for the Emergency."

She wanted to say more, half-remembered stories from her parents, but Lina was already asking Mrs Wong something that sounded more involved than what they'd been talking about. Revathi considered going out for a cigarette—no need to worry about them talking behind her back, they could do that right in front of her. "What's going on?" she hissed, not caring that she was interrupting.

Lina looked harassed. "She keeps breaking into Hakka, and I only know Cantonese. I'm trying to work out what she means."

Revathi felt momentarily guilty, then immediately mistrustful. Why would Lina have any more loyalty to her than this woman? Her English was fluent, but in Chinese she was just as alien as the rest of these people, swooping through tones Revathi would never be able to hear, words she'd never be able to decipher. "The Chinese aren't on your side, any more than the white people," she imagined her father saying.

"What do you want to know?" asked Lina. "I told her you wanted to tell people in the West what really happened here. That's right, isn't it?"

"Just the truth," said Revathi, keeping her face neutral.

"She says so many people have asked her questions, the police and all, but they already seem to know what they want her answers to be. She's not even sure about Mr Leng. He says he's on her side, but lawyers can be like that. Persuasive."

"Ask her to tell me, please, in her own words, what happened on the night of 11 December 1948."

Lina interpreted, and then there was a pause, during

which a car drove by noisily outside, and some sort of insect buzzed right past Revathi's ear. Mrs Wong spoke, slowly at first, then gathering steam, not even waiting for Lina to finish translating so they began to overlap, talking over each other, leaving Revathi to pick out the English from the stream.

"It rained that day, so we were home." ("She means they couldn't tap rubber because of the weather, the dripping water would have ruined the latex," interjected Lina, her voice a bit lower to show these were her own words.) "I was a bit worried because there'd been so much rain lately, the monsoon season was heavier than normal. Me and my husband were both tappers, everyone in the village was, so bad weather meant we all had no money. At least the rain made it nice and cool. My husband thought of going to visit his cousin in the next plantation, but decided he was too lazy. If he'd gone—"

Revathi nodded, her eyes fixed on Mrs Wong. Later on, she would find only one voice in her memory, as if Mrs Wong had spoken English.

"The men arrived around four something in the afternoon, maybe five something. They were all in uniform, two ang mohs and a Chinese. The ang mohs shouted at us, and he repeated in our language. I don't know why they all had to shout so much, it's a small village, you don't need to be so loud, but we were used to it. Everyone was very *kancheong*—" ("I don't know the English for that," murmured Lina, "it's something like anxious, but not quite.")

"We lived in plantation houses; everyone in Sungei

Remok worked for the estate. Our food came in a big lorry. We had to cook it ourselves, they delivered exact amounts, rice and oil and so on, just enough for the people who lived there. They said they didn't want us to give any food to the people in the jungle; they thought because we were all Chinese that we were all—"

("Bandits," supplied Revathi, when Lina hesitated. "I didn't want to use that word," she snapped back.)

"There were police everywhere. None of us dared to bring food out with us when we went to tap rubber, we all went without lunch, it wasn't worth the risk. Sometimes they came to ask us questions, had we seen something or did we know someone, we always said no, it was easier that way. We had food and work and a place to live, we didn't want to cause any trouble. My husband wasn't perfect, but he was better than a lot of people. He didn't deserve to be shot. I don't mean because he wasn't one of them, although he wasn't; no one deserved to get shot."

"The bandits killed people," said Revathi. The two of them ignored her.

"At first we thought it was just another inspection. That happened sometimes, they came and started asking questions, usually there'd been some incident and they were looking for suspects, or maybe someone reported seeing something. Maybe they liked making our lives difficult. As if giving us trouble would make us too scared to help the Ma Gong."

"So you were helping them?"

Mrs Wong shrugged. "Why not? They were all someone's

cousin, someone's brother. It was just a bit of food. Should we have let them starve?"

A fly settled lazily on the tabletop. Mrs Wong barely seemed to move her hand, smacking down a placemat crisply on it.

"I don't agree with what the Ma Gong did," she said. "Not everything. They shouldn't have killed the plantation owners, but maybe they were bad bosses. Most were all right, even good, but some of them... And it's our land, we just wanted to get our land back. When the Japanese were here, we fought to get them out. What's the difference?"

"We're getting off the topic," said Revathi, a little desperately. "Could you ask her again to say what happened that day?"

The older woman smirked, as if she'd scored a point. "I was cooking dinner. When the shouting came, I told my husband to go see what they wanted, usually it was nothing much, just shout a bit and then go. But it continued, so I went to the door to see, and the ang mohs were waving their guns, telling us come out, stand over there. All the men were already standing in a tight group, over twenty of them. I wanted to go back inside to turn off the fire but they said no, come straight out. I went back anyway, no sense burning the house down. When I came out they grabbed my hand and said you should learn to follow orders. Guns pointing right at us, guards on the paths away from the village. As if anyone would dare to run—" ("It was the law." Lina again. "They weren't supposed to shoot civilians, but if you ran, then you were automatically guilty. So they could shoot you.")

"My boy was bathing in the river. I thought maybe he could swim away and hide, but they saw him, the men, so they shouted again and he came out, him and his friends, pulled on their clothes and ran over to us. They were only small, maybe this tall—" She held her hand an improbably low distance from the floor. "He didn't know what was happening. Many years later, when I talked to my son, I don't think he remembered much about that night. But I didn't want to ask, I didn't want to talk about it. So I don't know, maybe it's all still in his head."

"Did you find out afterwards what they found so suspicious?"

"It was the food lorry, just the regular one, but they said how come this small village needs so much food, as if they couldn't see how many children were running around, children take up so little space but eat so much. *Are you stockpiling food for the Communists?* It all came from the plantation, they gave us the correct amount, just enough. Then more ang mohs came, a couple kept their guns pointed at us while the rest searched our houses, we could hear them breaking things, smashing furniture. My boy started to cry and I tried to keep him quiet, all while the Chinese uniformed man was shouting at us to keep still, follow instructions, it's all for our own good.

"Then an officer came out of one of the houses waving some rambutans. We weren't supposed to grow our own food, so how could these be here? The poor woman whose house it was said they were wild, as if anyone in the village had time to plant a rambutan tree, but if you came across one in the jungle wouldn't you gather some fruit? Otherwise they'd just go to waste, get eaten by monkeys or something, we might as well have it. If not, we just ate the same things all the time, the same few vegetables."

"So they had the proof they needed?"

"What are you talking about? They didn't need proof, no one was asking them to show anything, they just did what they wanted. Pushing us around all the time. A few years later, they put me in this village, barbed wire fence and everything, like prison. I never did anything wrong. They kept saying all of us were helping the people inside, none of us were good. How could we argue against that? If they thought we were bad, how could we convince them?"

"How long did they keep you outside?"

"I don't know, you think I had a watch? We were there until it got dark. The children were crying from hunger, or maybe fear. I could see my husband on the other side, with the other men, too far away to say anything. Now and then he looked up at me and the boy, nodding a bit like he wanted to say it would be all right, but this was worse than anything that had ever happened, and we all knew bad things happened constantly. We knew the stories: people were always getting arrested and tried, put in prison or deported, even killed, for no reason, just for having food on them, never mind that we got so hungry during the day, it's very hard work, out in the jungle or fields all day. This didn't happen in the cities; people there could just live like normal, they didn't know what was happening to us, or maybe they didn't care, as long as it made them feel safe."

"Why didn't you go live in the city?"

"My boy did, later on. I made sure he went to school, so they'd take him. But people like us, we could barely read or write, what would we do in a city?"

"So you were outside till nightfall."

"Eventually they pushed us into one of the houses, all the women and children, the men stayed outside. Maybe forty of us, in one small room. We heard more shouting outside. Gunshots. After a while, the soldiers came in with some milk and a bit of rice. They said one of the men was dead. We fed the children and told each other they were just trying to frighten us. It was so hot in that room. There was nothing to say, so we stopped talking. One of the kids had to pee. We put a bucket in the corner. Hung a sarong in front of it so the adults could go too. The noise from outside didn't stop. I hugged my boy and fell asleep, eventually.

"When I woke up, it was early morning, and there was a bit of light coming between the cracks in the walls. We were still groggy when the soldiers came again and said get all our things, we had five minutes, just take our most important possessions and get ready to move. No one understood why but there was no time for questions. We ran back to our houses and scooped things into bags. I took clothes and cooking utensils; we didn't have very much but I didn't know where we were going or what I would need. My boy was so good, he didn't cry or cause any trouble, he even tried to help, so I gave him some things to hold. They were screaming all the while for us to hurry, and when we came out they pushed us towards a truck on the other side of the clearing. We could see the men nearby, squatting with their hands over their heads, the soldiers still with guns saying don't you dare look up. I called my husband's name but there was so much noise, I don't know if he heard.

"We got into the truck—"

The pause couldn't have lasted more than a few seconds, but perhaps the absolute stillness was what made the time stretch. Revathi felt the air curdling around her. Ought she say something? None of them seemed to be breathing.

"The sun had risen a bit more but I still couldn't see clearly. My boy stumbled. Luckily I was holding his hand tight; if he'd fallen they might have shot him, they all had their hands on their rifles and we knew to go slow, no sudden movements. There was a man lying face down some distance away, not moving; I couldn't see who it was, but one of the women was sobbing, trying not to make too much noise. We got into the back of the lorry, lifting the children up then climbing in ourselves. Then the vehicle started to move. Up to that moment, I'd actually believed the men would be joining us. Stupid. Some of the women screamed, tried to jump out, but others held them back. One of the soldiers in the lorry pointed a gun at us, kept it there until we got to the end of the road. I wish I'd done something, but I was holding my boy, and I felt like—if I just kept still enough, then—"

She hadn't looked at Revathi this whole time, she wasn't looking at anything. Her voice was so quiet it seemed to fade away, Lina's too, almost no sound.

"I heard a gunshot, I swear I did. Maybe they started shooting right away. Then we turned the corner and I couldn't see them any more. A minute later, I saw smoke rising. They'd set fire to our houses. There were thick black clouds of it. I kept looking back, and the smoke kept growing. In my memory, it filled the whole sky. Maybe it did. We kept moving, and I knew then we had nowhere to go back to."

She stared at the back of her hands, spread on the table.

"Where did they take you?" said Revathi, after a moment.

"The next village. It was about twenty minutes away. They pushed us off the lorry and drove away. When we said what had happened people came out to give us food and a place to lie down, they knew it could just as easily have happened to them, so they took us in. We were there for a few days. Eventually I took my boy and went to live with my husband's aunt, her husband was dead and there were no children so she had room for us. Then they took away her house too, that was what they were planning all along. They put us in this place, with the fence around it."

"I'm so sorry that happened to you," said Revathi, despising herself for slipping into familiar rhythms. She could hear what she was doing, the respectful pause, the dip in the voice to signal empathy. Tics honed in a thousand interviews, the same words for everyone.

Mrs Wong nodded. Her face was expressionless, and Revathi found it impossible to remember the timbre of her voice. It had been snatched away by Lina's ventriloquism. Without asking permission, she took out her camera and snapped a picture. The flash went off, but she already knew this wouldn't come out well, the hut was too dingy. She should have asked Mrs Wong to step outside into the sun, but her voice failed her. No point. Let her face fade. If the paper didn't like it, they could use a file photo. Palm trees or something.

"And your husband—" she began, but Mrs Wong shook her head, just slightly, and cut the thread. She angled her body away just a little, enough to make it clear the interview was over. She remained in exactly the same position as Revathi and Lina made their way out the door.

•

Back in the sun, they blinked, eyes adjusting. It was actually dizzying, like a physical blow to the head.

"I'm a Communist too, by the way," said Lina conversationally. "You probably guessed."

"Does Mr Leng know?"

"I don't try to hide it."

"But you're not a bandit."

"I'm not one of the people inside, obviously."

Revathi stumbled walking towards the car, glinting nastily in the sun. She looked around, but there was nothing she could have tripped over.

"Are you all right?" said Lina, taking her elbow.

Not all right, she wanted to cry, *there's nothing all right about this. I'm six thousand miles from home in a climate that makes no sense to me any more, right in the middle of a war that's not a war, that's stretching on even though it ended ten years ago. This is one day, twenty-two years ago, and lives are still being destroyed over it. What can I say? I'm not the right person for the story, except somehow I'm the one who's here.*

"It's a lot to take in," she said feebly.

Lina led her to a sort of shack nearby, a makeshift food stand, muttering something about how it was a lot more to actually live through this. "I can't go back to Singapore, even now," she said. "They might still be looking for me. I have no way to find out, but I know comrades still being detained. I can't take the risk."

"Did you do something?"

"Of course you're taking their side. We did nothing, just fought for a better world."

"Fought how? Like, by force?"

Lina ignored her, ordering a cup of coffee that came underlined by a thick layer of white that swirled greyish trails through the dense liquid when she stirred. It was strong and sugary, exactly what Revathi needed. She took a large gulp, gratefully, clinging to the sensation of comfort.

"How do you know what's right?" she said, more to herself

than Lina. "The soldiers believed they were shooting bandits. They were at war, they just wanted to do their duty."

"Duty is an excuse for many bad things."

"What do you think they should have done? What would you, if you were in that position?"

Lina turned to the man dozing behind the counter. "*Cik masih ingat Sungei Remok tak?*"

He grunted a response, and Lina said something back, slipping in bits of Cantonese, English and mime when her Malay failed. Revathi recognised the odd word, but not enough to make sense of it.

"He wants to know what you're doing here. I told him you're from the government."

"Lina!"

"No lah, I didn't really, don't worry. I said you've come all the way from England to find out what's happening, and he said it's about time."

"About Batang Kali?"

"Everything. The whole Emergency. All the people still inside. His house was in Kachau. He wants to know if you're going to write stories about him too?"

"What's Kachau?"

"A village. The British burnt it down, the same month as Batang Kali."

"Why?"

"Similar reasons. The Communists were there, or they were helping the Communists, something like that. They didn't kill anyone, so you didn't hear about it."

Revathi hadn't heard of Batang Kali, or Sungei Remok, whatever it was called until a week ago. She scribbled down a note to herself. "*Terima kasih*," she said to the man, and to Lina, "Was that right?"

"Close enough."

"Lina, where were you while all this was going on?"

"I was going to school in Singapore. We had study groups, supported the workers. It's different in the cities. A lot of the people who went inside come from the small towns and villages."

"So you don't actually know anyone—"

"My friend Siew Li is inside," said Lina. "I can tell you her name, it doesn't matter, she'll have changed it. We were at school together. She had to leave her family. Small children. What kind of government would separate a mother from her children?"

"I'm sorry."

"I hear about her, now and then. She was a real fighter. I wish I could be like her."

"Why do you say 'was'? Is she—"

"She's not well," said Lina. "I don't know more than that, I—" She broke off and stared angrily at the ground, then glanced at Revathi's cup. "Finished?" She stomped towards the car, Revathi scuttling after her.

This is ordinary, Revathi told herself. Everyone in this part of the world was touched by history, just like anywhere else. Her parents had their own Emergency stories, insulated as they were, why wouldn't people here? It was a war like any other, she'd heard things from her English friends in the same vein, relatives caught selling butter on the black market during rationing, neighbours who may or may not have been a bit too friendly with the Enemy.

Lina started the car. The windows were down, and soon a strong breeze was blowing past them. If not for the occasional branch slapping the doors, she would have stuck her head out, but the jungle encroached too close. She let her hair loose from its bun and allowed it to billow.

On an impulse, she turned to Lina. "Why are you so angry? The British have left, isn't that what you wanted?"

"The people they left in charge are still running things. How is that better? Just because the people stepping on our heads have the same skin colour as me?"

"So what are the Ma Gong doing about this? You blamed me for not knowing the struggle was still on, but what's actually happening?"

A long moment of silence. "I don't know," she finally said.

"Do you think the Ma Gong are doing the right thing?"

"I don't know what they're doing either. We've been abandoned," said Lina, hands gripping the wheel. "Last year, May thirteenth, we marched through the city. We wanted a Malaysian Malaysia. Everyone equal, no special privileges for the Malays. The government doesn't listen to us, there was nothing we could do. We were attacked with *parangs*. Fighting everywhere. We knew the Ma Gong were up near the Thai border, but with all the chaos, we thought they would come back. It was the perfect time to take charge again.

"I saw bodies curled up under the roadside trees, floating in the canals. Some of them had been shot dead. None of us had guns, so it must have been the police. Even when we were dying in the streets, the Ma Gong did nothing."

"What are they waiting for?" said Revathi carefully.

Lina wiped her eyes. "No one will tell me."

"Have you thought of joining?"

"No, I'm too scared. I'm not like my friend. They need people on the outside to help them, I pass messages and get supplies to them. But I couldn't go inside. Once you're inside, you're there forever. You can't come out. They'd kill you."

"The police?"

"The Ma Gong. If you try to leave, they kill you."

"That's terrible."

"They have to. Otherwise people will join just to learn all their secrets, then turn around and betray them. You don't know what people will do, when the government is offering such big rewards."

"How long did it go on for?"

"May thirteenth? Weeks. Till the end of July at least. Hundreds of people died."

"I wonder if my parents knew this was happening. They never said—"

"There was a curfew. No one was allowed outside. From my window I saw a dog running down the lane. I knew that dog, it belonged to the family a few doors down. The man ran out chasing it but he got shot after a few steps. There must have been a police marksman nearby. The family tried to hold the wife back, but she shook them off and ran to the body. Of course they shot her too."

Revathi tried to say something, but no words would come.

"I thought there would be crying, shouting, but their door just shut. It felt like the whole street was holding its breath. The dog stood by the bodies, quietly, all night long. When I looked out again in the morning, the lane was empty again."

"I didn't know things like that were still happening."

"Why would you? It took Batang Kali more than ten years to get into your newspapers, and that was with white men doing the killing. Guilt, I suppose. We kill each other all the time. No one cares about that. They declared another Emergency, did you know that? People have heard about the long one, but there've been more."

"There are bandits to the north. I can see why this isn't over yet."

"If it wasn't them, there'd be some other excuse. There's always an emergency somewhere."

•

The rest of the trip was fairly uneventful. Lina drove her out to the actual site of Batang Kali, where there was not a lot to be seen, but she took pictures of the crumbling wrecks of buildings, and the spot where the mass graves might have been. There were a few other people to interview. Now and then, she asked after a name that had been mentioned, but mostly it was easiest to let Mr Leng line them up.

The article was written in scraps of time, between snatched moments of sleep. *This can't be normal*, she thought, exhilarated, typing away in her slip at three in the morning. She'd been brought up to believe in regular work that took place in nice, clean offices, between fixed hours. Yet here she was, in a hotel room that could be anywhere, weaving a story into being and feeling like if she stopped for a second to breathe, the whole thing would fall apart. As long as she got the next sentence out, and the one after that, she'd be all right.

It felt good, all of it. Everything about this felt urgent, something that would burst into the world with the force of truth. She didn't need to plead this case, just lay the facts out clearly, and allow the British public's sense of justice to do the rest.

On her last night, Mr Leng picked her up at the hotel and took her to dinner. She tried afterwards to remember the name of the place but never could. It was hard to tell how posh it was, rickety tables beneath trees with fairy lights threaded through their branches, stray cats gnawing at discarded bones in the ditch. Revathi slapped at mosquitoes and ate delicious things tasting of coconut and shrimp, flavoured with spices she couldn't identify. She asked what each dish was called, intending to ask her parents about it afterwards, but by the time she got back to London, she'd forgotten all the names.

This isn't real, she thought, *this is a respite*. Heavy air prickled against her skin as she smiled at Mr Leng. He was so pleased she'd found what she needed, he told her, a voice of the Malaysian people on the other side, someone who could tell the British what really happened in their name, not just here but all over the world.

There were too many strands, all the threads of history, everything that ever happened, more than a single person could grasp. The settled story was only one version. She'd seen how the game played out, the *Herald* did it sometimes, deciding to support Tollingforth in Tollingforth vs. Conswith, just because the *Times* was supporting Conswith, Lars arguing that the public deserved to hear the other side.

She allowed herself to daydream a little. Perhaps she could ask to stay out here for a while, maybe even write a book. So many compelling stories here, had anyone done a history of the region? *One step at a time. Get this done first.*

There would be more work to do over the next few days, facts to check and more sources to pursue, but with Mrs Wong she knew she had dynamite, a compelling voice to put at the centre of her story. A human face for the tragedy. The dead husband, the missing son. It would be hard to mess this one up. Whatever else might have gone wrong with her career, Revathi had a newswoman's instincts, and she knew this was absolutely red hot. She smiled and clinked her glass against Mr Leng's, scribbling sentences in her head, each one pinging off every bell in her mind.

•

As she'd known would happen, the article caused a sensation.

They had to run a special reprint, and more than one MP raised it in parliament, calling for an enquiry. She was giddy with it, allowing herself the pleasure of having it framed over her desk, so she could look up at it when she should be working. Her parents bought every copy at the newsagent's and spent the next month distributing them amongst friends and relatives. Her mother stopped suggesting she might look for a more respectable profession in order to attract a husband.

Something strange happened, in the weeks after Revathi's success. People took her seriously, a novel sensation. Such an important story, they told her, so grateful for the part she'd played in uncovering it. To start with, she'd given credit to Lars and his leap of faith in sending her—but they weren't interested in that, and so she fell back on an enigmatic nod, a modest smile. This was exactly right, and gained her even more respect. *So humble*, they whispered, *that's how you know she's the real thing*.

It felt unearned, and she had to tell herself this was hers, she deserved it. The idea had been hers. Spender would have squandered the opportunity somehow, blundered in at the wrong angle. She felt a fraud for not having had to dig particularly hard. She'd simply turned up and listened—they'd been so eager for their stories to be heard. And yet, no one had done even that. No one had thought of going, till she'd pushed.

She allowed this to become her cause. Why not? It was an obvious injustice, and no one in Britain was doing anything about it. Her voice would be harder to ignore than the ones from that part of the world. Why not do what she could? To start with, she lay awake some nights worrying that she was doing this for self-gain, but finally decided that motivations are always murky, even to yourself, and as long as good is done then it doesn't matter. *You should always get on the horse that's running,* her father said. She was moving now. She wanted to keep moving.

There was nothing hollow about what she was doing. She marvelled that she could feel this, absolute rage and pity for the people she wanted to help, in whatever small ways she was able to, but also pleasure at ordinary things, the smoothness of an orderly life proceeding on its tracks. A promotion and a raise, grudging praise from Lars, a desk in a better part of the office. A bedsit in a slightly nicer part of Earl's Court.

When the election came round, she wrote a series of columns predicting a Conservative victory, which were widely regarded as a stunt. It had seemed certain that Wilson was going to stay in Number Ten, and hers was the only prominent voice pulling the other way. Cassandra of the *Herald*. When asked how she'd known, she would only say it was a lucky guess, and then if pressed, that she'd listened to people. That was all. Enough of them were uncertain, and with every other paper assuring Labour voters they needn't worry, who would bother to turn out?

In the meantime, she kept an eye on the Batang Kali survivors, exchanging the odd letter with Mr Leng to see if there was the need for a second piece. There wasn't going to be another enquiry at the moment, but Scotland Yard was talking about the possibility of a prosecution. Between her piece and so many of the Scots Guards confessing, it was hard to see how they could do otherwise. She had her opening paragraph planned, something about how justice long delayed must taste the sweetest. Or words to that effect. She'd come up with something better.

The bad news came from her own newspaper, buried in the back pages. She stared for a long time at the small item, a few lines stating that the Scots Guards had no case to answer, their reputation was intact, and therefore the government's conduct during the Malayan Emergency was once more above reproach. She went upstairs to speak to the court reporter but he didn't have much to add. There was a new Attorney-General with the new government, and it was perfectly natural that he'd want to start with a clean slate. "It's for the best. Why give our boys a hard time?" he called after her as she trotted away.

She looked it up in Hansard, and it was as he said. The Attorney-General announced he was taking the advice of the Director of Public Prosecutions, who believed there was insufficient evidence to warrant criminal proceedings.

And there was Marcus Lipton, Labour MP for Brixton. "Does the Attorney-General nevertheless agree that, in view of sworn statements by four ex-guardsmen claiming to be present at the scene, which were published in the *People*, it was necessary to have the inquiry even though after all these years it is generally accepted that it is impossible to collect sufficient evidence for a prosecution?"

And the reply. "I do not wish to make any comment about the necessity of this inquiry."

She let the sentence run over and over in her head. That was all there was. He did not wish it, and therefore it would not happen. Of course, that's how it had always been. She understood this at one level, but at another felt horribly naïve at having allowed herself to believe in the possibility of justice. There had been no further discussion. A token show of resistance, and the chamber moved on to other business.

"What's wrong?" said Ian Spender, stopping by her desk. The men, she noted, were treating her better now, as if she'd needed to accomplish all she had merely in order to be taken as an equal.

"Nothing. Some bad news."

"Not too serious, I hope?" His pallid face was actually mildly concerned, as if he really did care.

"I'll survive, thanks." And she would. She would be fine. How had this come to mean so much to her? Her life would continue just the same, she knew that.

"We'll be down the pub, if you're coming."

"I'll be there." She waited for him to go, and rubbed the heels of her hands into her eyes, trying to ease away the incipient headache. Something heavy was settling onto her, an unpleasant awareness that the world was aslant and she was at the higher end. What could she do?

She looked at the article, at the shadowy picture of Mrs

Wong. Keep going. The world would always be unfair, and mostly unknowable, but she had the leverage to make a little more truth come to light, and that would have to be enough. One step, then another. She carefully put the cover on her typewriter, and walked out into the summer's evening.

5

They were waiting for her at the airport. She noticed them as she got off the plane, right after the corridor of smiling stewardesses in silly tight uniforms, thanking you for flying Singapore Airlines. There were two of them, men, not in uniform but you could tell from the way they stood awkwardly in their badly-ironed shirts, unsmiling, that they were waiting for someone. One of them whispered something to the other, and they approached.

"Stella Remedios?"

"Yes?"

"Please come with us."

One of them flashed an ID, too quickly for her to read. It looked official enough that she followed them, one on either side of her, as if she could be thinking of running away, down this narrow passage full of tired, jetlagged people trying to ignore them.

"I didn't get your names," she said, trying to be friendly, but they said nothing, like actors who've spoken all their lines and just want to get to the end of the scene. Both were in their thirties, she guessed. Bad haircuts and thuggish faces. She wondered who they worked for, the police or something else.

At customs, they were met by a man in uniform who escorted them through a side gate. Stella thought, *Well, this looks official, at least that means I'm not being kidnapped.* Then, irrelevantly: *I won't get a stamp in my passport.* They waited patiently as she picked her suitcase off the carousel, and one of the men even carried it to the boot of the car they ushered her into.

"What's this about?"

Instead of answering, one of them said, almost apologetically, "You'll have to put these on." He removed her cat's-eye glasses and stuck on plastic ones with something, maybe foam rubber, where the lenses should be. Was she being arrested? They were supposed to read out her rights. Had she done anything?

"Where are you taking me?" She was ignored. What was the point of the goggles? Singapore was too small for secret prisons.

The car thrummed along the road. She tried to work out where they were. There was only one road from the airport. She normally enjoyed it, straight and wide with blossoming shrubs on either side. For the tourists, of course, but that didn't make it any less pretty. They turned, and then again, until she lost all sense of direction.

To calm herself, she thought about the things she would

do when she got home. First, call her father, he would be expecting her. Unpack, put winter clothes into storage, sort through the mail that had arrived while she was away. But first, food. She'd slept through all the meal services on the plane and was now ravenous.

The journey seemed extraordinarily long, but then she had no sense of time any more. There was just the motion of the car, the loud breathing of the men beside her, and occasionally a garbled sound from the relay radio mounted on the dashboard. We could be underwater, she thought, we could be driving into the past. She was woozy from the long flight, and this seemed like a waking dream.

She'd dozed off when the car braked, and one of the men grabbed her elbow to get her out. She was walked across what felt like grass, and then—"Steps," said the man in warning—into a building. This was ridiculous, she felt like ripping the opaque glasses off to see where she was going, but didn't want to make them angry.

They brought her into a small room, and finally removed her blindfold. It was ping pong balls, she realised, cut in half and stuck over each lens. Her own glasses were still with them, so everything was blurry. As far as she could tell, this was a government building of some kind, the walls that institutional green you only see in schools and hospitals. A woman came in with some forms for her to fill in, but she couldn't see to write, and had to dictate her answers. It was just things like her address, and which schools she'd attended, surely information they already had. She wondered where they'd taken her luggage.

A little later, they brought her to a dimmer room. There were some people standing about, she wasn't sure how many. They seemed to have been waiting for her. Someone said her name again, with a harsh emphasis, and when she answered yes, the interrogation began.

•

Stella's childhood was unexceptional. The journalists who tried to find some kind of flaw in her upbringing were disappointed—she was mixed-race, of course, but you weren't allowed to point at that as a defect. Her mother's early death was a point of interest, but as she was under a year old at the time, and her father remarried not long afterwards, it again seemed unlikely this was to blame.

Her cousins Henry and Janet also lost their mother early, and she grew up very close to them. She'd drifted apart from Janet, who became more and more like her scary father, Stella's Uncle Jason, as she moved into adulthood. Henry was still one of her best friends, one of the few people who understood why so many things about this place made her dissatisfied.

Like nine-tenths of the population, Stella grew up in a government-provided HDB flat. She went to a primary school within walking distance of her home, and did well enough at the age of twelve to win a place at Methodist Girls' School. She was from a religious family, and later on there would be many pictures of her friends praying for her, saying they knew she was innocent, asking God to bring the truth to light.

She was only twenty-three at the time of her detention, not long out of university. Much as she admired her cousin Henry for winning his place at Oxford—indeed, she had just returned from visiting him in England when she was taken—she did not have the courage to uproot herself and move to a cold country of unfriendly people and bland food. Her father was a man of decided tastes, and she had grown up with the distinctively-spiced Eurasian curries that are so hard to find anywhere else.

So she ended up at NUS, the National University of Singapore (formerly Malaya, but a new name had to be found after Separation), doing something with history, and sociology. Afterwards, she found herself drifting towards teaching. Many of her classmates ended up there too—there were not many career paths open to those trained in the arts, especially those not overburdened with ambition.

It was easy for her to find a place at her old school, teaching keen Methodist girls the history found in their textbooks. She didn't fully agree with the narrative of benevolent colonialism giving way to a thrusting, vibrant city state, but that was the syllabus, and it made a pretty story. It helped that her cousin Janet was teaching at the same school and was able to show her the ropes.

Stella herself was not a Methodist, but Catholic like her father. She enjoyed the ritual and order of Mass, which gave her a great sense of peace. It was as if things had been this way since the beginning of time, and even though she knew that at some point, men had devised these ceremonies, she persuaded herself they must be inspired by God, and in any case, anything that brings you closer to divinity can only be positive.

She was a shy girl, less than a decade older than her students, whom she found near-impossible to control, even these well-behaved Christian girls, and as a consequence felt herself constantly judged by her colleagues. More than once a fellow teacher had come to investigate a commotion, and found Stella cowering behind her desk, ineffectually raising her voice against a boisterous, hormone-driven racket. In the staffroom, she sat and ate her sandwiches in a corner on her own, unless Janet happened to be free.

It was in church that she made her friends. They were equal before God, she felt it exhilarating that a young person like her, so broken and unpractised in the faith, was considered worthy of saving. She joined the small groups, and did volunteer work. It felt good, like she was making a difference to the lives of others. She became aware they all lived on a small island, and it was necessary to pull together and help each other out, rather than competing all the time. She wished everyone in the world would learn this lesson.

She could remember pockets of poverty when she was growing up, homeless people one tried not to see on the way to school. Nowadays, so many people had government flats, great featureless blocks springing up all over the island. People had money now, there were shopping centres along Orchard

Road and the MRT, which she found that terribly exciting, trains moving at great speeds beneath the feet of a city going about its business. That was one of her reasons for wanting to visit London, to see for herself the monstrous, wormlike tube network, the very one ridden by Mrs Dalloway.

But there were people left out of Singapore's headlong rush towards prosperity. She saw them in the streets, lying on park benches like they'd been there all night. Thousands more came in from other countries, Indonesia and the Philippines, working in people's homes for insultingly low wages. Her own family employed a domestic helper called Veronica, a devout Catholic girl. When she protested, her stepmother said: *Do you want to do all the housework yourself? I've never seen you so much as lift a broom. Should we send Veronica back to Cebu? She was unemployed for almost a year before this.*

Stella found it hard to meet Veronica's eye. She tried to clean up after herself, but Veronica was always there first with her broom and dustpan, trying to make herself indispensable. She slept on a mattress in the kitchen floor. Stella asked her to come to church, but she said she preferred to spend her rare days off with her fellow countrywomen. When Gregory at church asked Stella to serve on the maid welfare committee, she answered yes immediately. It felt like the least she could do.

•

"Can I have my glasses, please?" said Stella. A ripple around the room that felt a little like laughter. "Why did you bring me here? Can someone tell me what this is about?"

A man's voice, high-pitched and thin, cut in. "You don't ask us questions, we ask you questions. That's how this works."

"What do you want?" She tried to keep her voice neutral, but it shook.

The same voice, amused. "Another question. You don't understand, is it? Clever girl like you. Teacher some more. How come you don't understand simple English?"

She tried to place his voice, then she realised why it seemed familiar: he was a stranger, but his voice was the same as the school bully, as the sadistic student leaders at her university orientation who'd made them crawl through mud. The voice of someone with power but not authority.

She stayed silent. Best to let him do the talking.

"Stella." The same voice. "You know why you are here?"

"No."

"Are you sure? Reflect on what you've done."

It was disorientating not to be able to see them, or even how many of them there were. Apart from the spokesman, she could see blurs of movement just beyond the circle of lamplight. The room was not large, and sparsely furnished.

"Do you know who we are?"

"No." She was getting tired of this, but the voice wanted to play games.

"Guess." The hint of laughter, again.

"The police?" She knew that couldn't be, but she wouldn't give him the satisfaction.

"Stella, you're in the Internal Security Department. Do you know what that means?"

"I haven't done anything."

"Then why are you here? Stella, we can detain you for as long as we like, you know. You'd better think about why we've brought you in."

"I don't know."

"Better think harder. Or are you saying the government makes mistakes?"

"Why don't you tell me what you want?" She ground her teeth in an effort to calm down. Anger would be the worst thing. She had to stay in control.

"Tell you? Of course we can tell you. But it's better that it comes from you, don't you think so, Stella?"

"What's your name?"

"Why do you want to know my name? You want to marry me, is it? Forget it, I know you're desperate, teachers like you can never get married, too strict, frighten all the men away. All your life you've never had a boyfriend. You see, Stella, we know more about you than you think. We know everything."

"Ask me anything you like. I have nothing to hide."

"That's better, Stella. You see? Things will go easy for you if you co-operate with us."

One of the shadows came forward and resolved itself into the shape of a short Malay woman. She took the lid off a bottle of water and tipped it into Stella's mouth. Half of it went down her shirt, but even that was refreshing. There were no windows here.

"Stella, are you ready?"

She nodded.

"Who is Jackson Cheng?"

She stared. "I don't know."

"Are you saying you don't know who Jackson Cheng is?"

"I don't know who he is."

"Are you saying you've never met him?"

"I don't remember anyone of that name. Who is he?"

"Stella, I'm very disappointed in you. I thought you were going to co-operate with us."

"I'm telling the truth."

"Aren't you a good Catholic girl? Don't you go to church every Sunday, every week praying, praying for what? And you say you don't know Jackson Cheng."

"Is he something to do with the Catholic church? I don't know everyone in the church."

"Think harder. You surely know this man."

She bit her tongue, trying to stay calm and think. "Maybe if you tell me who he is, I might be able to remember."

"Stella." The voice was scolding now. "You can't bargain with us like that. Either you've met him or you haven't. Surely you should know? A handsome man like Jackson Cheng, you will surely remember, right? I know you Catholic girls, pretend to be so pure, but actually you're all hot stuff."

She refused to rise to the bait. "I don't remember meeting anyone by that name."

"Who is Low Woon Leng?"

"Woon Leng? She's in my church, we've volunteered

together a few times."

"Volunteered doing what?"

"A counselling service for domestic workers."

"What for? What counselling?"

"Just, you know, giving them advice."

"What kind of advice can someone like you give them? What do you know?"

"Some of them are scared and lonely. Actually, most of them are. They're far from home, and some of them are very young. We tell them what their rights are. Where to go if they need help. Sometimes they just need someone to talk to."

"So they come to you?"

"A lot of them are Catholics, especially from the Philippines. It's natural for them to turn to the church if they're lonely."

"Lonely." A snort. Laughter? "You think Singapore is a holiday camp? The Pinoys come here to work. Why don't you leave them alone to get on with their jobs?"

"We see them on their days off. We're only trying to help."

"So noble. You and Low Woon Leng help them together?"

"We both volunteer with the group, sometimes we're on the same shift. Has she done something wrong?"

"So quickly you try to push the blame to your comrade? Stella, all of you are in trouble now. You better tell me all about it."

"I don't know what you want me to say."

"We have Woon Leng next door now. If she confesses first, then we'll let her go, and we'll keep you here forever.

Do you want that?"

"What do you mean? What have we done that we should confess?"

The voice became grim. "If you're so determined to play dumb, then we can do this the hard way. I thought you Catholics would know how to confess."

Unseen hands behind her lifted her from her chair, began to drag her towards the door. She tried to walk, but they were going too fast for her to find her feet. She had to fight the urge to vomit. "Wait," she cried, aware she sounded pathetic.

Faintly, behind her: "It's too late, Stella. You've had your chance. We'll have to do things the hard way now."

•

First they made her take a shower. She was glad to feel clean again. There was only cold water, but that didn't matter in such warm weather. The hard bar of soap they chucked at her didn't smell unpleasant. When she got out, there was only a prison uniform, light blue, on a chair. "Can I get my suitcase, please?" she called.

A plump face appeared in the grille. She held the towel in front of herself. "What you want?" demanded the face.

"I'd like to take some clothes from my suitcase, please." She smiled as ingratiatingly as she felt able, pushing her wet hair out of her eyes.

"Your uniform is there. No outside clothes allowed."

"I meant—underwear." She felt herself blush.

"No outside clothes allowed," repeated the face, and banged the grille shut. She got dressed as quickly as she could, pulling the uniform over naked skin. It was made of cheap, shiny material. There were no fastenings, she noticed, only elastic around the waist. The wardress banged on the door. She shuffled out in flimsy plastic slippers, still damp, and they took her to her cell.

It was smaller than she had imagined, a cement cubbyhole with a mattress on the floor and not much else. A toilet with no seat behind a thin partition. It was clean but stained the colour of rust. Tiny slits in the wall let in sunlight—she was silently cheered. A room like the other one, with no natural light, would have been death.

She walked in and heard the door clang shut. A series of grinding sounds told her how many locks there were—as if she could have thought of escaping. She lay down on the floor, letting the tension from her body leach into the cool concrete. The floor was far from clean, but she was too tired to care. Her head ached. She tried to elongate her neck to ease it, and reached her arms and legs out as far as they would go.

Something stirred in a corner of the room. It was her aunt Siew Li, the one she'd never met, arms folded and in school uniform, like she was in the only photo they had of her; Uncle Jason had destroyed the rest, but Henry had clung on to this one. "They're going to break you," said Siew Li, and faded into the wall. Stella rubbed her forehead. What was happening?

There had to be some misunderstanding. Had Woon

Leng done something wrong? Had she been accused? She understood that detention without trial worked differently from normal arrest, but there were still some limitations, surely. Eventually they would have to tell her why she was here, and she'd be able to see a lawyer. She didn't like the way they were talking to her, but they were used to dealing with all kinds of hard nuts here, it wasn't their fault she was so sensitive.

When the wardress brought her dinner, an armed guard stood outside the door. She wondered if anyone had ever tried to escape from here, for there to be so much security. She thanked the woman politely, as her plate was slapped down on a stool. "What will happen to me?" she asked.

"You should have thought about that before."

"I only meant, what's next? Are they going to ask me more questions?"

"That's up to them. Don't try to be so clever."

"Do you think—I know, sorry, it's probably not up to you, but do you think I could ask someone for my glasses? I can't see at all without them."

"I don't know anything about that."

"Maybe there's someone I could ask? If it's no trouble. My glasses, and I'd really like one of the books from my suitcase, just if—"

"You'd better stop asking for special treatment." The woman's face settled into a snarl. "I know people like you, think you're educated so there are special rules for you. When will you learn that you have to follow the law like everyone else? Trying to be so clever, now look, you're going to be here for a long time unless you stop trying to be different. Why can't you think? It's your parents who will suffer." That delivered, she waddled out of the cell, and once again the locks ground shut.

Stella was still for a very long time, before she had calmed down enough to look at the food. She should eat to keep her strength up. How often would she be fed? Bringing her face close, she smelt over-boiled meat and old, dry rice. The green vegetables were swimming limply in grease. She choked down as much as she could, then went back to lying on the floor. The only other place was the bed, and if she lay down there, where would she go at bedtime? She tried to work out if that was logical, or if she was already losing her grip.

When the woman came to take the plate away, she turned her face to the wall and pretended to be asleep. She thought about crying, but decided to pray instead. She said some Hail Marys, just for reassurance, then asked for patience, and strength, and understanding. These people were just doing their jobs. It was wrong of her to be thinking of things she would like to say to the wardress, to the man with high-pitched voice. It wasn't their fault. This was the system. She had implicitly signed up by accepting the security of Singapore, the safe, clean streets.

She could tell when the sun set by the long shadows on the wall. Before the light faded altogether, the guard came in and flicked on the light in her cell.

"Thank you. But you needn't bother, I was just going to sleep," she said.

"Lights on at all times." And then he was gone. She lay on the mattress and stared at the ceiling until the light left burnt orange squiggles in her retina. What would happen to her? She folded a corner of the blanket over her eyes and tried to sleep.

●

The interrogation room was freezing cold the next time they brought her in. The people behind the light looked bulkier, and she realised they were wearing jackets. It reminded her of her staffroom, where teachers would leave cardigans and sweaters over their chairs, for days when the air-conditioning was especially fierce.

"How are you today, Stella?" A different man, taller, dark-skinned. His voice was deep and hoarse around the edges.

"Good, thank you." She was determined to start again, give the right answers, and secure her release as quickly as she could.

"Did you sleep well? Was your bed comfortable?"

Was he making fun of her? She quashed a flicker of anger. "I slept very well, thank you."

"So you're not feeling guilty?" He chuckled, to show it was a joke, and she smiled too.

"Could you turn the temperature up a bit?" she asked bravely, and held out her arm to show the gooseflesh.

He laughed again. "So sensitive, Stella. Didn't you just come from England? You should be used to the cold by now."

"I was only there for a week."

"Why did you go to England?"

"I was visiting my cousin. Henry."

"Did you ask your cousin why he doesn't want to study here? Our university not good enough for him, is it?"

"There are just more opportunities over there."

"So you're saying Singapore has no opportunities? Then why are you still here?"

She was silent. Anything she said could be twisted round.

"And you, Stella? Do you like your country?"

Surely this, at least, was safe to answer? "Of course I do. It's my home."

"Are you sure?" Two of the figures were conferring, and another was taking notes. She was becoming used to the half-blind twilight world, and found that by squinting she could almost make things out. She was still disorientated, unable to read the facial expressions of the speaker.

"Stella, I'll ask you again. Do you know why you're here?"

A sudden paranoid spasm. She voted for the Workers' Party three years ago, in 1984—her very first election. Her vote had helped JB Jeyaretnam win his seat at Anson. Letting in the opposition. Did they know that? The ballot papers had serial numbers which they said couldn't be traced, but what if—she shook her head, snapping the thread. Of course that wasn't it, they couldn't go after everyone who hadn't voted their way, that would be thousands of people. Why would they care, anyway? There were only two opposition MPs in Parliament.

"Well, Stella? Have you had enough time to reflect?"

She thought about the previous day. "You said something about my outreach work for the church. Is that it? Have we done something wrong?"

"Who said anything about 'we'? Don't worry about 'we', just think about your own actions. What have you done?"

"We help them," she answered, deciding to take the question at face value. "There are thousands of maids in Singapore, and we give them information. Sometimes we pay for treatment if their employers don't want to. Just last month there was this one, Sri Lankan, she'd had bad toothache for weeks. Her boss didn't want to take her to the dentist, so we did. She had three teeth extracted. They were rotten all the way down. Some people just don't care, they think they can treat their maids like—" She realised she was making a speech, and shut up. It had felt good to speak without constraints, just for a minute, but she needed to be more careful. She pressed her thumbnails into the flesh of her palm, to remind herself.

"So sympathetic."

"God tells us to help the poor. We're just trying to do that."

"Why don't you help your own countrymen? Where is your patriotism? Do you think there are no poor people in Singapore? Why are you so concerned about foreigners?"

She judged it better not to speak. It had been a mistake to say so much. The automatic reaction, from years of having to explain her work to others, had taken over. Better give them nothing to get hold of.

"These people come over here to exploit our system. Do you know how small their money is, how little they will earn at home? The salary here is like a fortune to them, and still you want to talk about welfare."

She could have said a number of things then, about domestic workers burnt with hot irons, fed nothing but biscuits, made to sleep with the bins. She could have told him about forced abortions and the scars she'd seen, but somehow she knew that none of this would help her case.

"Maybe you're right," she forced herself to say. "We should never forget that charity begins at home. When I see my group again, I'll tell them that. We should do more outreach work for local families."

There was a thin hush, and she realised it couldn't be that easy, there must be more to the story that she wasn't seeing. What did they want? The room seemed to draw in its breath, a cessation of air broken by the tall man's voice, now a lash.

"You think we're stupid? You just tell us what we want to hear and we'll let you go? You better be more sincere, okay? We're not your little schoolgirls. This is the real world."

She had been idiotic, she thought in despair, to think that would work. But if the truth was twisted round and lies were too transparent, what was left but silence? She looked around the room, hoping for a clue, but the figures grew blurry as tears came, even as she tried to resist them. She tried to see the walls but couldn't. She no longer had any idea what size the room was.

•

The first bucket of water almost seemed to burn, even though it was icy cold. How odd, said a detached part of her mind, that the two sensations should be so similar. They flung a second bucket that left her gasping stupidly for a few moments, before she regained control and pushed her sodden hair back. There seemed to be no more for the moment. Everyone else in the room had moved well away, so as not to be splashed.

"Why did you do that?" she demanded, forgetting not to be provoked.

"You looked as if you were falling asleep, Stella. You had to be woken up."

"There was no need to do that." Her voice found a note of the schoolteacher.

"Stand up, Stella." From behind, she was pulled to her feet, and shunted a few steps forward. She heard her chair being pulled away into a corner of the room.

She was directly beneath the air-con vent, and realised what they were trying to do. The cold air now seemed arctic, meeting her wet clothes and skin, driving the damp into her bones. Trying to move away, she felt strong hands dragging her back. The spotlight grew in intensity until she could no longer see anything outside the stark white circle. She wrapped her arms around herself and tried to calm her breathing.

"Are you ready to answer the questions honestly, Stella?"

"Please, can I get dry? I'm awake now, I really am, and I'm

trying to co-operate."

"How can we trust you?" The voice sounded bored, as if she were wasting their time. "Since you got here you've been trying to hide the truth from us. Don't you know that we always find out in the end?"

"Yes, Stella." The high-pitched voice. "We only treat people like this if they need persuasion. Otherwise we'll be here all day and you still won't tell us. I want to go back home and see my kids, you know, otherwise my wife will scold me."

"I don't want to keep you from your family."

The tall man walked into the light, his face close to hers. "Listen to me, Stella. This is serious. Stop playing around. If you want to mess around with this kind of thing, then of course trouble will find you."

"I'll tell you what you want to know." They were capable of keeping her here until the cold overwhelmed her altogether. Could she catch pneumonia from this alone? It was genius in its own way, a form of torture that left no marks.

"How many people were working together with you?"

"You mean at the school?"

"Pretending to be stupid again. Of course not at the school, what were we talking about just now?"

"The outreach work. There wasn't a fixed group, just whoever had free time." She was gabbling, the words sliding into each other clumsily. The thin uniform clung to her all over, everywhere its clammy coldness touched her skin a fresh agony.

"Do you want me to arrest your whole church?"

"No."

"Then you better give us names."

"You mean anyone I name will be brought in for questioning?"

"We have to make sure, right? You weren't working alone, were you? There must have been other people in this conspiracy. I tell you honestly, we already have some of them here. It will be better for you if you just tell us their names, so we know you're dealing straight with us. Then maybe we can relax a bit."

"What conspiracy?"

"You really don't know or you're bluffing? Maid welfare. If you really care about maids so much, why don't you do their work for them? Follow them home and wash dishes for them. Scrub the floors. Hang out washing, fall from the top of a block of flats. You don't want to do all that yourself, right? So why don't you just let them get on with their job instead of talking all this nonsense?"

"We don't try to stop them working, we just want to make their lives a bit better."

"Then why do you complain when they do their jobs? Why do you care what they get paid? Don't you know that we live in a meritocratic society? It's very fair. If you work hard, you'll do well at school and next time you will earn more."

"It's not fair for them." Her teeth were chattering, and she could hardly think straight. "They don't get a choice." Was that the correct thing to say? Perhaps this was the real point of the cold, to take away defences. She was no longer able to concentrate enough to worry about supplying the right answer—she spoke the words that came into her mind, hoping they would be the ones that clicked, her key back into warmth.

"Do you want us all to be the same? You think everyone in society should earn the same money? That's not possible. Some people work harder than others, some people are cleverer. If we did what you people want, then our society will never progress, and soon our women will have to go and be maids in other people's countries. Stella, we know who you are, you don't have to pretend any more. Other people in your ring have already confessed. You want to destroy our society. You want to bring us all down to your level. Stella, we know that you are a Communist."

•

Sometime later, perhaps a week, perhaps more, her parents came to see her. She had been allowed a comb that morning, although it was taken away after she'd untangled her hair. The uniform she had on was freshly laundered. What did she look like, she wondered, before deciding she was better off not knowing. It was a mercy her cell had no mirror.

She was on the other side of a glass panel from her visitors. There was no one else in the long room, which disappointed her. She'd hoped to see if anyone else she knew was being held, as if that would explain what was going on.

Her father looked exhausted, as if he had been sleeping no better than her, and perhaps he hadn't. Her stepmother merely looked annoyed. She was sitting on the very edge of her plastic chair, afraid of dirtying her white silk dress. Both hands were folded over her handbag, as if ready to leave.

The guard showed them how to use the intercom—it was like a telephone, two receivers coming out on either side of the glass. It might as well be two tin cans attached by string, thought Stella. She had done that experiment with her class once, just for fun, because they didn't believe her when she said that's what children did in her parents' day. She put her hand up to the glass, and was unexpectedly moved when her father put his hand directly across, almost like touching.

"Daddy." She would only be able to talk to one of them at a time.

"Are they treating you all right?"

"Yes, they're—" She had already decided to tell no one about the cold water, standing there for hours, being slapped across the face. Easier to pretend that was a bad dream.

"Of course they're treating her all right." She could hear her stepmother, even through the glass, a voice like nails on a chalkboard. "Do you think we live in some kind of third world country? Don't worry about her." She grabbed the receiver. "Stella. Stella. Do you hear?"

"Hello, Ma."

"Your father's not well. Look at him. Why are you making him worry like this?"

"I don't want to be here, Ma."

"You must have done something wrong, the police don't just anyhow pick people off the street and lock them up here. What's going on? They won't tell us anything."

"I'm just helping them to answer some questions."

"How long are they going to keep you for? What about your job? The school holidays are almost over. How are we going to explain to the principal if they don't let you out in time? Don't expect us to support you if you lose your job."

"I'm sure they'll talk to my employer, Ma."

"Typical. Don't care about anyone but yourself."

"Vanda." Her father took the receiver from the manicured hand. "Stella, your mother's just worried about you." Vanda didn't look worried, she was sulkily applying lipstick, peering into a little gold compact mirror like a wicked step-mother.

"Are you all right, Dad?"

"Just my blood pressure. The usual. Nothing wrong with me but oldness."

"You mustn't worry about me, you know. Nothing's going to happen."

"But Stella, why are they holding you? They're being tight-lipped, but you must have some idea. Something to do with the church? That doesn't make any sense."

"They think I'm a Communist."

"Why? You're not, are you?"

"No, of course not. But they think a Marxist group has infiltrated the church, and I'm part of the conspiracy. They think we're trying to bring down the state."

"Why on earth would they think that?"

"It's the outreach work. They said, why would someone like me with a good job want to spend so much time worrying about foreigners? They said, my salary is paid by the government, how can I question my employer like this?"

"Ridiculous."

"Be careful, they may be listening. And they said, only a Marxist would be so worried about inequality in society. So here I am."

"Barnaby? What's she saying?" screeched Vanda. Even muffled by glass, she sounded like a thwarted cat. He ignored her, pressing his free hand over his other ear.

"This has all got to be a misunderstanding." Her father looked old and baffled. She felt suddenly weak with what she was doing to him. Nothing they said could touch her as much. "Should we get you a lawyer? Will they let you see a lawyer?"

"This won't go to court or anything. They're just going to hold me here until—"

"Until?"

"I don't know. Until I've told them what they want to know."

"But you don't have anything to tell them, do you? I trust you. I'd know if you were in some kind of conspiracy. Even if there is something going on, you're not part of it."

"Thank you. Now I just need to convince them."

"Shall I get Father Gregory to write a letter on your behalf? Do you think that would help?"

"Daddy, I think it's best not to do anything for now. I don't want to make them angry. Let's just wait till the situation becomes clearer."

"Are you sure? I can call our MP, or write a letter to the papers."

"No!" Vanda's voice again. "This is a family problem, don't you dare make it public."

"It's fine, Daddy." She rested her forehead against the glass, pleasantly cool, and let her hair fall forward. "Don't worry."

"How can I not worry?"

She had no answer for that. She thought it best not to speak for a while, in case she started crying.

"Do you have everything you need?" There was a wobble in her father's voice too. She nodded. "Be sure to ask if you want us to bring anything. They said we can come next week."

"Maybe some books. They've given me the ones from my suitcase and—" And my glasses, she had been about to add, before remembering they were on her nose. They'd given them back, almost as an afterthought, a day ago. "But I think I'll have finished reading them by next week. Not much else to do here."

"Books," he nodded slowly. "Any particular books?"

"Nothing too political. Don't want to give them any ideas."

●

They treated her better after the first few days. No more drenchings, no more slaps. Perhaps they thought they'd softened her up. She was no longer truculent, now, but smiling and natural as a schoolgirl. It seemed easier. They were just doing their job, after all, and making their lives difficult would be like rudeness to a waiter. Was this how it had been for Aunt Siew Li?

She told them the names of the other people in her outreach group. They would be able to find that out easily enough, after all, and surely they wouldn't all be hauled in and drenched in ice water. She had been unlucky, or complicit in some way she hadn't worked out. The man with the high-pitched voice was called Cheng Mun, and there were times when he seemed quite fond of her. Once, he told her he had a daughter her age.

Some days the questions seemed repetitive, but she knew you had to ask the same thing in different words to trip up liars, and didn't mind. It still seemed unlikely the church was harbouring a conspiracy to bring down the state, but then a good plot would be well-hidden, and she was not an observant girl.

She told them about domestic workers she had helped, and the problems they faced. Sometimes they had to write letters to the Ministry of Labour, and it could take a bit of persistence to get a response. At least one of the maids had fallen pregnant and, refusing an abortion, been summarily deported. She even talked about their low wages, but guardedly, careful not to draw any comparison with Singaporean pay. Her politics were socialist, not communist, but she wasn't sure if her interrogators knew the difference.

Most days, it felt like they were just chatting. She talked about her work, her studies, happy to tell the truth. She had nothing to hide. In some ways it was a relief, not to have to worry about deadlines or timetables, just talking about herself. "Some people pay money for this kind of therapy," she joked once, and was relieved when Cheng Mun laughed full-throatedly.

The tall man, Devin, was less forthcoming. She couldn't work out whether he was higher or lower in rank. It wasn't like the regular police. He sometimes probed for exact dates and times, people's full names, and when she stammered and said she wasn't sure, shut his notebook theatrically. "Stella, I'm very disappointed in you. You're not being helpful today." She didn't even mind that, you had to play the good cop-bad cop game.

When they asked her about her family, she grew circumspect. It seemed distasteful to talk about her mother, crushed to death by falling bricks. Did she blame the government? they wanted to know. "Of course not," she replied. "It was obviously an unpreventable attack. And anyway, I was only a year old." Was her father a left-wing element? "You'll have to ask him that," she said, then bit her tongue, worried they'd bring him in next.

What about Henry? "He's my cousin, doing his Masters in London. I've just been to visit him—you know that, of course. He's doing very well." Was he a left-wing element? "I don't think so. He told me he voted SDP in the last election, but that means something different over there."

What else did she do in London? She was tempted to mention paying her respects at Marx's grave in Highgate

Cemetery, but sarcasm wouldn't work with them. "I don't know anyone there except Henry. We went to the British Museum and the National Gallery. He wanted to show me the zoo but it rained that day, so we went to a tea shop instead. I sat at the back of one of his lectures. About Regency Bath. He's very good. I understood all of it."

Anything else? "Second-hand bookshops on Charing Cross Road. Saw a play on the West End. Not much else. I wasn't there long."

Did she meet any of Henry's friends? "He's just moved to London, he doesn't have many friends yet. I met some of his classmates. Oh, and we had tea with a journalist named Revathi. I don't know how they met. She seemed nice."

Did Henry have a friend called Jackson Cheng? "You asked me about him before. I don't know anyone called Jackson Cheng, and I don't think Henry does either." Was she sure? "Well, you'll have to ask him, but if this Jackson is some kind of Communist, I don't think Henry would be spending time with him." Could she take a look at this picture? "Is this him, Jackson Cheng? I've never seen him before. I'm sure. He's quite handsome. I would have remembered."

She'd better be telling the truth. "I wouldn't dare lie to you."

●

They moved her to a larger cell after a month or so. There was a proper chair, with a back, and a shelf for her books.

They only allowed her three at a time, which was fine if she rationed herself. She drew up reading lists—things she'd always meant to get round to, new books by writers she liked. One long book in every list. The whole of the *Avignon Quintet* in a single volume, or *War and Peace*. Getting round the regulations in simple ways made her happy.

Sometimes her father came alone, and they would sit in companionable silence. The guard teased her about not talking to her father after he'd come all this way, and she would smile, not being able to explain that your real friends are the ones you don't need to chatter away to, afraid of what silence would reveal. Mostly, though, he brought Vanda with him, or perhaps she insisted on coming, afraid that Stella would infect him with badness. Vanda came alone once, when Barnaby's back was hurting him too much to move, but that was so awkward for both of them they knew it would never happen again.

The questioning became less regular. She heard sounds from other parts of the building, so she knew she was not the only one there. What was it they wanted to hear? She felt like a slow pupil, trying to give the right answer, but always falling short. Would it be better to say there *was* a conspiracy? But then it would look like she'd been lying before, and she'd never be able to make up enough detail to convince them. Who should she say was masterminding it? Where would they get instructions—Soviet Russia? It was hopeless. Entire days drifted past when they didn't bring her out from her cell, but instead of feeling pleased at being left alone, she felt guilty, as if she were a disappointment to them, as if they'd given up on her.

In the first weeks, she kept almost frantic track of time—*I was taken on a Wednesday, June seventeenth*, she would say to herself. *Then there was the day of the questioning, and the day of cold air, and another day of cold air, then normal questioning, so today must be the twenty-second. Monday. It's Monday, and people will be going to work.*

After this, it became too much effort, too many days that were hard to distinguish. She gave them all names, to start with—*the day I got an egg with breakfast, the day I killed a cockroach with my shoe*—but there were too many. Were there three or four days when she woke up and it was raining? Was one of those the extra mug of tea? So she just did numbers, day thirty-seven, day forty-three. Even that was difficult. She would wake up and be unable to remember if fifty-one was where she had stopped. If she'd thought of it soon enough, she could have put a line on the wall every morning, like a comic-book prisoner, but she had nothing to write with, and they would probably have used that against her. *A vandal as well as everything else*, she could hear Devin sighing.

If only Singapore had seasons, she might have been able to tell where she was in the year. One sunny day after another, they all seemed the same. Rain made her think, *Are the monsoons here yet?* But then it would be fine the next day, leaving her no less confused. During her visit, all of London had been excited by a single day of sunlight, unremarkable in itself, but to them a sign that summer was on its way. *Why did they care, surely summer would come anyway?* she asked Henry, and he said, *Ah, you have no idea what it is to suffer the cold and wet of an English winter, when it seems the sun might never come back.* So she said, teasing, *Maybe you should move back, then.* They both knew she didn't mean it.

Did the outside world know she was here? Was her salary still being paid? She wondered if there was leave for this, or if she'd lost her job. She could have asked her father to find out, but didn't want to face his disappointment if she had, and worse, the sadness he would feel in bringing her the news. She asked the guard for newspapers, but they never materialised. Could she have her violin, then, to pass the time? No, they told her, this wasn't a holiday camp. *But what do you want me to do all day?* She received no reply.

The questions grew more esoteric. Her aunt Siew Li was a known terrorist. Was that how she had become radicalised? "I've never met her." Then who radicalised her? "No one radicalised me." But she agreed with Marxist theory? "I don't know a lot of Marxist theory. Did he call for armed uprising? I don't agree with that." Was her ideal society a classless one? "I suppose, but isn't everyone's? Is it Marxist to think everyone should have a fair chance?" She shouldn't ask them questions, her job was to answer questions. "I'm trying. I've answered all your questions, haven't I?" She had, but not all her answers were good ones. "I'll try harder." Good, try harder. "I will."

•

The first time they mentioned Jessica, she felt a thrill of recognition, as if she had been waiting for this all along. It was inevitable—everyone she'd had more than a passing acquaintance with had been brought up and forensically examined. Was this person left-wing? Was this other? Who was it who recruited her? She tried to answer neutrally, and not incriminate anyone else. Was being left-wing bad in itself? She didn't know any more.

They talked about dangerous socialist ideals. "But the PAP used to be socialist," she said, mildly. What was she talking about, they wanted to know. "The PAP called itself a socialist party." Really? Was she sure? "Oh yes. I mean, they even worked with the Communists to start out with." Ah, no—the voices grew certain, they were on surer ground here—the PAP only worked with the Communists to bring them under control, to keep our country safe from them. "Well, sure, but even after they'd locked up all the Communists they kept saying they were socialist, until they had to leave Socialist International. In the seventies." How did she know all this? "I read books."

For the most part, they weren't interested in talking about ideas, only people. They had a big file, full of lists. Every classmate she had ever had, people she was—as they put it—known to have associated with, obscure relatives she had never even met. Each time they were able to process a name, cross it off the list or circle it for future questioning, she felt a hum of satisfaction round the room, as if they had whittled a little more away and were circling closer to the truth.

And so they came to Jessica. Who was she? "We shared a dorm room at university." Why did she need a dorm room? "Lots of people have one. Sometimes we studied late, and it wasn't always convenient to go home." She must be a rich girl, to stay in dorms when she had a perfectly good bedroom of her own. "I wasn't the only one, most people in halls could stay with their parents instead. The buses aren't very frequent, it can be hard to get to school for an early lecture."

It was Cheng Mun doing the questioning that day. "Stella, we have information—" She was familiar with this formulation. That meant someone else had told them, or else they simply suspected something they wanted her to confirm. "You've had an unnatural relationship with Jessica Lim."

She stalled. "Unnatural relationship?"

"Please, Stella." Cheng Mun looked pained. "Don't pretend you don't understand. Are you a lesbian? Is Jessica Lim your girlfriend?"

"Does it matter?" No response. Stupid question, she should know by now that everything mattered. Had they spoken to Jessica? "I suppose," she began, picking her words carefully, "we might have experimented a bit. Young girls often do. I don't know if you could say we had a relationship."

"I'm not here to judge you, Stella. We're just concerned that if someone knows about your unnatural relationship, they could use it to blackmail you. Is that what happened? Did someone blackmail you into joining this conspiracy?"

"No, of course not. It was hardly anything."

"You shared a room for two whole years."

"She's a very dear friend."

There was a kind of grim satisfaction as he took his next few notes. She tried not to reveal anything of herself beyond a kind of bland wholesomeness, and her interrogators seemed aware of this game, constantly on the alert for any chink of personality she let slip.

"Are you still a lesbian, Stella?" She had no answer to that, and found that she couldn't meet his eye. "Do you have a girlfriend now?" She could at least shake her head to that. "What happened to Jessica?"

"She's married to a nice man now, a teacher. I went to their wedding."

"Do you ever wish you could become normal, Stella?"

"I am normal."

"Stella, you're supposed to be a good Catholic girl, remember? What would your God say about this?"

"God is compassionate. I think God wants me to be happy."

"Doesn't God want you to be obedient first?" She said nothing. "Stella, what would your father say if he knew what you've done?"

She could say nothing to that either, but to her horror she felt her eyes twitch, and then her nose. Tears threatened to spill, but she was afraid to wipe them away in case he hadn't noticed them. She stayed very still, feeling his eyes probing away at her skull.

He leant back. "Enough for today," he said, not unkindly.

•

After a while, they seemed to trust her, and Cheng Mun even allowed her into his office. "No point going to the cold room," he smiled. "Much more comfortable here." He made her coffee. He only had instant, but it still felt like a special treat, a hot drink made just for her. She watched childishly as he stirred in the condensed milk, then placed the mug in front of her.

He let her drink in silence for a bit. When she seemed relaxed and settled, he began. "Stella, we know you're not a Communist." She nodded. They must know she was no danger, or they would not be treating her so gently. "You're not a bad girl. But we think you're naïve. And that's risky, it's very easy for people to make use of you."

"I don't think anyone is making use of me."

"Of course you don't think so. They won't make it so obvious."

"Are you still talking about the church? No one would do a thing like that."

"Stella, you don't know the people we're talking about. They will infiltrate anywhere, yes, even a church, in order to achieve their objective. I know you don't want to believe me, but some of the people you think are your friends are actually manipulating you to get what they want. Of course you're too young to remember the Emergency."

"We talked about it in history. I know what happened."

"I was there. We saw what these Communists would do.

For them, it's like a religion. That's why Communists don't believe in God, they have their own gods. Every day we would read in the newspaper, so many people killed. They shot police, plantation owners, anyone who got in their way. And they also did this—not just openly fighting the state, they also joined legitimate organisations and tried to subvert them from within."

She was silent, absorbing this. "But that sounds like a thriller, not my life. All we do is have meetings. I make the tea."

"Stella, you have a good job, why would you get involved in this? If you spent more time on your work, you could be a department head in a few years."

"I don't want to be a department head. I like teaching."

"Is that what they told you to say? Because you would earn more money as a department head? Stella, you mustn't be ashamed of that. We live in a meritocracy. If you earn more money then it's because you're clever, you work harder than others. Why do you talk about being fair all the time? Do you think some people earn too much?"

"I never said that."

"But you complain that these maids, these people you are trying to help, they earn too little. If some people earn too little, then some people must be earning too much. Am I right?"

The feeling of helplessness that she felt in each session was growing on her. Was that really what she was saying? It was impossible to argue. Every word that came from her mouth could be turned round to condemn her further.

"Stella, I know you mean well, you're doing this out of the kindness of your heart. But these things you're doing can be used to destabilise the government. People in your group are talking about organising protests. Holding rallies to raise awareness. Can't you understand that Singapore is a small country, we can't allow anti-establishment forces like this to proliferate?"

"We're not anti-establishment."

"You think Singapore has always been like this," he went on, as if she had not spoken. "We used to be poor. In one generation we have improved so much. Look at our airport. Look at our housing. They've just opened the new MRT network. When you get out, you'll be able to ride on it, and think how far we've come. Why are you attacking our progress? Why do you want to throw all this away?"

He seemed genuinely angry. She carefully put her coffee, now cold, barely touched, on the edge of the desk. "I couldn't see suffering and not do anything about it."

"You think these people are suffering?" His face was an ugly sneer. "Foreign workers. They come and tell you all kinds of sob stories. You think they don't laugh at you behind your back for believing them? And then you fight for all kinds of rights for them. What rights do they deserve? They're already lucky that we let them in here. We pay them more than they could ever earn in their own country."

"Even if you're right, that's just a difference of opinion. It doesn't make me a traitor."

"Stella, still so stubborn. I must say I'm disappointed in you. I'm trying to explain to you that this is how the Marxists work. The United Front. They will get all these workers on their side, until they have enough support for their so-called uprising. And then blood will flow and they will bring down the government. Do you want to be part of that?" She shook her head. "Then go back to your cell and think hard whose side you are on."

Later that night, she heard music—a choir, singing hymns, from some distance away. Was it people from her church? She tried joining in, but her singing voice was rusty from lack of use, so she just listened, her face pressed against the cool cement of the outside wall. After a few minutes, she saw flashing lights dip in through the narrow window. The bark of a police loudspeaker, and then silence.

•

The nature of time seemed to change. When she was in the questioning room, it seemed to stand still or jump at random. Sometimes she was surprised to get back to her cell and find it was dark. Other times, she'd ask how long she'd been there and it was only a couple of hours. They could have been lying, of course, but she didn't think they'd stoop to that.

She was in court, they brought her there blindfolded again. The judge handed down a detention order, as expected, and she was back in her cell. Mid-Autumn came and went. She was given a mooncake with her lunch and allowed an extra family visit. "Do you celebrate the Lantern Festival?" Devin asked, as if testing how Chinese she was. Then she was in court again. The detention order was extended.

Siew Li and Mollie popped into her cell now and then, mostly silent, holding her hand when she felt unwell. She tried to conjure up Jessica too, but that wasn't very convincing, maybe because the real Jessica was outside, and it was too easy to imagine her walking freely through the open air, pushing a pram through the Botanic Gardens, living a whole life that didn't include Stella. Better to stay in the dark with the dead, let her aunt and mother comfort her.

The questioning started to feel circular. She was very consistent in her answers, and hoped they believed her. It was easy to be consistent if you stuck to the truth. Sometimes they mentioned Jessica, which was upsetting, and sometimes her dead mother, which didn't bother her as much as they seemed to think it would. What did they want? She began giving them all the names they wanted, it didn't matter, her stepmother said they'd been to her room and taken her diaries, her address book, all the loose bits of paper that looked important. They'd even been through her wastepaper basket.

It was a confession they were after, it seemed, but she had to say the right things. She maintained that there had been no conspiracy, or at least none that she had been aware of. Then how had she been exposed to Marxist ideas? "I haven't been exposed to Marxist ideas." How would she recognise Marxist ideas, if she hadn't read any Marx? "I don't know."

So she could have been exposed to Marxist ideas. "I suppose it's possible."

Devin was asking the questions, which usually meant they were going to be difficult. "Stella," he said. "Do you know how long you've been staying here with us?"

As if she were a guest. "I'm not sure exactly. A few months?"

"Five months, Stella. If you were pregnant, you would be showing by now." He chuckled, and then his eyes hardened. "But of course you can't get pregnant, can you? How can you get pregnant if you only play around with other girls?"

She said nothing. There was no point reacting, this was just one of the random jibes they would fling at her from time to time. The pointless cruelty of a bored child poking a caged animal.

"Stella, all your friends have confessed. They've all betrayed you. There's no point denying it any more. You're only making trouble for yourself. Who are you trying to protect? No one is protecting you."

She felt, more than any other emotion, sheer exhaustion. "Which friends?"

"Jackson Cheng, your ringleader. Kevin de Souza. That girl from your church, Frances Ling." And he went on, listing people she had heard of and people she hadn't. So many people detained? She lost count after sixteen. "I don't know most of them," she said.

"Do you know where these people are now, Stella?" She shook her head. "Packing their things, ready to be released. Soon it will be only you left, Stella. I get paid to be here, I can go home in the evening to see my family. But you?

"Why do you keep saying you don't know them? When we show them your picture, they said yes, she's part of the conspiracy."

"That's not true."

"How many times must I tell you, Stella? These people are so good at infiltrating that you can be working for them without knowing it. What was it that made you join the group?"

"I was concerned for the foreign workers. I could see that they weren't being treated well. We had a maid at home. She had one day off a week, and that was considered quite generous of my family."

"A lot of people have maids, Stella, and they don't become Marxists. Who invited you to join the group?"

"I can't remember exactly. I was talking to some people over coffee after service, and a couple of them volunteered."

"Was Charlie Jay in the coffee shop?"

"He joined us sometimes. I can't remember if he was there that day."

"So isn't it possible that he was the one who invited you to join?"

"It's possible. Why does it matter?"

"Stella, I thought schoolteachers were supposed to be clever. If Charlie Jay was the ringleader, then of course this is how he would recruit people. Do you think he would be so obvious, come up to you and say, hey, do you want to be a Communist? No, he is more subtle." He pronounced it sub-tel. "He knows you have a kind heart, so he tells you society unjust this, society unfair that, and before you know it you have been radicalised by him."

"I don't think I've been radicalised."

"But you always say, society treats these people badly, society neglects those people. That's how Marxists talk. If you're talking like this, then it must be because someone has infected you with left-wing sentiments."

It was always like this, the circularity, the dead-end logic. She felt her brain rebel, refuse to think of another argument. What was the point? And perhaps placing her in this state was their goal. A further prison in the mind.

"Then say that's what happened. Why don't you let me go? If I didn't know what was going on, if I was innocent, if you say everyone else has already confessed, why do you still need me?"

"You have to confess as well, Stella. A proper confession. Everything you've done. You've already been here for so many months. If we let you out now with nothing, it will look like we made a mistake. The old man will lose face. Do you think he'll be happy about that?"

She said nothing.

"It's your choice. We can apply for another detention order if we need to. We'll get it. You're a danger to society, we can hold you for as long as we like. You don't look rehabilitated to me, Stella, you aren't being very co-operative today. Do you know how long Chia Thye Poh has been in detention now? Twenty-one years. And we'll hold him for longer, because he's stubborn and won't confess. He says, how can he renounce communism if he's not a Communist? But only a Communist would be so stubborn. He was young when he came in, now he's not. Do you want to be like him? It's up to you, Stella. Everything is up to you."

●

Her cousin Janet came to see her one weekend. "I brought you biscuits," she said without preamble, patting a blue tin of butter cookies. "And your dad said you want books. I brought you *The Screwtape Letters* and this Peter Marshall one. Don't write in it, it's Winston's."

"Hello, Janet."

"Why do you look so surprised to see me? Your dad's not well—don't worry, it's just pneumonia—so I said I would come."

"Pneumonia?"

"He's fine, they sent him home from hospital. Vanda's looking after him. I suppose you'd rather see me than her, anyway."

"Thank you, Janet. It's very kind."

"How can I pass you these things through the glass?"

"You'll have to give them to the guard afterwards. They'll go through them before I get them."

"Go through them? What for?"

"Afraid you've hidden something in them, I guess. Secret commie messages in the books. A hand grenade in the tin.

You shouldn't have bothered with the biscuits, you know. They'll eat them in the office."

Janet half-rose to look for the guard, but he was looking studiously out of the window. Seeing her in silhouette, Stella realised she was pregnant.

"How long—?"

"This? Four months. Four and a half."

"Congratulations."

"Have to get started. The government changed their mind and said don't stop at two, have more if you can afford it. Winston has to lead by example. I don't mind telling you this one was an accident."

"Life is never a mistake, Janet."

"Sorry, I forgot you're Catholic."

"You'll love it when it's here."

"Of course I'll love it, what's wrong with you?" She stared around the room. "Are you the only one here? I thought prison would be a lot bigger."

"This isn't prison."

"Can you go home now? No? Then it's prison." There was no point contradicting Janet and her teacher's voice. Not for nothing was she the Discipline Mistress.

"How are things at the school?"

"Same as usual. They've got a relief teacher to teach your classes. They're pretending you're on no-pay leave."

"Will they let me come back?"

Janet leaned forward, almost touching the glass. "You dad says they're just waiting for you to confess. Is that true?"

"I don't know. They imply that if tell them everything about the conspiracy, they'll let me go. But I was never a part of the conspiracy. I'm not even convinced it exists."

"Does it matter? Do you know what the papers are saying about you?"

"I'm only allowed a newspaper very occasionally. They go through them first and cut out some of the articles."

"You're dangerous, carried away by poisonous ideology. People like you infiltrate these organisations and then use them to carry out your own ends."

"Janet, you don't believe that, do you?"

"It doesn't matter what I believe. It's in the *Straits Times*. All these Marxist Conspiracy people, everyone detained under Operation Spectrum. They've been running these stories for months. Everyone knows about you now. All the leftists have to be weeded out. Same in Malaysia, they just had their Operation Lalang. Copying us, as usual."

"I don't know how to prove that I'm innocent. How do you prove a negative?"

"You don't prove it. You confess. What do you think would happen if they let you out now? For the rest of your life people will say you must have done something, they wouldn't just lock people up for no reason. You'll be under suspicion forever."

"But if I confess—"

"Then you can say sorry, you've learned from your mistake. And the government will say you've been rehabilitated. Then at least some people will think that you deserve a second chance. Why are you making a stand like this? Who do you think you're helping? You shouldn't have gone against the government if you don't want to pay the price."

Stella felt breathless, and it was only with an effort that she stayed sitting. "Are you suggesting I should say I did it, just to get out of here? Make the whole story up? I never went against the government."

"Those foreign workers. Why must you get involved with such people? The government sets the terms and conditions, they all know the rules when they come over here. Who are you to say no, this is unfair? If that isn't going against the government, what is?"

"Janet—" It was like trying to stop a tsunami.

"Have you seen what you're doing to your parents? Uncle Barnaby looks terrible, really terrible. And have you thought about me? How will Winston get elected if they know his relative is mixed up in all kinds of trouble? They might even drop him before the next GE."

"Because of me?"

"They have to be clean, that's why they all wear white. You make him dirty. How will it look, he's up there making big speeches about the way forward for this country, and his wife's cousin is sitting in jail for being a Communist. If he doesn't make it in this election, there won't be another one for four years. And if you're still here then—"

"I won't be." But she might be. Her heart dropped within her at the thought. They could keep her here as long as they liked, hauling her to court every month to get an extension that no one doubted would come through. And all for what?

"My father doesn't want anything to do with you. I can't even tell him I came to visit. You know what he thinks about Communists. Only my crazy brother still supports you. He phoned. Says he can't visit till he's finished his PhD, though he hopes you'll be out before that. But of course he's in England, they can't touch him."

Janet's eyes were pleading now. She was frightened, Stella realised. It was like when they were growing up, Janet the prefect, her tie always straight, terrified of getting into trouble with authority. "This isn't just about you. We're all involved now. Please, Stella. Do the right thing."

●

She signed the paper in the end. Everyone signs the paper, sooner or later. What other choice is there? Nobody wants to spend the rest of their life in a dusty cell, not even a martyr, nor a symbol of resistance. What principle are you proving, when everyone's forgotten you?

At first they told her to write out in her own words what had happened. After so much questioning, she was familiar enough with the desired narrative to reproduce it glibly. Two pages in, Cheng Mun told her to stop. "You can't just say this happened, and then this happened—this can't only be description. We need to feel you're sincere."

She nodded, and began again. It became easy, as if

she were back in school, writing an English composition. The smell of the ballpoint pen, the thin lined paper, like an exam. She remembered the rules—have a beginning, a middle, and an end. Be sure to count the number of words. Don't use words you can't spell. Never end with "and then I woke up and it was all a dream".

It took her two hours to get it all down. Cheng Mun snatched away each page as she finished it, and worked his way through it, his lips moving, nodding in approval. "Do I have to mention Jessica?" she asked, and he shook his head. Jessica was irrelevant, convenient only as a goad. She saw now how many weapons against herself she had unwittingly provided.

"Make sure you mention who was your mentor," he interjected at one point. "Don't try to protect anyone. How did you meet the other members of your conspiracy? Whose flat did you meet in? Be sure you include all these informations."

And she kept spinning, like Scheherazade, telling stories to save herself. Who she'd talked to. Who had coerced her. All those picnics, late-night sing-alongs, everything could be made to take on a darker significance. Any roomful of people could count as a conspiracy, if you imputed the right motives to them. A gift of a book became an act of subversion. She had a bookmark with a Bible verse: *The righteous considereth the cause of the poor.* Now she could see that it was a coded call to arms.

When she had finished, her hand felt stiff, curled into

a claw. She tapped the papers to align them into a neat pile, and wished she had a stapler to fix them together. Her handwriting had always been good, teacherly—small, neat, just enough flourishes to be elegant. She waited docilely for her examiner to take away her answer script. She had done her best now, and could only hope to pass.

Cheng Mun's eyes were approving. "Do you want to read through it?" She shook her head, and his smile deepened. The right answer. "Good, we don't want you to have second thoughts. You mustn't doubt yourself, Stella. You're doing the right thing now. I'm glad you've come to your senses."

As he escorted her back to her cell, he said, "Doesn't it feel better, to finally tell us the truth?" and she felt a spasm, right across her chest, but managed to hold herself upright and not fold into tears until she was alone.

A few days later, they told her she was wanted for an interview. "You're going to be a TV star, Stella," sneered Devin. "They want to film your confession."

"Who does?" she asked, stupefied.

"SBC, who else? How many TV stations are there?"

"What for? Isn't it enough that I've signed a written statement?"

"So many questions. Haven't you learned to shut up and do what you're told? Quick, put this on." He flung a pale yellow dress at her. It was one of the ones from her suitcase— from that holiday in London, how long ago was that now? He stood there as if he wanted to watch her change, just long enough for her to grow pale, then stepped outside the door with a nasty laugh. She climbed into the dress quickly. It was too big for her. How much weight had she lost? It was a little grubby and wrinkled, but she didn't think of asking for an iron.

They put the blinders on her again as soon as she got into the car. She didn't bother protesting. It was restful, not being able to see, sandwiched in the back seat of the car between Cheng Mun and Devin. The air-conditioning was strong, and with the radio on and the familiar traffic sounds beneath it, it was easy to forget that she was anything other than a normal person going somewhere in a car.

Their destination was an old bungalow, one of the black and white colonial ones. They gave her back her glasses so she could see it properly. There was only one cameraman inside, with all his equipment already set up, pointing at a pair of rattan chairs. One of them was occupied by a handsome man she recognised from TV—a newsreader? Something like that. He was wearing a light coat of foundation, she noticed. No one offered her any make-up.

Cheng Mun offered her a quick look at her handwritten confession. "Will you remember what to say?" he asked, anxious as a father before the school play. Yes, the story was etched in her. She felt utterly serene, almost blank, as she took her place.

She hardly needing any prompting. It was like teaching, the click of approval when a class is going well—she seemed to soar, fluid and convincing. She remembered when to look penitent, and to smile radiantly when she talked of how the state had shown her the right way. She found that she really was sorry for her actions—for where her actions had brought her. Now and again the interviewer nudged her— "don't just say ideology, say Marxist ideology. We need the audience to remember what it was that brought you here. Don't say friend, say comrade. Say co-conspirator. Don't say fair society, say classless society." When she hesitated, stumbled, he smiled forgivingly. "Don't worry. We'll edit this. You're doing fine. Keep talking."

She was still calm at the end, but her dress was soaked with sweat. It wasn't that hot a day—the host even had a jacket on. He was talking to the cameraman now, going over a list of points in his hand. She looked around, wondering if she could go. So this is what it felt like. The men talked amongst themselves, then took her back to the car.

A few days later, she was summoned to Cheng Mun's office. "Your detention is extended," he told her, as if this were good news.

"I thought I would be released, after the confession."

"You will be. Why are you in such a hurry? What's another few weeks? Of course we can't let you go right away. How will it look if we just throw you out after you said you've done all these things? There has to be a deterrent."

It made sense. She was well cared-for here. Three meals a day. One of the wardens even found her an old pack of cards and taught her a new version of solitaire. She couldn't say she had suffered.

"The time will pass very quickly, Stella. Take the chance

to reflect." His face beamed with pride and benevolence. She found herself smiling too, and then laughing hard.

•

Vanda came to pick Stella up on the last day, only weeks later. She stood in the awkwardly-shaped entrance hall, her suitcase at her feet. It felt like the last day of term. Almost Christmas time, almost 1988.

"Be careful what you say to journalists," warned Cheng Mun, waiting with her.

"I won't talk to journalists."

"There's no harm—of course people will be curious. But don't tell them we mistreated you."

"I'll just say no comment."

"If you say anything bad, it will affect the release of the others." She didn't ask what others. She no longer wanted to know. It made her feel a little better, knowing she was not the last to be released.

"What will you do?"

"I'm not sure." She wondered if she would ever see him again. "I don't think the teaching service will take me back."

"That's too bad. But you can't take a chance where kids are concerned."

"Maybe I'll give tuition. I'd like to travel—" She bit her tongue. The terms of her release prohibited her from leaving Singapore. He seemed not to notice.

"Look, here's your mother." And sure enough, Vanda

was stumping bad-temperedly across the car park. She was wearing giant sunglasses, as if afraid of being recognised. "Goodbye, Stella," said Cheng Mun. "Don't be a security threat in the future." Was that a joke? She didn't know if she should laugh, and compromised by smiling vaguely. He shook her hand very gallantly and helped carry her suitcase down the stairs.

Vanda continued to be grumpy as she started the car. "Had to cancel my hair appointment," she muttered. "And now I'll have to wait another week. I'll look like a fright at the Wongs' party this Sunday."

"Thank you for coming, anyway."

"No joke. I almost told them to keep you in there another night. Why don't they give more notice? Calling me this morning, saying come get you."

"That's how they do things. We knew it would be around this time."

Vanda wasn't listening. Her brow furrowed as she negotiated a badly parked van. The car slipped through a gate, which slipped shut unobtrusively behind them. They turned a corner, and suddenly they were on a busy road. It was early, probably the dregs of rush hour. And there they were, two women in a car, going home.

Stella had prepared herself for this. She knew it would be difficult to reacclimatise. This is what agoraphobia must feel like, she thought. The great trees, the rushing traffic, it was all too much. How did people cope, every day, with all this noise? She wondered if she still remembered how to cross a road, or if she would be mown down at the first attempt. Did cars really go this fast all the time?

"Looked stupid on television," Vanda was saying, and Stella realised she was talking about the confession. "It was on during the news. Everyone saw it. The neighbours were shocked. When you were arrested they said it must be a mistake, you were such a nice girl. But to hear you admitting to all those things. You've let us all down."

Stella said nothing. She wished her father had come, but of course he wasn't well enough.

"What are you going to do?"

"I haven't thought about it."

"I hope you don't think we're going to support you forever."

"I'll find something to do."

"No one will want to marry you now. Oh, your friend Jessica came to see us. She was very angry. She said you told them you had some kind of relationship, and then they took her for questioning. They didn't put her in the papers, but now she's lost her job too." She looked at Stella, demanding a response. "Why must you get everyone into trouble?"

The good thing about being inside was she'd learnt to hold a silence. It was easy to let Vanda talk herself out, before saying, "Maybe I'll help Janet look after the baby."

"Oh." Gears shifted in Vanda's head. "That could be good too. They have a maid, of course, but they can always do with more help. I'm glad you haven't forgotten your family. Winston's doing very well, you know. They say he'll definitely get in."

"Good for him."

"All your friends have surrendered. Just recently. The Communists, the Ma Gong. All the way up in Thailand now, still fighting after so many years, as if anyone remembers them. It's finally over, no more Communists left here."

"They're not my friends."

"Anyway, you must put this behind you." Vanda's lips compressed. "You made a mistake, but nothing really happened. Thank God you didn't really bring down the government. You must pray in gratitude, that it didn't go too far. You still have your family. You must go on living your life."

Stella nodded, numb. Then— "Can we go home by Orchard Road?"

"What for?"

"I want to see people."

Vanda said nothing, but turned the car in that direction. Stella stared in fascination at the busy pavements, even on a weekday morning. The overhead gantries were festooned with giant snowflakes and pink-faced Santa Clauses. She'd have to come back at night, to see them all lit up.

When they passed the red cube of MacDonald House, she didn't feel the usual sadness, thinking of her mother's death, but only resignation. It comes to everyone, she thought, the bolt from nowhere that shatters your life. If Mollie had lived—

"We should go home," said Vanda. "Your father will

be waiting."

It was remarkably easy to slip back into normalcy. The flat was smaller than she remembered it, her bedroom tiny. Was it actually the same size as her cell? The school was, unsurprisingly, reluctant to have her back. She didn't search for another teaching position—something told her there would be none available for her. Church was out of the question too—she was too afraid of running into the other people who'd been taken. She started staying in her room most of the day, re-reading novels or staring at the ceiling. When her father mentioned at dinner that she hadn't left the flat for weeks, she nodded but didn't see what she could do about that.

A few months later, one of the others phoned—they were planning a press conference to tell their side of the story. They'd been mistreated, and wanted the world to know. People thought their confessions had been voluntary, that they were all meek and repentant now. Had she been slapped, kicked, deprived of sleep? The officers weren't supposed to do that. Would she stand with them? She said she'd think about it, and whenever they called after that, she got Vanda to say she wasn't in.

In the end, only nine of them put their names to the statement. As Stella had feared, they were rounded up and put back in detention almost right away, along with their lawyer. The government said their actions proved they hadn't really been rehabilitated, that the Malayan Communist Party, the Ma Gong, were trying once more to gain a foothold amongst the English-educated intelligentsia. The newspapers were agog. Another plot to overthrow the government, so soon after the last one?

Stella and the rest were summoned to Phoenix Park, and ordered to sign a declaration refuting the allegations. Devin was there, grim-faced. He was glad to see them looking so well, he said. "We hope you'll co-operate with us. We don't want people to misunderstand. Weren't you all treated nicely? Free meals from the government! I think some of you even put on weight."

Stella couldn't stop thinking about the nine who'd spoken up. It seemed likely they would be held for years this time, not months. She ought to feel pity or guilt, but instead she resented them for putting her in this position. What was she supposed to do? She couldn't go inside again, she knew that. There was so little left of herself, she couldn't afford to lose any more. When her turn came, she felt Siew Li's disapproving eyes on her, but still—not knowing how she would atone for any of this, trying not to think what she was doing—she picked up the pen.

6

"My father died last night," says Henry on the phone to Revathi. "Also, Ralph is gone. For good this time, I think."

"Ralph is an arsehole. I'm sorry about your dad."

"I should have gone back sooner. I didn't think he'd…"

"Are you all right?"

"Yes, I think. We weren't close or anything. Still…"

"How's your sister doing?"

"Janet? You know, indestructible."

"Can I do anything?"

Henry lies back on the sofa. "No. I don't know. Talking helps."

"When are you going back?"

"Day after. Saunders can take over my classes. I might be gone a while."

"The funeral?"

"Friday. There's the whole flat to be cleared out, and probably all sorts of paperwork. I should give myself a bit of time."

"Sensible."

"I don't feel sad enough. It comes and goes in waves, but even at my saddest, it doesn't seem sufficient. I don't really feel much of anything. Is that normal?"

"Your boyfriend dumped you and your father died. You're allowed to be discombobulated."

"He left yesterday, before I got the news, for the record. He's not that much of an arsehole."

"Why do you care how much of an arsehole I think Ralph is?"

"Rev, what's happening with my life?"

He hears crunching, and she says indistinctly, "If I could give you the answer to that, I'd be a lot wiser. You'll be all right."

"You don't know that."

"You're right, I was just trying to make you feel better."

"Will you feed my cat while I'm gone?"

"I've got a better idea. I'll come with you."

"What, to Singapore?"

"I'm due a trip anyway. Haven't been for a couple of years, and you know I need to stay in touch with what's going on." Revathi's books and articles very much depend on her being ahead of the curve on Southeast Asia, packaging trends and developments into neatly understood gobbets for consumption in airport lounges and board rooms. "Hey, I have air miles and an expense account, I'm happy to come. You sound like you could use the company."

"I really could. But are you sure?"

"What else would I be doing?"

After hanging up, Henry remains prone on the sofa for quite a while, watching the waning sun paint long shadows across the ceiling. When it's almost too dark to see, he shambles to the fridge and mechanically starts eating the most perishable things, using a spoon for propriety's sake but still spilling brown sauce down his front.

It doesn't take him long to pack. Most of his clothes are completely unsuited to the tropics, so it's a simple matter of packing everything short-sleeved and lightweight. More books than he could possibly read on such a short trip, but he doesn't know what he'll be in the mood for. The cat starts sulking when she sees the suitcase, and he has to placate her with an extra treat. He sends an e-mail, arranging for a grad student to feed her. His phone pings—Revathi, checking his travel details so she can book herself on the same flight.

This is a good opportunity to move Ralph's detritus out of his flat. There is nothing valuable enough to return, so he bags up the random garments and trashy paperbacks for Oxfam, and bins the extra toothbrush. The relationship wasn't long enough to be worth mourning, but he still feels—not sad exactly, but weary. It would have been nice, just for once—But never mind, a trip away will scrub this ridiculous episode from his mind.

When Henry first moved away from Singapore, he didn't go back for a long time. There was something about the thought of returning that filled him with claustrophobia, as if he might somehow be prevented from leaving again.

He's more secure now, after the many decades here and the "indefinite leave to remain" stamp in his passport, though recent developments have made him nervous—there have been some horror stories, people deported for the tiniest infraction. Still, Singapore doesn't allow dual citizenship, and he isn't yet prepared to cross over completely to the other side.

Each death is the severing of a connection, though there are too many of those for him to become completely untethered. He searches his e-mail for a photo of his father, and finds one Janet sent a few years ago, at one of the boys' birthday parties. He is smiling vaguely, perhaps not completely sure where he is, as a slab of cake is placed in front of him. A harmless old man.

Now, finally, tears prickle his eyes, and he lets them flow where they will. No point thinking about the conversations they never had. Both of them had decades in which to reach out to each other. There were terse phone calls, birthday cards approximately once every three years, and messages passed on via Janet. So much lost. Questions are already forming in his mind, things he wishes he'd asked when there were answers to be had. Never mind. Make the best of it. He cries himself empty, and drags himself to bed.

The next day passes in a welter of errands, and then he is meeting Revathi at the airport. The rigmarole of security, judicious use of the sample moisturisers at Duty Free— "Airplanes dry out your skin," he says defensively, as she raises an eyebrow at him—and onto their Singapore Airlines flight, which may or may not still be the best in the industry, but is comfortingly familiar. They are flying eastward, into the night, and not long after take-off it has grown completely dark.

•

"You only come home when someone dies," says Janet at the airport, and Henry can think of no rebuttal. He was last in Singapore for Uncle Barnaby's funeral almost a decade ago, but he didn't stay long enough to visit. He's been terribly negligent, only seeing his nephews occasionally on Skype, and briefly when Kevin was over in London on a school trip. There's so much that can be deferred indefinitely.

He hands over the bags containing her demands: lemon biscuits from Fortnum and Mason's, Earl Grey from Whittard, blackcurrant jam from Harrod's. Janet has very specific tastes. She nods thanks, and slings them into the boot along with their suitcases. She could probably have got all of that on Amazon, but she also has old-fashioned views about familial duty, one of which is that her brother is obliged to supply all her British needs, otherwise what's the point of him living there?

Janet has a civil servant's car, clean but cluttered with papers and books. Revathi has to shove some garish hardback folders out of the way to squeeze into the back seat. When he asks what's in them, Janet rolls her eyes. "Policy documents. I need to read them to know roughly what's happening, in case Minister happens to ask me in a meeting or something. Waste of time, they'll change it all in a couple of years."

"Do you miss teaching?" Revathi asks.

"No. I don't like kids."

There is a silence as they purr down the long, straight road from the airport, the arrays of pink flowers on either side fetching in the early morning light. They've gone straight from air-conditioned airport to air-conditioned car, and thus been spared the sharp burst of heat to the face that tells Henry he's home, though the shimmering haze on the road ahead reminds him of what he's in for.

He asks Janet about her husband and children, treading carefully so she doesn't discover that he only ever skims the long e-mails she sends anatomising their lives. He remembers the highlights: the younger nephew's exam results and Winston's ministerial position, but otherwise her messages are a blur of banal detail, sandwiched between forwarded jokes and Christian tracts.

"So how do you two know each other?" says Janet, in a tone of voice that indicates she doesn't really care. Henry says something about all the Singaporeans in London being acquainted, swapping tips about where to find the best laksa, which is the cue for Revathi to launch into an anecdote about how they first met at some ghastly Singaporean Chinese New Year event, god knows why she was even there but good luck trying to find anything for non-Chinese Singaporeans, and Henry was the only one who'd looked as appalled as her by the emcee's awful jokes, so they'd bonded over that.

"We're going to the Tiong Bahru flat, by the way," says Janet. "It's Henry's idea. Not that we have room to put you up anyway. I hope you're okay with that."

"It's fine," says Revathi, "I'm not superstitious."

"He didn't die there, if you were afraid of that."

She turns off the highway, wrenching the wheel a little harder than necessary. The buildings here are low-rise—shophouses and four-storey apartment blocks—and the streets named after people who were once famous. Eng Hoon Avenue. Yong Siak Street. Who were these men? He has never bothered to look them up. Revathi would probably know.

"They'd like to tear all this up, but it's a conservation area. Waste of space, all this prime land." Parking makes Janet short-tempered—she is enraged by anything she can't do well.

The open-air car park sits enclosed by the horseshoe-shaped block, shaded by old trees. Emerging from the car, Henry feels the moist humidity, smells the sweet sap of seed pods crushed underfoot. Funny to think of Englishmen, two hundred years ago, embarking on an adventure to this small island, many dying from the smothering warmth and vicious diseases. The Victorian novels he used to devour barely mentioned the colonies, yet all their wealth was plunder.

"Come on," says Janet brusquely, and he shakes himself free of his jet-lagged thoughts to help with the bags. The flats are old enough not to have lifts, which seems eccentric in high-tech Singapore. He struggles with his suitcase while Revathi, the seasoned traveller, has shown up with no more than a light rucksack and her capacious handbag.

The flat is more crowded that he remembers. The old furniture is still there, dark wood shelves stuffed with books and papers, but there is now a secondary layer of furniture in front of it, shoddy chipboard things, also crammed full. Stacks of newspapers fill any spaces the furniture doesn't. It's dingy until Janet savagely jerks a curtain, letting in bright tartrazine sunlight that haloes all the dust in the air.

The kitchen cupboards are full of tinned food, some of it several years past the best-by dates. There are drawers full of light bulbs, matchboxes, cough mixture, sensible things to have on standby, apparently bought in bulk. All the rooms in the house are similarly crowded. Janet's old bedroom is a warren of cardboard boxes (he looks inside one: instant noodles) and bin bags containing mothballed clothes.

Henry opens the door to his old room, and is overwhelmed by a smell of decay, emanating from a plastic bag of what might once have been fruit. Sifting through the bags underneath in case there are other perishables, he dislodges a large brown cockroach, which scuttles for cover. Reflexively, he steps on it, and then has to scrape the white ooze off his shoe. The room seems uninhabitable, but perhaps he'll be able to clear a path to the single bed he last slept in more than thirty years ago.

"Do you want me to book you a hotel?" he murmurs to Revathi, and she widens her eyes.

"Are you kidding? Pass up the chance to witness a real-life *Hoarders*? Anyway it's much more fun in the heartlands."

His father's room is no less occupied, but the bed can at least be seen, and it seems reasonably hygienic. He puts Revathi's things in here and takes the sheets out to the washing machine. There's no detergent anywhere to be found.

Revathi asks where the bathroom is. While she's gone, Janet turns to him and says, *sotto voce*, "I've seen the will, by the way. There isn't much money left, and he left me the flat." She looks like she's expecting a fight, and deflates a little when he simply nods.

"That's fair. You took care of him."

"We couldn't have put him in an old folks' home—how would that have looked? Anyway, we haven't decided what to do with this place, either sell it or leave it for the boys when they want to move out. We'll have to sort all this out." She gestures at the mounds of rubbish, which look alarmingly permanent.

"Well. I'm grateful."

She nods, mollified. "How are you, anyway? Everything fine with—your male friend?"

"We're not together any more."

"I'm sorry." She pulls her hair back into a ponytail and turns her attention to one of the drawers. This is an improvement—it took her years to even stop wondering aloud whether her brother might suddenly switch to dating and, hopefully, marrying women. Now that they are in their fifties, she seems finally resigned to at least acknowledging, if not accepting, who he is.

"If you need to get to work—" he offers.

She takes the opening. "Thanks, yes, I only took half-day leave. You should know where everything is, but if not, text me." She hands him the keys and then, awkwardly, fishes a parcel from her bag. "I made this for you. All that time in the hospital. Maybe it will be useful in the winter." She clatters out the door before he can look. When he pulls the paper off, it's a scarf, clearly hand-made, the colour of the night sky with flashes of brightness.

•

Having decided not to nap, they start sorting through his father's belongings, but this quickly becomes overwhelming. To start with, Henry sets aside anything Janet might remotely be interested in, but very soon he is tossing everything he can into bin bags from a roll he unearthed in the kitchen. He had no idea things had gotten this bad, and wonders why Janet didn't say anything, didn't try to intervene.

After a couple of hours, he starts to feel like a bad host and suggests a walk around the neighbourhood. The sky is completely overcast, and the light has a glassy, heavy quality. Henry and Revathi stop at a provision shop for washing powder and cockroach spray.

Walking around Tiong Bahru, Henry realises he was wrong. The buildings might be the same, but it has unquestionably changed. Of course it has, he's been gone so long. Several times, he sees faces that seem familiar, only to stop himself just before waving. His memories of the area are two or three decades old, and the people he holds in his mind couldn't possibly look like that any longer. A whole new set of people have moved in, smartly-dressed and wielding iPhones.

The ground floor of these buildings are taken up by shops, but very few are as he remembers, just the occasional tze char restaurant with its sizzling wok smells, kitchens spilling out onto back alleys where cats lurk for scraps. They walk past a yoga studio, a bookshop, even an art gallery. He sees cafés with outdoor seating, trendy expat mums and teenagers with Macbook Airs. They have cappuccinos and little French pastries. *It became Hoxton when I wasn't looking,* he thinks. It's disquieting, but Revathi shrugs each time he apologises. "I'd be surprised if gentrification somehow missed Singapore, it happens everywhere else."

"This isn't the heartlands any more," he says.

"Of course not, I was joking earlier. Flats around here are going for a million dollars. You should seriously come back more often; the country you have in your head isn't there any more—everything's moving on."

He's thinking like an old man. *Stop*, he admonishes himself. *It's good that things are getting better.* What he wouldn't have given, as a teenager, to have a bookshop on his doorstep. And now here is one, a whimsical little place with orange crate bookshelves and a cat on the counter. He wanders into its coolness and is seduced into buying a small stack to add to his reading pile.

The afternoon feels empty. The funeral is the next day, but Janet has made it clear he doesn't need to do anything beyond turning up. He's not in touch with anyone else in Singapore, outside of his family. He cycles through names from school, from national service, from the neighbourhood, but has no idea where any of them are now.

Revathi is the one playing tour guide now, pointing out glimpses of the old neighbourhood, the art deco features of the architecture. "Someone told me they wanted to apply for UNESCO World Heritage status, but they'd have had to restore the façades, which would mean getting rid of the aircon units. The residents said no."

"That sounds about right. Never get between a Singaporean and their aircon."

"Can you blame them? If you lived here, your brain would melt without it."

"My dad, though. He just had fans."

"Henry, I don't want to speak ill of the dead, but your dad was—eccentric."

"I'd noticed. It's strange, there are all these things I thought were normal, and it was only when I was grown up that I realised they were just my family."

"Lots of people have that."

"It's so strange that he's gone. I think I expected him to outlive me."

They walk past hoardings for a new condo development, the outside painted with optimistic renderings of poolside idylls and retro interior design, populated by ethnically ambiguous but light-skinned figures. "This used to be a field," says Revathi. "I guess it was too much to expect, that they'd actually leave the empty space alone."

"Singapore property developers abhor a vacuum."

"Silly. Come on, let's get some food."

Tiong Bahru Market is where he remembers it. They have done it up, fresh paint, even escalators, but the building remains essentially the same. Fresh food downstairs, cooked food above. Revathi is more up to speed with the current etiquette—put a packet of tissue paper on an empty table to claim it, then go order your food.

The food stalls are laid out in three long rows, joined in a triangle, surrounded by functional plastic tables. The central airwell keeps things cool, as do slowly turning fans on the high ceiling. Suddenly wanting to experience all the tastes of his childhood, Henry orders too much food: chicken rice, simmered in fragrant stock and served with chilli; double-boiled herbal soup; fried oysters in an omelette; and a shaved-ice concoction for dessert. At the cold drinks stall, he watches as the lady pushes thick stalks of sugarcane through a mechanical crusher, squeezing out sweet green liquid.

"Are you starving or something?" says Revathi, eyeing his spread over her plate of fried noodles.

"I got carried away."

He eats too fast, and too messily. A mouthful of rice, a spoonful of soup. Thinly sliced shallots, crisp edges of fried egg, and the syrupy cool of the ice. Food spills down his shirt, but that can go in the machine later. There is an ominous crack, and torrents of rain begin to fall outside. He has a memory from boyhood, walking through this warm, fat tropical rain. If it doesn't stop soon, perhaps they'll go out into it; home is only a short distance away. He has another spoonful of dessert, and finds a buried piece of yam, crushing it against the roof of his mouth, sweet and powdery.

●

The funeral takes place in a church. Janet insists that their father accepted Christ just before his death, which Henry does not find very likely, but it seems to make her happy. "We'll see him again, he'll be waiting for us," she tells him, almost gaily, as if that's not a terrifying prospect. He tries to tell her again that he hasn't been a believer for a long time, but Janet hears only what she wants to. When an in-law asks Henry which church he attends in London, Janet jumps in with, "Henry hasn't found a church that suits him yet," and then "He works too hard. I always tell him he should make the effort to get up early on Sunday, but he's so lazy." He lets it go. We must find comfort where we can.

They are in Janet's church in Queenstown, a large modern building with stark white walls and a lot of tinted glass, although from the train he was startled to see a banner reading "Homosexuals Can Change" unfurled across the roof in bright colours. The whole place hums with air-conditioning and a heavy floral scent. Walking in, the visitor is seized by two greeters who proffer a hymnal and a photocopied order of worship. Other ushers take over to seat people, filling up from the front. It is a well-drilled operation, and scaled to deal with large numbers, with radio mikes and video screens projecting close-ups of the pulpit to all corners.

Janet frets at the low attendance. "I told everyone," she fusses. "His old colleagues, all the cousins, but so few of them got back to me." The five occupied rows do look a bit sparse in all that space. She waves, smiling tightly, at each new arrival. Most of these seem to be her friends, middle-aged Chinese men and women with the pale, dutiful look of the professional bureaucrat.

Henry is in the front pew with Janet and her family. He shakes hands firmly with his brother-in-law and admires his nephews—young men now, taller than him, at the age when they're a little embarrassed to be related to old people. He nods at them and they smile back, perfectly friendly. He is a distant figure to them, while he's watched them grow up through the pictures Janet sent. He regrets not having reciprocated with more e-mails. Stella comes late and takes a pew at the back, earning a scowl from Janet.

The pastor is a squat Chinese man with a kindly face, though his eyes gain a hint of steel when he talks about God. He reads from a sheet of paper, something about the life and career of our brother Jason Low, and speaks some words of comfort for the family. There is a reading from the Bible. Janet's face is solemn, like her husband's, but there is a sparkle in her eyes, as if she is being told something of great value. Henry wishes Revathi were here, to make him feel less like the only heathen present, but she said it would be weird to go to the funeral of someone she'd never met.

Afterwards, they have tea and sandwiches in the small Sunday School room. Janet has allocated half an hour for this. Foam play mats are stacked in a corner, with quantities of colourful books. He picks one up. Stories from the Old Testament, in comic form. On the cover, a square-chinned Daniel faces down the lions in their den.

There are not many people he knows, but strangers come up to him and express their condolences. Everyone is bracingly unsentimental, which he appreciates. There is little to be said about a death when the family's feelings can best be summed up as guilty relief. They ask him about life in London, and seem genuinely interested in what he has to say. Janet hovers, passing food around: curry puffs, plastic beakers of weak squash. When she judges enough time has passed, she chivvies everyone downstairs, where a chartered bus is waiting.

Henry finds himself sitting next to a young woman who turns out to be the daughter of a second cousin. She is an optician now, and meets Janet regularly for coffee. "Your sister holds the family together," she tells him. "She organises a dinner at least once a year." Not that Jason ever went to these gatherings; to be honest, she confesses, she was rather frightened of him. His quick temper. Once, Henry would have responded with stories of being hit with a belt as a child, of his father's volatility and implacable rage, but now he judges it better to smile gently and say nothing. The good thing about age is the accumulation of injuries reaching the point where each individual hurt seems less significant.

The bus drops them off at Mandai Crematorium. They file into the windowless room. It looks like a lecture theatre at one of the newer universities. The coffin is already at the front, with a glass panel through which Jason's face is visible. They have shaved his face and combed his hair in a strange way. He looks like he is made of wax. Sitting down, Henry feels tears beginning to come, and looks across at Janet to see her also red-eyed and blurry. She nods grimly at him.

The pastor says a few more words, and Janet rises to make a speech thanking everyone for coming. Again, she talks about her father being reunited with his wife, their mother, in the next world, and both parents waiting there for their children to arrive. People nod, and Henry feels he has to nod too. Fortunately no one seems to expect him to speak.

Then they are on the move again, up a staircase, past an indoor waterfall, and into a gallery overlooking a featureless room, panelled in wood like a squash court. Two attendants push the coffin in on a gurney, then slide one of the panels open to make a door just wide enough for the coffin to glide in onto a hidden conveyor belt. It disappears from view, almost an anti-climax.

Downstairs, Janet hands out packet drinks. People come up to shake their hands, and then disperse. Stella hugs Henry and says something about meeting properly another time. Winston leaves to ferry a gaggle of aunts to the nearest MRT, and then it is very quiet. They are far enough from the road to be insulated from traffic noises. Henry and Janet sit on a wooden bench in the lobby, waiting for their father's ashes.

•

The MRT has sprouted all kinds of new lines since Henry last rode it. The stations are like something out of science fiction, gleaming palely with underground light. TV screens on the platforms show public-service videos between announcements. A group of bad actors notice someone furtively leaving his bag beneath a seat. What are they to do? It could be a bomb! The next train arrives before they can take action, so Henry never finds out whether they were blown up.

Revathi accompanies him a couple of stations, because she wants to see the new line, then bails. He tries to get her to join them for dinner—Janet won't mind, probably—but she has a lot to do. He'd been afraid of leaving her alone while he did family stuff, but it turns out she wasn't lying about this being primarily a work trip. Her schedule is full of meetings of all kinds—she seems to have an endless number of people to interview and events to attend. His friend, he is discovering, is a different person here than she is in London, where she is quite happy to hang out in pubs with him for entire aimless afternoons.

Janet and Winston live in Sengkang, near the top of one of those unfeasibly tall new private developments with a faux-European name. He has to change trains twice, the second time to a driverless light-rail that runs alarmingly close to the buildings on either side, all steel and exposed concrete like a Brutalist nightmare. He wonders what it must be like to live surrounded by so many people stuffed into identical little boxes, but bites back the thought. At least people have somewhere to stay, for the most part.

He gets lost trying to find the condo—the blocks seem laid out randomly rather than sequentially—and arrives breathless and late. Winston pats him hard on the shoulder and takes the flowers he brought. "Chrysanthemums!" he smiles. "Is this a funeral?"

Janet takes the bouquet to put into water. "Henry doesn't know all this," she says, "He's been living in ang moh land too long. Never mind, we're not *pantang*."

Vaguely aware of having made a faux pas, he takes off his shoes and pads into the living room. He hasn't visited since they moved, and is impressed by how sleek the furnishings are in this new place. Ministers earn quite a bit here, he remembers. There is a handsome bookcase in pride of place, though its contents are mostly business manuals and management guides.

The boys are out—"I told them to stay and see their uncle, but young people are so busy"—and Henry can't be hurt by this. He ought to have made the effort to know them better, if he'd wanted them to stay home for him. Instead, he has

Janet's pinched good cheer and Winston's bonhomie. "So, Henry, you've been so-called writing," booms his brother-in-law. "Is that going well?"

The maid brings out the food. White rice and a few simple dishes. Henry wonders if she'll join them, but she retreats into the kitchen after making sure they have everything they need. Conversation over dinner is surprisingly uncontentious—what the press is saying about Winston's latest speech, how well the boys are doing. He'd thought they might talk about their father, but other than complaining about the funeral catering, Janet doesn't bring up the subject, and he finds he doesn't want to either. Maybe that's for the future, when they've had more time, or maybe they've already said all that ever needed to be.

He looks across the table at his twin and thinks, *If there was ever an argument against genetics—our faces aren't that different, but everything else is. Is it just all our different choices, cumulatively, or something more fundamental?* He feels it like a physical void between them. As if he could reach out and still not be able to touch her.

To be honest, this feels flat. This dinner, like the funeral, like this whole trip, is hollowed out. What did he expect, closure? The rest of the evening is the same, amicable, less stressful than he'd expected, but still he feels like he's only skating over the surface of ice too thick to crack. He remembers many dinners with their father, he and Janet sitting in tense silence, afraid of angering him. Now that they can talk, it turns out they never had that much to say to each other in the first place.

Revathi is still out when he gets back to his father's flat. He wonders if she's met someone. She has a non-exclusive arrangement with another journalist back in London, a younger man whom she refers to as her toyboy—but that barely seems to slow her down, as if she's determined to age as disgracefully as possible.

Needing to be active, he starts tidying up again, wondering why he's doing this, when the flat now belongs to Janet. There's something about the ritual that feels necessary. Like a laying out of the body, as if his father had put himself into these objects he'd felt compelled to accumulate, scared to lose anything more.

He works to the point of exhaustion then lies down, but cannot make his eyes shut. The night swirls around him, traffic noises and a child somewhere practising piano scales. Probably too early for bed, but he feels something cold clutching at him, and being very still seems the best way to slough it off. How much longer, he wonders, but there can be no answer till he formulates the rest of that question. It's a relief when his phone chirps, and he can sit up again. It's a text from Stella, asking him to lunch the next day with some of her friends.

●

The address Stella gave them turns out to be a shopping centre so run-down Henry is surprised it still exists. It's perfectly sound, but he's come to expect malls in this country to be fortresses of marble and gleaming glass with all the usual high-end chains, not this unremarkable three-storey white-and-tangerine slab. There are no brand names at all here, just small businesses, tailor shops and maid agencies, and at the far end, a Chinese restaurant that hasn't been redecorated since at least the eighties. Stella stands outside, waving.

"So glad you came," she says. Her partner Maryam, whom Henry hasn't seen for years, grins widely. He introduces Revathi, and they go inside, where it looks like there is a party of some sort going on. "Is this a wedding?" asks Henry, before realising they are the youngest people here— everyone else is closer to seventy, or maybe older. Yet it does look like one, a few dozen guests seated around numbered tables covered in heavy damask, their centrepieces co-ordinated to the streamers over the raised stage. They all seem to know each other. Is this some sort of club?

Stella has saved them seats at one of the far tables. She introduces the others, whom she seems familiar with. "This is Geok Leong, she was quite senior in the General Labour Union. This is Halim, he's a historian these days, wrote a book recently about the movement, you might remember it. And over there, that's Ng Lay Kuan, maybe you remember her? She was an MP very briefly in the sixties, before your time of course. Never got to take her seat."

The old leftists, she explains, meet for lunch once a year. She only found out about this a few years ago, and now she joins them regularly. When Henry continues to look bemused, she shrugs. "Sure, I guess it must seem a bit strange to you. I first heard about it a few years ago and thought I'd see what it's like. Everyone's really lovely."

"Do they mind outsiders joining?"

"Don't be silly. Anyway, you're not an outsider, you have family connections." And indeed, he is surprised by the outpouring when Stella mentions who his mother is. Ng Lay Kuan embraces him, and says Siew Li was one of the best ones they had, such a shame—

He braces himself, but their stories are sweet and not particularly revelatory. He already has all this information, about her work with the unions, her detention. As for what happened after her disappearance, there is nothing—these people weren't in contact with her any more than he was.

Everyone is keen to chat as the food starts to arrive, course after course. There is lots of gossip, rehashing of old episodes and catching up on each other's latest ailments. Revathi is beaming—there's an article in this, he can see her thinking. Henry catches up with Stella's life—she's still making ends meet giving tuition, not doing much else. Halim asks Henry if he's still angry with the government for what it did.

"I haven't really thought about that in a while. It's all in the past."

"The ISA is still around today."

"They say they only detain terrorists, though."

"They called us terrorists too, you know. If there's no trial, no need to produce evidence, you can call people anything you want."

"Your ma was right to go," says Lay Kuan, suddenly looking fierce. "Otherwise, locked up like us, no chance. Some people are still outside. Can't come back. How can you say everything is in the past, when there are still people trapped outside? You mustn't blame your ma, whatever you do."

He can only nod, and is fortunately saved from having to reply as the performances start just then. A trio of erhus drone out a melancholy tune, and then someone does card tricks. There are some songs, and a skit from the old days, something about a girl almost betraying her village but coming to her senses just in time.

Next are the speeches, some in English in deference to the few non-Chinese comrades, the rest in Chinese. Henry finds he understands enough of the language to keep up a whispered commentary to Revathi. Not much of what they're saying is important, anyway. This has the feel of ritual, of words being spoken not only because they are true, but to keep them from being forgotten.

Afterwards they sing a chorus of "Unity is Strength", then rise to mingle. Revathi is in her element, going up to people and charming their stories from them, even though they barely have a language in common. Stella wants a cigarette, so Henry goes to stand outside with her.

He hands her a framed photo he found on top of a bookcase: Janet smiling, him nervous, and Stella trying to look rebellious, all black clothes and cropped hair. "Thought you'd like this."

"This was just before you left for London, wasn't it?"

"Must have been." He wonders if she'd already guessed, back then, that he had no intention of returning. "So, you're okay?" He has asked this before, several times, but he doesn't know what else to say.

"All right. I mean, not really, but also yes. Everything's fine."

"How's your step-mother?"

"Vanda? She remarried, a while ago. Stockbroker. Always lands on her feet, that one."

"I'm glad you have these people to hang out with."

"I'm not really one of them—I came much later, and to be honest I'm probably not ideologically pure enough. But it's always nice to see them. People seem to have forgotten what happened back then, and I need to be with people who still remember. We don't even have to talk about it. They all know. The others I was in detention with, my batch, many of them are still fighting. Writing books and standing for Parliament. I—" She spreads her hands helplessly. "I survive."

"That's already something," says Maryam, who has appeared from round the corner, taking her arm. "You're doing very well."

"Come visit London," says Henry, not knowing what else to offer.

She grimaces. "Not likely, that last trip ended pretty badly."

"That wasn't London's fault," protests Henry, but she is shaking her head and he doesn't want to press too hard. *If only we could have been closer*, he thinks with some sadness. But there was all that distance, both geographical and the other sort, harder to define, that grew between them.

Revathi rejoins them, glowing. "What fascinating people! Thank you for inviting us."

Stella smiles, they all hug again, and she leaves, walking slowly, holding herself very straight, Maryam a step ahead of her. "It's good that—" says Revathi, but leaves the thought unfinished.

●

It's in the mornings that he's most aware Singapore is a tropical island. Before the blunt force of noonday heat, when the just-risen sun feels clean and strong, and the streets look burnished. As Henry strolls through Tiong Bahru, everything from the pink roadside bougainvillea to the small clumps of palm trees sparkle as if fresh-minted. They'll be wilted and dusty by mid-afternoon, but for now are refreshed by the cool of night.

The woman at the bakery recognises him. "Your dad showed me your book," she explains. "I remember your picture on the back." She's sad to hear that Jason has died— he was a regular customer. On an impulse he can't explain, Henry asks what his father would usually get, and picks up a loaf of the same sort of bread.

Back in the flat, he takes a closer look at the shelves, and sure enough his authored books are all there. Not exactly prominent, but less dusty than the ones around them. Did Jason read them, or just show them off around the neighbourhood? Either way.

After breakfast, he and Revathi get back to clearing. Janet has begged off, claiming first work commitments and then dust allergies. Fair enough that she simply doesn't want to be here, thinks Henry, he can hardly complain after all his years away. She offers to send her maid over to help, but he says that won't be necessary.

They get into a rhythm of shovelling things into plastic bags—armloads of yellowing paper, milk turned lumpily solid in its carton, appliances grown rusty and unusable. These get hoisted out the back door, down the spiral staircase to the bins in the alleyway. The clothes that look like they might be salvageable go into cardboard boxes for the Salvation Army to pick up.

Everything in the flat teems with angry life. A jar left out overnight smells odd by morning, and has a film of blue mould over its surface within a couple of days. Getting rid of the rotting food is a low point, but having invested in rubber gloves and a box of disposable masks, Henry manages. Did Janet simply give up on their father? He was in the hospital for weeks, but some of this stuff has clearly been around much longer.

By afternoon, the outlines of the home he remembers show themselves, like an excavation carving out a ruin. Once they've got rid of the more recent makeshift furniture, the durable stuff from his childhood is visible again. They can see the floor too, scuffed terrazzo. There are plastic boxes everywhere, filled with what turn out to be newspaper clippings.

"I had no idea he was still doing this," says Henry. "He'd read the papers, then cut out anything that might be of interest and file it away. If you visited and mentioned, say, yoga, he'd disappear for ten minutes and come back with a lifestyle piece about yoga from six years ago."

"But it's all on the Internet now," says Revathi. "Newspapers don't even have morgues any more."

"We tried to explain that, but—" He gestures around, letting the lack of a computer speak for itself.

With its cupboards emptied, the kitchen looks piebald. There are ingrained dirt and food stains to be scrubbed away, and the pots on the draining board host their own ecosystem. The walls are moderately dirty up to just above head height, after which they are filthy. Jason must have made some attempt to clean the place, but only as far as he could reach without standing on anything.

"If your sister can be bothered to renovate, she could rent this out for a fortune," says Revathi, looking out the window at the weekend brunch crowds, who are queuing patiently outside the trendiest joints downstairs.

"She'll probably do that, she's not sentimental."

"And you?"

Henry runs his fingers over the counter, the texture calling back something like memory. "I won't be here. Don't know if I'll ever come back again. Silly for me to want this to stay the same. A museum to what?"

"You grew up here."

"Everything I grew up with is gone. I went looking for the National Library, and there was just a tunnel in the side of a hill. Might as well lose this too."

He upends another drawer, spilling wooden implements he can only guess the use of. He holds one up for Revathi to inspect, a toothed semi-circle.

"That's a curry puff mould. Did your dad make curry puffs?"

"Not that I know of. Must have been left over from…"

He trails off. There is something stuffed into a napkin-holder, carefully folded papers, some still in envelopes. He opens them and sees letters, age-spotted paper covered in spidery Chinese writing, and rough-edged photographs in faded sepia. He holds them up to the light. Pictures of his mother, he's sure of it. It's the schoolgirl from the one photograph he has of her, here all grown up, dressed in khaki fatigues, holding a rifle casually by her side, as if she's forgotten it's there. He flicks through the others, and there she is, pointing at the sky, looking at the camera with determination. They are all heroically posed.

He turns the last one over, and scribbled on the back in rough Chinese characters is her name, Siew Li. It's her.

Revathi is silent for a while when he shows her. "You knew she'd gone inside, didn't you."

"We suspected. My dad just said she ran away, didn't want to talk about where."

The pictures are faded, easily half a century old. "I've

seen ones like these before," says Revathi. "I don't know why they keep mementoes like this, but I suppose they wanted a record, just like everyone else."

"Why didn't he show them to us?"

"Maybe he thought that wouldn't have done any good."

"That wasn't his choice." Henry feels a stab of anger, then lets it dissipate. What's the point now? He carefully unfolds the letters. There's a small stack of them, the paper spotted brown with age. He brings the first one close to his eyes and reads, piecing together the Chinese writing with difficulty: *I hope you are healthy, I hope you are safe, I hope you have not been taught to hate me.*

•

When he tries to remember the next few hours afterwards, they become a blur. The world is suddenly askew, and he can only keep moving, hoping to find his balance again. His plan has practical difficulties to be sorted, which mercifully keeps his mind busy.

"What do you mean you never learnt?" demands Revathi. "I didn't think it was possible to live in the twenty-first century and not know how to drive."

Henry shrugs. "Never needed to. I've only ever lived here and in London."

"Is there a train or something?"

"There's a bus as far as Ipoh, and I guess I can get a taxi from there."

Revathi looks at the map. "There's more than fifty miles."

"I don't see what else I can do. I called Janet, she doesn't want anything to do with them. Leave the past buried, she said. I'm on my own here."

"It'll cost a fortune."

"You have any better ideas?"

"Rent a car. I'll drive."

"Really?"

"Why not?"

"It's a long way to go. Are you sure?"

"It's an adventure, isn't it? I'm not getting any younger."

And just like that, they are speeding down the North-South Highway. He's never gone on a trip without planning ahead, but he'd quickly combed the letters for clues—the postmarks, the topography—and after some quick Googling, despite his mother's subterfuge, was able to roughly guess where she must have been. Revathi got on the phone to the car hire place while he tossed some clothes in a bag, and thirty minutes later they were passing through Malaysian customs, handing their passports over to a bored counter clerk who barely glanced at them. There was a bit of traffic over the Causeway, and they got momentarily lost in Johor Bahru's warren of narrow streets trying to find a money changer. Now they have ringgit in their pockets and the expressway before them—plain sailing. The speed limit is 110kph, but he's pretty sure everyone around them is going faster.

Henry continues reading the letters as Revathi zooms

along, yelling at anyone cutting into her lane, which happens frequently. "There isn't a lot of information. She keeps saying she can't tell us where she is—she's not allowed to, but also she doesn't really know, it's just somewhere in the jungle."

"Are you sure we're even going to the right place?"

"I hope so. By the seventies the Communists weren't controlling many areas, so this is one of the few locations she could have ended up in."

"How was she even getting these letters out to you?"

"They had people on the outside who brought them supplies, medicine and things like that. She got one of them to post these for her."

"Wasn't that dangerous?"

"Probably."

"Are you going to show Janet?"

"I photographed them on my iPad and e-mailed her the copies. Technology!"

"What did she say?"

"I don't have a data plan, so who knows."

"There's a KFC up ahead. Maybe they'll have Wi-Fi."

"We've only been on the road a couple of hours."

"So? It's lunchtime."

At the rest stop, Revathi eats fried chicken as Henry checks his messages. Janet's response is surprisingly mellow. She has already gone through all the letters, having forced Kevin with his A1 in Higher Chinese to translate. *No new information,* she says, *but it's nice to know Ma was thinking of us*. She doesn't know what Henry thinks he's going to gain from this trip, but she wishes him the best of luck.

"You sure you don't want any of this?" says Revathi. "Hot and crispy. If they had this in London, I'd be the size of a house. A chilli sauce dispenser at the table? People keep telling me KFC is better in Asia than elsewhere, but I never believed them till now."

"I'm not hungry," says Henry.

"Are you nervous?"

"I don't know what I am. Janet's right, I don't know what I think I'm going to find. But it seems important to go."

"You want primary sources, that's all."

"I don't know why I didn't do this before, but I also don't know why I'm doing it now."

Revathi wipes off her fingers with a moist towelette and pats him briskly on the shoulder. "We're excavating. Let's get back on the road."

The landscape is featureless, mountains in the distance, scrubby plains and run-down buildings along the road. The highway rips right through the country, a long thread up the spine of the peninsula. Palm tree plantations give way to paddy fields. When he sees grazing water buffalo, he knows he is a long way from home.

His father took them on a couple of holidays when they were children, only to Malaysia. Back then, it was all trunk roads, and they'd crawl for hours behind timber lorries while their car soaked up the sun like an oven. Janet was prone to carsickness and had to clutch a plastic bag the whole time, while Henry tried desperately to forget where he was by never looking up from his book. Jason would shout at them to navigate, but as he'd never taught either of them how to read a map, they weren't able to do much more than stare helplessly at him. On their last, disastrous trip, they'd gotten a flat in the middle of a monsoon, and had to stand in pouring rain as Jason changed the tyre, swearing with such abandon that it was almost funny.

When he tells Revathi this memory she raises an eyebrow. "No wonder you're so anti-holiday." It's true, he realises, he can't remember the last time he went somewhere for pure pleasure—too easy to find some purpose for each trip, research or a conference. They reach Ipoh in the evening and decide not to go any further. Revathi is starting to look exhausted, and Henry feels pointlessly guilty about not being able to share the driving. He's tired too, jetlag and his recent lack of sleep starting to hit him. Luckily, it's out of tourist season, and easy enough to find a cheap hotel. The owner assumes they are a couple, and even when they ask for separate rooms, leers, "You had a fight, is it? I'll give the madam a double bed, in case the sir changes his mind." Revathi glares at him hard enough that he stutters into silence, and hands over their keys.

They'd passed by some hipsterish coffee places on their way in, but this hotel is in the old part of town, and starting to fall apart. A section of the lobby ceiling is actually crumbling, though instead of repairing it, they've chosen to fix a net beneath to catch the falling flakes of plaster. In his room, the high ceiling has damp stains across it, and the arrow pointing towards Mecca has peeled so it droops towards the ground. When he mentions this to the owner later, the man smiles, "It doesn't matter, sir, nowadays people have an app to tell them where Mecca is."

The air-conditioning gives him sinus trouble, so he turns it off and sleeps with the windows open, even though that lets insects into the room that hum and buzz around him. Finally, he fumbles through the drawers for repellent, and finds instead a single plastic-wrapped mosquito coil. Popping it on top of the little metal prong, he lights it and breathes in the chemical scent. When did he last smell this? Probably not since that last Malaysian vacation. A thin wisp of grey smoke rises and diffuses around him. When he turns the light off, he can still see the bright ember.

•

The next morning, Revathi knocks on his door and thrusts a brown paper packet at him. "Here, breakfast."

They sit at his rickety table and eat their *nasi lemak*, which tastes slightly unfamiliar. More pandan? And chicken curry instead of fried chicken. Revathi rolls her eyes at these observations. "*Please* don't become one of those people who list all the ways Malaysian hawker food isn't as good. Those are the worst kinds of Singaporeans."

He gets out the map and they trace the day's route. A little farther along the expressway, then the road toward the Thai border, and onwards into the hills.

"If you change your mind, we can just go look at temples instead," says Revathi.

"Why would I change my mind?"

"Finding out about the past doesn't always work out the way you hope."

"Thank you, professor."

It's only later, when they've wandered out in search of coffee, that he thinks to ask, "Have you ever wanted to find out about your own family?"

"There's nothing to find out. We're very boring."

"Once you start looking, though—"

"It felt like a big enough deal, the first time I came back to Malaysia to see where my parents had come from. I didn't think about looking further back. My grandfather was brought over by the British from Jaffna—they wanted him to run a general post office in Selangor. One colony to another, so the systems were the same. I've never even been to Sri Lanka."

"It's not too late."

"Who knows what there is left to find? Anyway, I don't have anyone to tell, and I'm not that curious myself, so what's the point? Live in the present."

"I wish I could."

"I didn't mean you. Do what you have to do."

They start driving again, and despite the blazing sun, there is something sombre about the day. He is short of breath, and can't get the temperature comfortable no matter how much he adjusts the car's ventilation system. They leave the highway and continue along dusty roads. The sky seems bluer here, and he wonders if that's his imagination or if there's a scientific explanation, lack of pollution or something. Traffic is thinning out.

When they pass a small town that is little more than a row of shops by the side of the road, Revathi says she needs a break and pulls over. They walk to a tiny *kopitiam*—just a wooden shack with plastic chairs beneath a picnic umbrella outside—and get coffee, good and strong with a layer of condensed milk at the bottom. As children, Henry remembers, before he and Janet were allowed coffee themselves, they'd fight to be the one to swirl the white into their father's drink.

"Almost there," says Revathi. "Are you all right?"

"Of course I'm all right, why do you keep asking me that?"

"Because you look like a nervous wreck. You're doing that thing where your leg keeps twitching."

"I can be anxious and still be all right. I've had a lot of practice."

The table they are sitting at has cracked lino nailed over it. None of this has changed in decades, he can tell. Nothing at all different but the price of the coffee. Henry is crying a little, and has no idea why. Revathi kindly pretends not to see.

The Thai border is staffed by a single guard, and they have to rap at the glass to get him to take their passports. Betong is not all that different—Henry hears a lot of

Chinese and Malay being spoken, along with Thai. He wonders how many Malayans ended up here after everything that happened, recreating their lives on the other side of the line.

The town is rather worn, but shows signs of recent prosperity. When they ask for directions, the locals point proudly at the squat pink lozenge of the Merlin Hotel, looming over the skyline. Just look for that, they say, you'll never get lost.

They have lunch at a street-side stall—fishball noodles. He is able to order in Mandarin, and while waiting for the food to arrive, he asks the owner, a grey-haired woman, where to find the Ma Gong. She looks up from what she's doing, dunking dishes in a plastic bucket of water to clean them. "You want the Peace Villages or the Friendship Villages?" she asks, smiling. Her front two teeth are missing.

"Friendship, I think. Is there a difference?"

"Two groups. They don't agree about some things."

He has questions about factions and ideologies, but can't remember the Chinese words for these things. Instead, he asks for directions, and she points at the peaks around him, explaining what lies where. She speaks crisply, her accent more like a Mainlander than a Malaysian. Her expressions are old-fashioned, a little formal.

"My son-in-law works on one of the farms up there. He'll be stopping by in a while, if you're looking for a lift."

He glances at Revathi, and she apparently knows what he's thinking. "No, you go, I'll stay down here," she says. "I'd like to check out this pink hotel, see if it's as good as all that. Maybe I'll join you in a day or two, if you stay that long, but you should do this on your own. Text me if you need anything."

"Are you sure?"

"I might write a piece about this place. Look at it. I love border towns. All sorts of meetings happen here."

"Thank you, Revathi."

"You'd do the same for me. All right, you Chinese people go and have your drama. By the time you come back down, I'll have found out where all the good food is."

•

The Thai name for the villages is Piyamit, or "dear friend". On the back of the son-in-law's motorcycle, Henry rises into the hills. The metalled road soon peters out, and then they are rocking along the same red soil that makes up the exposed flanks of the slopes. A recent landslide has blocked half the road, and they have to move slowly, honking the horn before rounding corners.

Land for agriculture has been hacked out of the hills. Spindly rubber trees stand on terraces, next to durian and rambutan groves. "People come to Piyamit especially for the durians," the son-in-law tells him. "Eating durians in the mountain air is a special experience." There is no sign of human activity—the farmers are probably sheltering from the noontime sun, having been up since dawn.

There are four Friendship Villages, a short distance from

each other. The first one they pass looks semi-deserted—there are only a couple of kids out in front, glaring at him as they zoom past. The second is more promising. When they show up, a thin middle-aged woman comes out onto the road, while other faces peer from the large building behind her. "This is Gaolan," says the son-in-law. "She'll take care of you."

"We don't get many visitors this time of year," says Gaolan by way of greeting. She is already taking his rucksack and ushering him into what looks like some sort of guesthouse. He hasn't said anything about wanting to stay here, but fair enough, there probably isn't anywhere else. "People used to rent out rooms in their houses," she says, "But then we had a meeting and decided to build this hotel. I think you'll be comfortable here." They negotiate a price that includes all his meals, to be taken at the attached restaurant. He asks if she's the owner, and she looks at him as if he is mad. "It belongs to the village."

She scurries ahead of him to air out one of the rooms, and when he walks in she is painstakingly arranging a towel on the bed in a fan shape, individually wrapped guest soaps amongst its folds. It's a rustic place, latticework on the top parts of the walls to provide ventilation, sturdy furniture and sheets that smell of starch.

As soon as Gaolan puts the room key on the table and leaves, he lies down on one of the twin beds fully dressed, and falls immediately to sleep. He rouses himself three hours later with a slight headache and the mild panic of waking up in a strange place. Too late to do much more than wander round the village, taking photographs of the wooden houses and neat vegetable patches in the fading light. (Such an early sunset, he thinks, then remembers that Thailand is an hour ahead of Malaysia.)

When he gets back to the restaurant, a dozen or so people are there. They want to have dinner with him— they're curious about the visitor. It's not tourist season. *Is he here for the hot springs, or the rambutans? What does he do? Oh, a university professor, visiting from London?* "I knew you couldn't be local," says one of the women, "Your Mandarin is so terrible."

He hasn't ordered any food, but Gaolan says, "I made you something simple," and brings out soup, rice, a few vegetable dishes sprinkled with meat. "We grow all our own vegetables," she adds. "Taste how fresh that broccoli is. Do they have greens like that in London?"

They are silent for a while as they eat, then the questions start again. *What is he here to find out, is he writing about this place for his university? Is he married, does he have children?* They are all older than him, the young people having left for further studies, for the bigger towns. Happy to have someone to fuss over, they put food on his plate, ask for news of the outside world. They have TV and the Internet, of course, but it is hard to understand how the world is changing when so much has remained the same here.

He asks how they live, and they tell him about the land they were given, for planting rubber, fruit, vegetables, so much they have to hire local labour come harvest time to get everything in. There is a flower garden named after the Thai princess Chulabom, who visits at least once a year. They grow more than enough for themselves, and the surplus gets sold in the market at Betong. It's a good, simple life, and the Thai government treats them with respect. "We didn't surrender, after all," they remind him. "We negotiated a peace."

"We came out of the jungle in 1987," says a tall man in glasses. "Two years sooner than the other lot. They spent more time haggling, so they got a better deal—we weren't allowed to enter Malaysia until later, but they could go right away. Doesn't matter. We just wanted to get out."

The other lot, it turns out, is the Communist Party of Malaya, who now occupy the Peace Villages. The people around him are from the Communist Party of Malaysia, a splinter group, comprising the Revolutionary Faction and the Marxist-Leninist Faction. "Did you believe different things?" asks Henry, and they mutter about this or that article, before a woman sheepishly admits, "We followed different people." Anyway it's all fine now: the Peace Villagers and the Friendship Villagers are on good terms again, partly because they have united in hatred of Chin Peng, the former leader who spent many of the post-Emergency years in China. "He should have saved us," snaps Gaolan, "but he didn't care, in the end."

When he reveals he's a professor of history, they're surprised he doesn't know more about them, and he has to confess his expertise is more the Hapsburgs. He has done some quick Internet research around the subject, but much of the literature is about the Emergency itself, not the decades after. He was vaguely aware that these men and women were in the jungle all the while he was growing up, but they barely figured in the papers, unless they had one of their occasional skirmishes with the Thai army. Yet from 1948 to 1987, there they were, for forty years. He asks, but none of them were inside all four decades; the ones who joined earlier on have all been martyred by now.

"Martyred?"

"Yes, if they were part of the Ma Gong when they died, we call them martyrs, even if it was from sickness or old age."

Gaolan particularly wants him to know about the great purge in 1970—when the leadership sent down lists of traitors to be terminated. By this point, they had radio equipment—no need for messages to be smuggled in tubes of toothpaste. "They said that was why there'd been no progress after twenty years of struggle, these traitors," she says. "But we knew these people, we'd grown up with them. They were just different, maybe livelier or more opinionated than the rest, that's all. So many of them were strangled or stabbed—they didn't want to waste bullets on them. Our own people."

"It was because of the Cultural Revolution," says a thin-lipped woman who was introduced only as "Ah Chang's lover". She shuts her eyes for a moment. "Central always wanted to copy China. They never understood that this country is different. It was a mistake to go into the jungle—that made us irrelevant. We should have been urban guerrillas."

Siew Li's last letter is dated 1974. Suddenly, Henry has a vision of the woman in the photographs—his mother, though he still can't quite think of her that way—being taken into a little shack, questioned by some uniformed thug with a machete in his hand, and then—

Before he has even thought about it, the picture is on the table—the one he'd been carrying around in his wallet. The best one—the rifle in one hand, her other shading her eyes as she stares proudly into the sunlit day. "Is this— Do you know—" He gestures helplessly.

Gaolan picks it up and stares, and they pass it around. Their eyes are not good, he realises. A couple have glasses, but with the nearest optician a bumpy ride down the hill, most of them probably haven't bothered. They peer at her so hard he feels strangely protective, and then they are saying a name. *Lifeng.* A couple are uncertain, after so many years, but Gaolan and others nod, definite. "It's her, it's our Lifeng."

"That's not her," he says, warily. Could this all be some sort of mistake? No, they explain, they all changed their names when they went inside.

"I used to be Ah Mui," says Gaolan. "Can you imagine? Like a little girl. I don't think about Ah Mui much, these days. She was a different person."

"What happened to Lifeng?"

"She's dead," says Gaolan gently. "How did you know her?"

"She was a family member." That's all he feels capable of saying at the moment, and they let it go. This must happen a fair amount, because they don't ask him where he got the photograph, or seem surprised that he has a picture of one of them in uniform.

"It was a long time ago," says Gaolan. "She had a friend in the next village. I'll take you to see him tomorrow—he can tell you more."

●

Henry sleeps well that night. This place is high up enough in the hills for there to be no mosquitoes, and the air is eerily still. When was he last completely out of reach of traffic noises, even distant ones? Real silence. It's unsettling. He reaches for his phone to text Janet, but there is no reception.

There is surprisingly good coffee the next morning. Gaolan serves him toast and soft-boiled eggs in a porcelain bowl, with soy sauce and white pepper on the side. "From our own chickens," she beams. "See how yellow the yolks are? That's how you know they're fresh."

Breakfast is just as delicious as last night's dinner. There's something appealingly simple about life here, everything pared down but of the highest quality. He knows a lot of the former Ma Gong were devastated not to be allowed back into Malaysia or Singapore, but he can also see why these people chose to stay here after the travel ban was lifted, on the land they were given. This place is monastic, stark without being austere. *If I stay here too long,* he thought, *I'll stop thinking about the outside world, because everything I need is right here.* But this isn't fairyland, and he can break the enchantment anytime, as he does now—taking in a lungful of sharp, fresh air, and shaking his head.

Afterwards, Gaolan offers him a lift on her scooter. They putter along the trail, heading higher into the hills so white that wisps of mist start blurring the way ahead. Should have brought a jacket or something, he thinks. He should have known—the hills were always where the British came to cool down, when they wanted weather that reminded them of home.

The road wraps around the overgrown slopes, and it's easy to see how the Ma Gong could have stayed hidden so long, beneath the green fog of vegetation. "They sent planes out—the Thai air force," says Gaolan when he asks, "but we always managed to avoid them. They just dropped bombs at random onto the canopy."

She drops him off not at the next village, as he expected, but in front of a cave just outside. He looks at her askance and she waves him in. "Xiongmin works inside. You'll see."

This is some sort of underground museum, it turns out. Not secret, literally underground, lit by orangey halogen lamps. He goes up to the counter for a ticket (priced in both ringgit and baht). The woman there also tries to entice him into buying some incense.

"I didn't know you Communists were religious."

"We're not, but you might be." She smiles at him. "The tourists kept asking for an Earth God shrine, so we set up one down the hill. It's a Malaysian-Chinese thing: wherever they go, they want to pray to the local gods."

He refuses the incense, and instead browses a rack of memorabilia—khaki caps with red stars on their crests, postcards of old propaganda posters. A little Mao statue seems like the perfect gift for Janet, and if it annoys Winston that's a bonus.

Xiongmin is waiting just inside, and is expecting him. They shake hands gravely. "I mostly look after the archives," he says, "but Gaolan says you're a special visitor, so I thought I'd show you round myself."

They walk down the tunnel, which Xiongmin explains was built as a refuge. "We had to hide from the bombs, and what if the army came? So we dug this with nothing, just a *changkol* blade and baskets to clear the soil away. We had to go back out every half hour for air, or we'd have fainted." Henry pats a packed-earth wall as he walks past. It is cool and firm, like a real cave. There are alcoves for sleeping in, storage niches, and even a larger chamber with a peaked roof. "The radio room," says Xiongmin. "We had a wire leading up to the surface."

There is a whole warren of these underground passageways, now fitted with information boards and displays. A map marked with different colours shows how the area occupied by the Ma Gong shrank over time.

There are entire walls of propaganda materials, posters and pamphlets emblazoned with revolutionary youths. And photographs, some posed, some candid—the comrades doing surprisingly ordinary things.

"Are those people…gardening?" It seems so unlikely.

"Yes," says Xiongmin. "You mustn't think it was just fighting all the time. We went amongst the Thai people, you know, helped them with their weeding and housework, sorting out domestic issues. The Thai police knew we were here, but they didn't do anything. Everyone trusted us. When we told them we were leaving, some of them held onto us and cried, but we had to go. The struggle was over."

They walk on a bit farther, in silence. The exhibition is amateurishly designed, the grammar imperfect in both English and Chinese. They have obviously done it all themselves, with no outside help. Four decades of fighting, and this is the only residue. There are newspaper articles too, including Revathi's famous one in the *Herald*. Xiongmin points at it with some pride. "That's my mother," he says, "That's her, in the photo. I didn't see that till years later, but I was happy to have that. I never saw her again." He says it without loss, as a fact. Henry thinks of mentioning that he knows the journalist, but what for? Another meaningless point of connection.

Xiongmin says, as if he has been holding this in a long time, "Gaolan tells me you knew Lifeng."

"In a way."

"Family?"

"My mother."

Xiongmin nods, absorbing this. Henry shows him the photograph, and he smiles, "Yes, she was so proud of her rifle, and rightfully so; she was one of our sharpest shooters."

"She sent it to us. Letters too."

"I knew she was doing something like that, but I chose not to notice. Why make trouble? She missed you terribly, you and your sister. I could tell, even though she hardly mentioned you. We weren't supposed to think about our old lives. I wasn't jealous, we all had things in our past. I loved her too, you see."

Henry looks at him, uncertain what he means. Xiongmin is wiry, light on his feet. Even though he must be past seventy, his hair is still quite thick, and mostly black.

"We didn't get married in the jungle. It was too bourgeois, part of the old society. But I was her lover. That's what we called it. I knew about her other family—you—but that didn't matter. We had a daughter of our own. I was with Lifeng until she died."

"That was in—"

"1975. Something was growing inside her."

"Cancer?"

"I suppose you'd call it that now. We didn't know very much. The medicine we had cured most things, but she was too sick."

"Couldn't you have taken her to a doctor?"

"We have medics here. They tried everything, cut her open more than once, but she kept getting worse, losing weight. Like she was being emptied from the inside."

"A hospital, then?"

"We couldn't bring her out—it was too dangerous. She didn't want to die in prison. Back then, there were amnesties from time to time—the army dropped safe-passage papers from helicopters, and if you held one of those, they wouldn't shoot you, and the police wouldn't dare arrest you. Special Branch took you in, even gave you a new identity, kept you safe from reprisals. More and more people did that, just to get out. But Lifeng had actually killed someone, you see, and that was the one thing that couldn't be forgiven. If you surrendered, everything else would be forgotten, but not—"

"Not murder."

"It wasn't murder. We were at war."

Henry says nothing. No point arguing. *Xiongmin's old*, he thinks, *and I'll be old soon. A few more decades in this world, at most. Just finish this story, and carry on.* This place isn't a museum, it's a memorial. Poor Siew Li. Did she really think she could change the world? In the end, it comes down to this—a dying village with nothing to offer but the past. Would she have been glad, if she'd lived to see this?

He isn't even that surprised about the killing—why would he be? He knew what that rifle was for. And the thought of his mother dying alone in the jungle—no, not alone, she had this man, and she had—

The thought fizzes in his chest. "Daughter. You said you had a daughter."

Xiongmin nods.

"She was born inside? Is she still here?"

For a moment Xiongmin hesitates, almost fearful. But what does it matter now? "You spoke to her earlier. She works here with me. Behind the counter at the entrance."

Her? Henry stares at the woman, now bent over arranging the little Chairman Maos. Her long hair swings over her face. When he can see her again, Henry thinks: *Yes, of course.* She is a few years younger than him, nut-brown from the sun, crinkled around the eyes from laughter.

Xiongmin is calling out to her, pointing at Henry. "Your half-brother is here!" he is shouting. His voice is wild. It seems impossible these words could exist.

The woman turns to look at them, gaping, then smiles with painful intensity, the same wide smile as in Siew Li's photographs, becoming unbearably like her. It's her face, Lifeng's, Siew Li's. She has Janet's nose, she has Henry's eyes. Before she opens her mouth, he knows what she will say.

ACKNOWLEDGEMENTS

State of Emergency has been in the works for more years than I care to remember, and I couldn't have done it without the kind support of many, many people. Apologies to anyone I have inadvertently left out below; my memory, like most memories, is all too fallible.

I owe particular thanks to Yu-Mei Balasingamchow. Not only was her *Singapore: A Biography* (co-authored with Mark R. Frost) a vital source, her wisdom and knowledge throughout this process have been invaluable.

Too many other books were consulted to name them all, but particularly useful were: Poh Soo Kai's *Living in a Time of Deception*, Teo Soh Lung's *Beyond the Blue Gate*, Han Suyin's *And the Rain My Drink*, Ian Ward and Norma Miraflor's *Slaughter and Deception at Batang Kali*, Agnes Khoo's *Life as the River Flows*, Chin Peng's *My Side of History*, Fong Chong Pik's *The Memoirs of a Malayan Communist Revolutionary*, and Tan Jing Quee, Tan Kok Chiang and Hong Lysa's *The May 13 Generation*.

I am indebted to the excellent journalism of Kirsten Han, and to the films *To Singapore, With Love* by Tan Pin Pin, *The Last Communist* by Amir Muhammad and *1987: Untracing the Conspiracy* by Jason Soo.

Gratitude also to those who agreed to be interviewed in the course of my research, including David and Janice Wong; Richard Lee at Seminyih New Village; Ling Yi, Liao Xiongmin and the other inhabitants of Friendship Village 2 at Betong; Father René Nicolas; Chua Shop Fong; and my parents.

Many others provided help and encouragement along the way, including Lydia Shah, Aditi Shivaramakrishnan, Dan Koh, Zhang Ruihe, Teng Qian Xi, Fikri Alkhatib, Christie Chua, Deanne Tan, Sarah Day, Kate McNaughton and Diana Wong. I'm particularly grateful for the inspirational support of Jim Crace and Maggie Gee, who saw an early draft of this novel come to life during an Arvon course they led.

Thanks to publisher Edmund Wee, editor Jason Erik Lundberg, line editor JY Yang, UK rep Kate Manning, marketing manager Winston Tay and all at Epigram Books, and to my agent Karolina Sutton.

And finally to Drayton, for all the rest.

ABOUT THE
AUTHOR

Jeremy Tiang is a writer and translator. His short story collection, *It Never Rains on National Day* (Epigram Books, 2015) was shortlisted for the 2016 Singapore Literature Prize. He has translated more than ten books from the Chinese, including novels by Chan Ho-Kei, Zhang Yueran, Yeng Pway Ngon and Su Wei-chen. He won the Golden Point Award for Fiction in 2009, and has received an NEA Literary Translation Fellowship, a PEN/Heim Translation Grant, and a People's Literature Award Mao-Tai Cup. He also writes and translates plays, and currently lives in Brooklyn.

INHERITANCE
BALLI KAUR JASWAL

A NOVEL

INHERITANCE BY BALLI KAUR JASWAL

- Winner of the 2014 Best Young Australian Novelist Award -

In 1971, a teenage girl briefly disappears from her house in the middle of the night, only to return a different person, causing fissures that threaten to fracture her Punjabi Sikh family. As Singapore's political and social landscapes evolve, the family must cope with shifting attitudes towards castes, youth culture, sex and gender roles, identity and belonging. Inheritance examines each family member's struggles to either preserve or buck tradition in the face of a changing nation.

ISBN: 978-191-2098-00-2
PUBLICATION DATE: MAY 2017

KAPPA QUARTET

A NOVEL

DARYL QILIN YAM

KAPPA QUARTET BY DARYL QILIN YAM

Kevin is a young man without a soul, holidaying in Tokyo;
Mr Five, the enigmatic kappa, is the man he happens to
meet. Little does Kevin know that kappas—the river
demons of Japanese folklore—desire nothing more than the
souls of other humans. Set between Singapore and Japan,
Kappa Quartet is split into eight discrete sections, tracing
the rippling effects of this chance encounter across a host
of other characters, connected and bound to one another in
ways both strange and serendipitous.

ISBN: 978-191-2098-72-9
PUBLICATION DATE: MAY 2017

NOW THAT IT'S OVER

a novel

O THIAM CHIN

NOW THAT IT'S OVER BY O THIAM CHIN

- Winner of the 2015 Epigram Books Fiction Prize -

During the Christmas holidays in 2004, an earthquake in the Indian Ocean triggers a tsunami that devastates fourteen countries. Two couples from Singapore are vacationing in Phuket when the tsunami strikes. Alternating between the aftermath of the catastrophe and past events that led these characters to that
fateful moment, *Now That It's Over* weaves a tapestry of causality and regret, and chronicles the physical and emotional wreckage wrought by natural and man-made disasters.

ISBN: 978-191-2098-69-9
PUBLICATION DATE: JULY 2017

THE LAST
LESSON

of

MRS DE
SOUZA

A NOVEL

CYRIL WONG

THE LAST LESSON OF MRS DE SOUZA BY CYRIL WONG

One last time and on her birthday, Rose de Souza is returning to school to give a final lesson to her classroom of secondary school boys before retiring from her long teaching career. What ensues is an unexpected confession in which she recounts the tragic and traumatic story of Amir, a student from her past who overturned the way she saw herself as a teacher, and changed her life forever.

ISBN: 978-191-2098-70-5
PUBLICATION DATE: JULY 2017

SUGARBREAD
BALLI KAUR JASWAL

A NOVEL

SUGARBREAD **BY BALLI KAUR JASWAL**

- Finalist of the 2015 Epigram Books Fiction Prize -

Pin must not become like her mother, but nobody will tell her why. She seeks clues in Ma's cooking and when she's not fighting other battles — being a bursary girl at an elite school and facing racial taunts from the bus uncle. Then her meddlesome grandmother moves in, installing a portrait of a watchful Sikh guru and a new set of house rules. Old secrets begin to surface, but can Pin handle the truth?

ISBN: 978-191-2098-66-8
PUBLICATION DATE: SEPTEMBER 2017

The
Gatekeeper

A NOVEL

Nuraliah
Norasid

THE GATEKEEPER BY NURALIAH NORASID

- Winner of the 2016 Epigram Books Fiction Prize -

The Gatekeeper tells the story of a ten-year-old Gorgon girl named Ria, who petrifies an entire village of innocents with her gaze. Together with her sister, she flees the jungle of Manticura to the underground city of Nelroote, where society's marginalised members live. Years later, the subterranean habitat is threatened when Ria, now the gatekeeper, befriends a man from the outside.

ISBN: 978-191-2098-68-2
PUBLICATION DATE: SEPTEMBER 2017

LET'S GIVE IT UP FOR
GIMME LAO!

A NOVEL

SEBASTIAN SIM

LET'S GIVE IT UP FOR GIMME LAO! **BY SEBASTIAN SIM**

- Finalist of the 2015 Epigram Books Fiction Prize -

Born on the night of the nation's independence, Gimme Lao is cheated of the honour of being Singapore's firstborn son by a vindictive nurse. This forms the first of three things Gimme never knows about himself, the second being the circumstances surrounding his parents' marriage, and the third being the profound (but often unintentional) impact he has on other people's lives. Tracing social, economic and political issues over the past 50 years, this humorous novel uses Gimme as a hapless centre to expose all of Singapore's ambitions, dirty linen and secret moments of tender humanity.

ISBN: 978-191-2098-65-1
PUBLICATION DATE: NOVEMBER 2017